A Chance Encounter . . .

He saw that Chabot had moved closer to her, his lapels all but resting on her bare shoulder. Like a ram in rut, he was staking out his territory.

Ferocious will power held Dragoner's feet in place, while all the rest of him thrummed with primal male instincts of the brutish kind.

"Ah, it is Dragoner," said the comte, unaware that he was moments away from an ugly death.

"I am here," said Dragoner, "to speak with my wife. You won't mind, I am sure, if I claim a few minutes of her time."

"Certainly not, so long as you return her to me." Chabot's long-fingered hand settled on her shoulder in an unmistakably possessive gesture.

Delilah smiled up at him. "I am counting on it, Gustave."

Black spots danced before Dragoner's eyes. Never once had she ever addressed her own husband as "Charles." He did not relish the idea of Delilah on intimate terms with another man. With *any* other man. . . .

Lord Dragoner's Wife

Lynn Kerstan

A SIGNET BOOK

SIGNET
Published by New American Library, a division of
Penguin Putnam Inc., 375 Hudson Street,
New York, New York 10014, U.S.A.
Penguin Books Ltd, 27 Wrights Lane,
London W8 5TZ, England
Penguin Books Australia Ltd, Ringwood,
Victoria, Australia
Penguin Books Canada Ltd, 10 Alcorn Avenue,
Toronto, Ontario, Canada M4V 3B2
Penguin Books (N.Z.) Ltd, 182–190 Wairau Road,
Auckland 10, New Zealand

Penguin Books Ltd, Registered Offices:
Harmondsworth, Middlesex, England

First published by Signet, an imprint of New American Library,
a division of Penguin Putnam Inc.

First Printing, October 1999
10 9 8 7 6 5 4 3 2 1

*For Chet Cunningham, a true hero
and his lovely heroine, Rosie*

Chapter 1

"They say, best men are moulded out of faults; And, for
the most, become much more the better for being a little
bad."

Measure for Measure
Act 5, Scene 1

19 June, 1814

The house at Clichy, old and somewhat dilapidated, did not
look to be the residence of the woman who had all of Paris
at her feet.

Charles Everett, Lord Dragoner, lingered at the door that had
just been opened for him by a footman, steeling himself to
make his entrance. Inside the crowded drawing room, the lights
and colors and half-familiar faces were swimming before his
eyes. Then, within the space of a dozen heartbeats, his vision
cleared and the sensation was gone.

Odd, that. He shook off the feeling that a shadow had followed him into the salon and looked around, taking his bearings. Plotting his exit.

Two sets of double doors, spread wide, led to adjacent parlors where some of the guests were engaged in lively conversation and, no doubt, even livelier flirtations. After escaping the
grande salon, he could make himself relatively inconspicuous
in one of those parlors.

There was no mistaking which of the ladies held court here.
And he must have been described to her, because she appeared
to recognize him. Seated on a Grecian couch, her black ringlets
dangling from a turban crowned with bird-of-paradise feathers,

Madame Germaine de Staël raised a gloved hand and beckoned him forward.

He wondered how much she knew.

"Madame." Bowing, he accepted her raised hand and brushed a kiss over her wrist. "You honor me."

"So I do," she said agreeably, addressing him in English. "You may ascribe your invitation to my unfailing curiosity. My friends tell me that you are not entirely respectable."

His gaze lifted to meet a look of high good humor in her eyes. "Do not credit everything you hear in Paris, madame. I am, I assure you, a perfect angel."

"*Quel dommage.* But I do not believe you, of course, for if I did, you would not be here. In my salons, you will discover, it pleases me to put the wolves to graze among the lambs. And what," she added with surprising coyness, "shall I expect from *le beau dragon?*"

"That rather depends, I suppose, on what you want. But if it is within my power, I shall most naturally oblige you."

"Then tell me how it came, sir, that I found myself banished from my home and compelled to wander abroad like a Gypsy, while an English prisoner of war was allowed to gambol here as freely as any Parisian nightingale."

He lifted his hands in a gesture of contrition. "An appalling miscarriage of justice, to be sure, which you may entirely ascribe to my insignificance. And I, you understand, could not bring myself to leave Paris before making your acquaintance."

Her shrewd eyes flashed approval. "And now that you have done so, will you return to England?"

"I'm not altogether sure that England will have me back." New guests had entered the salon, and he glanced over to see the Vicomte de Chateaubriand regarding him with unconcealed impatience. The time had come to make a polite withdrawal. "You must inform me, madame, if ever I can do you a service. May I hope to call on you again?"

"Oh, one may always hope. I grant that you amuse me, and you are undeniably ornamental. Nonetheless, I continue to wonder if there is truth to the alarming stories I have heard of you. Promise me, *cher dragon*, that when next you create a scandal, you will do so at one of my salons."

"As you command," he said, bowing. " 'To promise is most courtly and fashionable'."

Her laughter followed him as he moved away, under the bemused gazes of those who had overheard the conversation.

For the next hour he entertained himself in one of the smaller parlors, where the guests included several of his acquaintances and, providentially, none of his lovers. Wandering from group to group, he heard talk of the Bourbon Court and the disgruntled Bonapartist army, but for the most part, people were speaking with well-advised circumspection. In these unsettled times, it was dangerous to take sides. For that matter, it was practically impossible to know what sides existed to be taken.

"Not one of your usual haunts, Dragoner," said a cultured voice from behind him. "You won't find any gaming here."

Turning, Dragoner saw the handsome, slightly dissipated face of the Comte de Chabot. "Oh, dear," he said. "In that case, I shall certainly take an early leave. But no, I almost forgot. I have come here for the women."

Chabot laughed. "As have I, of course. Then may I assume my brother's pockets to be safe from you this night?"

"Well, that rather depends on my degree of success with the ladies," Dragoner replied easily. "Do you mean to warn me off Monsieur Batiste?"

"*Mais non!* Jacques must fend for himself, as must we all in this new regime. And you probably know that there has been no communication between us for several years. He is, I am afraid, a blot on the family name."

"A distinction I share with him," Dragoner observed, "along with our mutual taste for playing cards and tossing dice. For good or ill, we reprobates have a knack for finding one another."

"What's going on there?" said a man standing near the door.

Dragoner looked around. Conversations went on in the small parlor, but a hush had fallen over the grande salon. Moments later, there came a round of enthusiastic applause.

With a curt nod to Chabot, he crossed the room to pluck a goblet of champagne from the sideboard and expertly separate the prettiest young female in the room from her friends. She fluttered her blackened lashes at him and obediently took his arm.

"Mademoiselle Fanouelle, is it not?" he said, allowing his gaze to drift where she must have wanted it to be, considering how little of her gown had been allotted to covering her breasts. Yes, she would do nicely. He steered her firmly toward the door to the grande salon.

What he saw was entirely unexpected. A space had cleared around Madame de Staël, and dropped onto one knee before her, paying gallant and somewhat theatrical homage, was the Duke of Wellington.

Good Lord. Dragoner stifled a laugh. Not for a moment had it occurred to him that he should *kneel* to the woman.

"Is that *him*?" Mademoiselle Fanouelle whispered, tugging at his sleeve. "Oh, I simply *must* meet him! You are English, yes? Will you present me?"

"I'm afraid not, my dear." He drew her into the circle of his arm. "But if you flirt quite outrageously with me, he will notice you and perhaps request an introduction. Might I suggest that you gaze at me adoringly?"

Wellington had risen and was standing with his hands clasped behind his back, his eyes fixed on Madame de Staël. She said something that made him laugh, and his response brought general laughter from those close enough to hear.

"Are you ticklish?" Dragoner asked, lightly scratching Mademoiselle Fanouelle beneath her arm. She obligingly produced a high-pitched giggle.

Wellington turned, an expression of mild curiosity on his face, and acknowledged the girl with a smile. Then his gaze shifted to the man standing next to her.

Dragoner, looking back at him, saw the duke's eyes harden to a wintry blue. He clutched the girl's waist, aware of the blood draining from his face.

"I'd have thought you to be more discriminating, Madame de Staël," said the duke, his voice resonating in the silence that had fallen over the room. "How came this fellow into your salon?"

Replying only with a light shrug, she flicked open her fan.

The next move, Dragoner supposed, was his. Keeping the little blonde in tow, he made his way across the room and bowed to his commanding officer.

Wellington regarded him with manifest scorn.

"Oh, I do beg your pardon," Dragoner murmured. "I have been so long from the army. Ought I to have saluted?"

"Still hold your commission, do you?" Wellington fired back. "I shall soon see you stripped of it. A lieutenant, are you?"

"A captain, I'm afraid." Dragoner tossed back the last of his champagne and handed the glass to Mademoiselle Fanouelle. "'A worthy officer i' th' war, but insolent.'"

"So you are, by God. Horse Guards will hear from me on this matter. If I thought you worth the trouble of it, I would summon a court martial within the week."

"'Lay upon me the steep Tarpeian death'," Dragoner quoted solemnly.

"That will do, Captain. You are a disgrace to your regiment, sir, and a blight on your country's honor. You are never to appear in uniform. From this time, you may regard yourself as a civilian."

"Why, so I have done these last four years, Your Grace. And my regimentals long ago made a meal for the local moths. But I wonder at your astonishment to find me here in Paris. Did you fail to notice that I'd gone missing?"

Dragoner released the blonde to lift both hands in a conciliatory gesture. "I kept expecting to be ransomed, you see, or exchanged, or whatever it is you do to retrieve a captured British officer. Am I to blame for my country's negligence? And what is an abandoned soldier to do but keep himself pleasantly occupied? If that is a crime, sir, by all means assemble a court martial. Better yet, drag me home to London in chains. But the ladies of Paris won't thank you for it."

Stone-faced, Wellington looked him slowly up and down. Then he turned his back and walked away.

The room had gone stunningly silent. Dragoner stood alone, his face lit by the chandelier overhead, cold sweat sluicing down the back of his neck. Even his pretty blond accessory, no longer enchanted with his company, had distanced herself.

"I expect, Lord Dragoner, that you have another party to attend," Madame de Staël observed mildly. "You mustn't let us hold you here."

"No, indeed." Drawing closer, he gave her a mocking bow and lowered his voice. "But if you recall, my sweet, you *did* requisition a scandal."

"And you have generously obliged me. Unfortunately, you have also insulted a great man, one whose regard I happen to covet. It is unlikely that I shall forgive you for it. *Au revoir, mon dragon.*"

He felt the scores of eyes focused on his back like steel probes as he made his way, indolently, to the entrance hall and reclaimed his hat and walking stick. It had been impossibly worse than he had foreseen, and yet, in a perverse sort of way, he had rather enjoyed himself. By the time he reached the street, his taut lips had begun to relax.

It was early yet. The June night, pleasantly cool and scented with spring flowers, was long from over. He strode without hurry to his hired carriage and directed the coachman to the area of the Palais Royal and the cafés and clubs that had sprung up around it. That was where all the really entertaining people were to be found.

Le Chien Noir, blazing with lights and loud with music and laughter, stood between a wine shop and a haberdashery. It was Paris's most fashionably disreputable club, glittering with mirrored walls and gilt chandeliers, stinking of wine and beer and roasting meat. Dragoner nodded to acquaintances as he wove through the crowded dining room toward the wide staircase at the rear.

Minette was waiting for him on the mezzanine balcony, her full breasts spilling from the bodice of her crimson gown. "You are late, Vicomte."

"I am sorry." He planted a kiss on her cheek. "It was unavoidable. Later, I shall make amends."

"*Allons.* The Comte de Fervoux is in the Blue Room, losing heavily at dice. No? Then perhaps Jacques Batiste and some other of your friends playing cards. Will it be your special wine tonight?"

"As always, in the silver goblet." He moved against the ornate railing to let a waiter go by. "I would like you to remain close by. Are you at liberty?"

"All has been arranged," she said, smiling. "Will you win tonight, or lose?"

"Oh, win, I think."

Not long after midnight, with one set of fingers clamped on the back of his chair for balance, Dragoner used the other to trowel a large heap of coins onto a cloth napkin. "Another night, gentlemen," he said. "You will understand that I have plans for the rest of the evening."

Minette, busily tying the corners of the napkin together, looked up to smile at him, and three of the men laughed with good-natured envy. Only Jacques Batiste, who had contributed significantly to the contents of that napkin, scowled in protest.

"No gentleman leaves the table when he is winning," he complained. "It would be, as you English say, unsporting."

Dragoner lifted a brow. "But surely, my dear, unless all five of us contrive to lose, one lucky fellow must toddle home with his pockets jingling. Perhaps tomorrow night, it will be you."

Already the plump napkin had disappeared into a pocket under Minette's voluminous skirts, effectively closing the discussion. She waited until he had given each of the waiters a coin before leading him away.

On the stairs, in full view of the patrons thronging the dining room, he stumbled, flailed his arms, and grasped for the railing. His fingers touched it and slid off. Unceremoniously, he landed three steps down, on his backside.

Minette stood above him, clicking her tongue against her teeth while a fat bourgeoisie in a blinding yellow waistcoat, on his way to the mezzanine, made a wide arc around the drunken Englishman.

Unperturbed, Minette summoned a footman, and propped up between the two of them, Dragoner was transported without further incident to the street.

"You wish a carriage?" the footman inquired, letting go of Dragoner when he seemed inclined to wrap his arms around a lamppost.

"Lord Dragoner requires fresh air and a walk," Minette replied. "I shall see him safely home."

He broke into song as they navigated the crowded pavement, passing by the clubs and restaurants spilling over with people until they had left the Palais Royal behind and were winding their way through narrower, dimmer streets. He stopped singing then, but kept his arm at Minette's waist as they drew near the shabby, three-storied house where he lived.

Few of his neighbors were awake at this hour. Here and there between closed curtains, a slice of light could be seen, but none of it reached the street. He located the key in his waistcoat pocket, dropped it, and leaned against the door, laughing, while Minette crouched beside him to feel for the key on the pavement.

"Cochon!" she exclaimed, punching him on the shin. "Help me."

He bent forward and toppled onto his hands and knees. "What are we looking for?" he asked, his eyes searching the narrow alleyway that divided two blocks of town houses directly across the street.

Minette found the key and stood to open the door, muttering a number of savory French oaths while Dragoner pulled himself upright.

A brace of candles stood on a pier table just inside. Silhouetted by the light, he wrapped his arms around Minette and pressed her against the doorjamb. One hand stole down to lift her skirts.

"Patience, *chéri*," she trilled, slapping his hand away and drawing him into the house by his lapels. He kicked the door shut behind him.

When they had reached his bedchamber on the top floor, he used the candle he'd brought with him to ignite every lamp in the room. Minette went to the window that overlooked the street, drew the curtains, and raised the casement.

He joined her there for another embrace and let her untie his neckcloth and unclasp his starched collar. When his black evening coat hit the floor, he stepped back and began to unbutton his waistcoat. "Now you, Minette. Slowly, if you please. Remove your clothes."

Striking a pose in front of the open window, she raised a hand to the top of one long kidskin glove and drew it with careful grace down her arm.

Grinning, Dragoner slowly removed himself from the circle of light and slipped into the dressing room. "You are missing a remarkable performance," he said, closing the door behind him.

Edoard uncoiled himself from the room's lone chair and held out a manicured hand to receive Dragoner's waistcoat. "And because Minette is giving one tonight, shall I presume that you were followed?"

"Yes. Ineptly. And unless I am very much mistaken, by the same chaps who've been dogging me all week." Dragoner stepped out of his satin knee breeches and sat to remove his shoes and stockings. "Pass over the knife, will you? And some peppermints, if you have them. My tongue feels like the bottom of a peat-cutter's shoe."

"What do they want?" Edoard persisted, a frown on his thin face.

"If they keep this up, I suppose I shall have to ask them." Dragoner secured the leather strap of the sheath around his calf. "No, not the pistol. I'm going over the rooftops. And I don't expect they are in the least dangerous, my bumbling new friends. No more than an untimely nuisance."

"If you say so." Edoard, who had already laid out the snug black trousers, black shirt, and soft-soled boots that Dragoner was to wear, moved out of the way to let him dress. "How did it go tonight? Are we cashiered?"

"Well, *I* certainly am. Sergeant Edward Platt may yet be permitted to resign with dignity, should he one day elect to rise from the grave. Oh, good. Peppermints." Popping one in his mouth, Dragoner slid the narrow box into his pocket. "They'll ruin my teeth, I know. You needn't scold."

"Only a fool gives advice to a stone wall," Edoard said, tossing him a black knit cap. "How long should I keep Minette here?"

"Why, for as long as you want her. I don't expect our watchdogs will linger once the curtain is drawn. But when you take her to your bedchamber, don't put on any lights."

By the time Dragoner exited the dressing room, Minette was

bare to the waist, her skirts barely suspended by the swell of her lush hips. "Slow a bit, *poupee*," he cautioned, regarding her with open appreciation. "I'll need—shall we say?—four minutes."

With a wink, she turned her back and put her hands against the window casements, allowing her audience across the street a lingering view of her splendid breasts.

"I am seized with dark envy and foulest lust," Dragoner said, clapping his valet on the shoulder. "She is a goodly wench, my friend, and clever to boot. You should consider keeping her."

"Oh, aye," Edoard replied, lapsing into his native Yorkshire drawl. "'Tis certain Minnie is sizing me up for leg shackles. She wants to get married."

"Don't they all?" Dragoner said.

Leaving Edoard to enjoy himself, he let himself into the passageway and followed it to where a statue of Zeus held guard over a concealed panel in the wall. At a touch on the right spot, the panel opened soundlessly to the adjacent house that had stood empty since he leased it three years earlier.

Dust billowed under his boots as he made his way to a small room furnished only with heavy curtains over the window and a paint-spattered ladder. He propped it against the wall, climbed to the trapdoor, and slid out on his belly to the steep, slate-shingled roof.

A cool breeze had sprung up, feathering his cheeks as he wriggled up the steep incline and concealed himself behind a cluster of chimney pots. Then, raising his head, he looked down on the scene below.

From his bedchamber window, a rectangle of bright light angled across the street, and just beyond its reach were the shadowy figures of the two men who had been tracking him. They had pressed themselves against the walls that lined the alley, their faces lifted to the spectacle of Minette disrobing.

She was watching the clock on the mantelpiece, he knew. And when his own inner sense of time told him the four minutes were up, the curtains were abruptly pulled closed.

The street went dark. He waited. And then, instead of using the alley to take a discreet leave, the two oafs lumbered from their hideaway onto the pavement and made a turn at the lam-plit corner.

Amateurs. But who the devil had set them after him, and to what purpose?

Bent low, he picked his way across the roof to the last in the row of houses, dropped to his knees by a lead gutter, and swung his legs over the side of the building. He was, it seemed, a lit-tle drunker than he'd meant to be, because he had miscalculated the location of the balcony. Hand over hand he edged his way along the gutter, took a swift glance to be sure this time of his bearings, and let go.

He landed a long way down, his feet meeting the balcony with a bone-rattling thud. Silence again. The resident of the cor-ner house, an ancient woman who employed an ear trumpet when she was awake, had once again slept through one of his surreptitious exits. If ever he left his current lodgings, he thought, pausing to reward himself with a peppermint, he must remember to send her a gift.

Then, with careful stealth, he descended past the open win-dows of a cloth merchant's house to the lower balcony, jumped to the pavement, and set a course through the back streets of Paris to his destination.

An apple-cheeked aide-de-camp was waiting for him by the trademan's entrance of a fashionable hôtel leased by the En-glish government. "Captain Lord Dragoner?" he asked uncer-tainly when the figure emerged from the gloomy dark.

"Not for very long," Dragoner said, holding out his arms to be searched. "The captain part, at any rate. You may take the knife concealed in my right boot, but I want it back."

The youngster, flushing hotly, withdrew the knife from its sheath. "My apologies, sir. Orders, you understand. Follow me, please."

At the end of a long passageway, Dragoner was ushered into a room lined on three sides with bookshelves. Across from the door was a paper-strewn desk set between two curtained win-dows. And behind the desk, intent on sharpening a quill pen with a tortoiseshell-handled blade, sat the Duke of Wellington.

He looked up when Dragoner appeared in the doorway. "Good Lord, young man. Who is your tailor?"

Dragoner waited until the aide-de-camp had gone. "I beg your pardon, sir. It was necessary to elude the attentions of two suitors for my hand. Or so I presume them to be. Since they haven't killed me, they were probably sent to recruit me."

"To do what?" Wellington asked sharply.

"Oh, to make trouble, I suppose. On whose behalf, I've no idea. So far they have confined themselves to tracing my movements. Well, not the ones that brought me here, you may be sure."

The duke went back to sharpening his pen. "You will advise me, no doubt, when a significant contact is made. Do sit down. We need not observe ceremony here."

Restraining the nervous energy that had brought him this far, Dragoner lowered himself onto a chair across from the desk. He recognized his own handwriting on the papers scattered in front of Wellington, who had begun to gather them into a neat pile.

"I have read your reports," the duke said in an amiable voice. "Excellent work. And of no possible use to me."

"Spies can tell you only what *is,* Your Grace. To divine the future, I'm afraid that you require a gazetted prophet."

"Let me know when you find one, then. Meantime I shall have to make do with your educated guesses. How blows the wind in Paris?"

"Hot and cold, as always, while everyone stands around trying to decide which way to leap. Fouché has a scheme for every contingency, of course, and he had already set a few of them in motion before they became irrelevant. We expect trouble from the disappointed victims of his plots. They credited the rumor that Bonaparte would have his wrists slapped by the Allies, be told to behave himself, and find himself escorted back to the throne." After a beat, Dragoner met the duke's cool blue eyes. "You supported his reinstatement, I believe."

"In part," Wellington replied evenly. "So long as his fangs and claws are drawn, better a competent tyrant than disorder. But that's neither here nor there. You are informing me, politely, that there is little or nothing to tell, so we shall change the subject." He leaned back on his chair, gazing thoughtfully at his pen. "My brother says that I shall find diplomacy a very pretty amusement. Do you concur?"

Instead of leaving the subject, Dragoner noted with amusement, the duke was simply coming at it from another direction. "In the early going, yes, the new British Ambassador to the Court of the Tuileries may look forward to enjoying himself. The ladies of Paris are incomparable, and you will be much admired by them. Certainly you will be feted and flattered in public. But all the while, the discontented will be gathering behind closed doors and forming factions of every sort. It is certain that soldiers who cannot find work will riot in the streets. And if the Vienna Congress imposes strict reparations, I wouldn't be surprised to see open rebellion throughout the country."

"As bad as that?" Wellington laced his fingers together and propped them under his chin. "In that case, I shall most definitely put your services to good use. Unofficially, of course, as I have declared my intention to see you booted from the army. But the Crown has just granted me half a million pounds, did you know? I can now afford to pay you from my own pocket. Do we remain in agreement?"

The question, Dragoner supposed, was meant to be rhetorical. By playing his part in tonight's charade, he had already committed himself to what he expected to be a profitless endeavor. Even so, he itched to decline the offer of a salary paid by the duke himself, if only for his pride's sake. But his duties would require him to cut a dash in Paris, and as Wellington was about to discover, cutting a dash in Paris was devilish expensive.

"If you wish it, yes," Dragoner said finally. It wasn't as if he had anything better to do. "But if I may speak frankly, there seems little point to keeping me here. I doubt you will retain your post as ambassador for more than a few months."

"Well, well, you may be right. But the alternative was a command in the American war, and that's a bad business indeed. I mean to stay well clear of it."

Dragoner realized that his palms were sweating. Like the duke, he had been left at loose ends when peace was made in Europe, and this assignment offered no more than a temporary delay. Soon enough he would have to confront a future that stretched before him like an arid, featureless plain.

And before that, as much as he would rather defer the whole

business, an even more dismal prospect loomed in his path. "There is another matter," he said slowly, "that I must take up with you. Before I continue my work, sir, I must return for a short time to England."

"Must you, by God!" Wellington looked severely displeased. "Have you any idea what to expect? Exchanged prisoners have carried tales of your riotous conduct, and the scandal sheets were quick to spread the news in London. To set foot there during the Victory Celebrations would be sheer folly."

" 'No man cried "God save him!" No joyful tongue gave him welcome home'." Dragoner forced his suddenly cold lips into a smile. "I don't expect to be crowned with laurel leaves, Your Grace, and my reputation was hardly unblemished when I left England in the first place."

"Nonetheless, the situation is worse than either of us had counted on. The subterfuge that put you in the hands of the French has got out as well."

"Am I, then, to be tried and hung for treason?"

"Oh, nothing so irretrievable as that." The duke waved a hand. "I am speaking of general gossip. There is no evidence to bring you to court, and I would naturally forestall any attempt to do so. The point is, I cannot clear your name for so long as you remain of use to me here. You would be well advised to delay your journey until things are set to right again."

It was a good excuse, and Dragoner was greatly tempted to jump at it. But imprisonment, he had learned, came in several forms. One of his gaolers, the one he meant to confront, even now awaited him in London.

"*Can* they be set right, sir? I take leave to doubt it. Rumors are sometimes ignored, and eventually they will be forgot. But should you speak out on my behalf, it will only serve to make it official that I have been—not to put too fine a point on it— whoring for England."

Wellington fingered the papers on his desk. "Do you imagine, after Cintra, that I fail to understand how it is to be falsely disgraced? At present I cannot help you, but in future your name will be cleared."

Dragoner, aware from the duke's expression that the interview was at an end, came to his feet and saluted. "My errand will require only a brief absence, Your Grace. I shall depart in a few weeks, and you may expect to find me in Paris on your return."

"I *will* expect it."

Dragoner was at the door when Wellington spoke again, his voice curiously intent. "It went well tonight, don't you think?"

"Oh, indeed, sir." Dragoner shivered at the memory. "If I may say so, you are an exceptionally accomplished actor."

"As an ambassador, I shall need to be," replied the duke, seemingly pleased at the compliment. "But I've much to learn about dissimulation, while you are indisputably a master of the art."

Chapter 2

"A young man married is a man that's marr'd."

All's Well That Ends Well
Act 2, Scene 3

"I've come to take you for a walk," Lady Hepzibah Ffipps announced, sweeping into the upstairs parlor with two closed parasols and a pair of bonnets dangling from her hands. "He isn't coming, my dear. Not today. He doesn't even know where you are."

"Oh, I should imagine he'll have found out by now." Delilah unwrapped her legs from the window seat and stood on feet that immediately began to tingle, as if she had walked onto a carpet of needles. "It's only just four o'clock, Heppy. He may yet arrive, and what would he think if I wasn't here to greet him?"

"That you had better uses for your time, I would hope." With a snort, Lady Hepzibah dropped the parasols onto a Sheraton chair. "You are plucking at straws, Delilah. And if by chance you get hold of one, what is it that you will have? A piece of straw, that's what."

"Ah, but I want *all* the straws," Delilah said. "Then I shall spin them into gold."

"Fustian! Wherever do you come up with these noodle-headed notions? Now put on your bonnet, that's a good girl, and let's go find us a breeze."

Impatient, energetic Heppy. Delilah gave her an apologetic smile. "I'll wait here a bit longer, if you don't mind. He's bound to come by way of the river, and I wish to see him before he sees me. But by all means, do have yourself a walk. I've been afraid you were planning to meet him at the door with a loaded pistol."

"A horsewhip, more like. Well, keep vigil if you must, and perhaps the scoundrel will turn up after all. But have you any idea, child, how you look?"

"Oh, like a scarecrow wigged with a red mop, I suppose." Delilah ran her fingers through the corkscrew curls she had loathed since first she grew hair. "But he's seen me before, you know. He won't be expecting much. I will change my dress again, though, and wash my hands and face, if you'll watch for him in the meantime."

Grumbling, Lady Hepzibah crossed to the window and took up her position. "Five minutes, then. And it's a far sight more time than he's worth."

Keeping to her word, she was no longer there when Delilah returned six minutes later, wearing an apple green muslin gown that was already beginning to droop in the muggy heat.

Lady Hepzibah had arranged for a pitcher of iced lemonade to be placed on the buffet alongside the decanters of wine and brandy, and she'd left an open parasol on the cushioned window seat. Delilah carried a glass of lemonade to the bay window and settled herself, parasol raised against the sun, to wait.

Whatever would she do without Heppy? The elderly spinster had come all the way from Northumberland for her great-niece's wedding, and when the groom took his leave the very next day, she had stayed to console the bride. A half-dozen years later, she was still consoling the bride.

Sipping the cold lemonade, Delilah gazed out over the sweeping lawn that led from the flower garden to the river. In the humid air, a mist had formed over the brown, sluggish Thames as it curled around a wooded headland to her right and flowed in front of the house she had named Dragon's Lair.

Sooner or later, the dragon would find it.

He ought to have known where she was living, of course. She had never done anything of significance without writing to inform him. Nonetheless, his letter—the only letter she had ever received from him—had been directed to his London town house. The new owner had forwarded it to her solicitors, who enclosed it in a packet of business correspondence that had arrived at the Lair only a few hours earlier.

There had been no warning. Not even a premonition. She had been at her desk, methodically working her way through the thick stack of mail, and had almost reached the bottom when her gaze was drawn to the scarlet seal on a single folded sheet of paper. It was imprinted with a winged dragon, stamped in the wax by her husband's signet ring.

Light-headed, her fingers trembling, she had lifted the crumpled paper and broken the seal. One sentence was all he could spare her.

"Madam, I shall be in London on Wednesday, the twenty-first of July, and will do myself the honor of calling upon you at one o'clock."

The message was signed, in his jagged handwriting, "Dragoner."

She had wept then, but not for long. He was due to arrive within two hours. Besides, he would scarcely have confided his true sentiments in a letter. There was, she supposed, some reason yet for hope.

To be sure, she had been nursing that same fragile hope long past the time any sensible woman would have let it die a natural death. Ah, well. He was, at last, coming home. Perhaps he was coming home to her.

So she had bathed and dressed herself and taken up her place at the window, where she ruthlessly ordered her thoughts and made a few tentative plans. She had even permitted herself to airdream, a treat she had denied herself for a long time, but soon discovered that she had fallen out of the habit of it. Her fantasies refused to go the direction she wanted them to, much like her intractable life.

And all her dreams, she supposed, had come crashing down around her when her bridegroom stumbled into the church on a long-ago Saturday morning, sullen, resentful, and reeking of brandy.

He had come alone, she remembered, without family or friends. One of her brothers was recruited to stand up with him as groomsman—*hold* him up, as it had turned out—and he'd spoken his vows in a voice so low that she could scarcely distinguish the words. At the minister's direction, and after a good deal of fumbling, he had produced a ring from his waistcoat pocket and shoved it onto her pudgy finger, scowling because it didn't fit. Never once did he look directly at her face.

The ring fit perfectly now. Sunlight glinted off the plain gold band as she lifted her hand to examine it. She would never be beautiful, of course, what with her round face and humiliating dimples and impossible hair, but Heppy's regime of simple meals and vigorous walks had trimmed her figure.

She wondered if he would notice.

A small boat, propelled by oarsmen, was just rounding the curve. She could barely make it out. Shimmering in the cloud of mist that hovered over the water, the boat vanished and reappeared as if emerging from a dream.

There appeared to be two passengers, one seated in front of the other. She knelt up on the cushions, feeling suddenly cold. It might not be him, of course. Lots of boats had gone by that afternoon. She had hoped and despaired a score of times. But this time the small hairs on her arms were lifted in anticipation. Her heart had begun to pound.

When the skiff angled from midriver toward the small wooden dock, she was nearly sure. But she didn't let herself believe it until she could clearly see the lithe, slender man seated on the narrow bench at the bow.

He wasn't wearing a hat. His black hair, damp from the mist, shone like polished ebony. He rose when the boat came near the bank and jumped lightly out when it nudged against the watersteps. For a moment he stood, his hand bladed over his eyes against the sun, and gazed at the house. Then, leaving the others to secure the ties, he strode purposefully up the hill.

She drew back from the window. It was now. Oh dear Lord. But there was time for a short, heartfelt prayer, and another minute or two for her to regain her composure. She had made sure of that. A footman would greet him at the door and summon the butler, who was instructed to be slow in responding. If Heppy was still in the house and unable to resist a caustic welcome, so much the better.

Delilah remembered to close the parasol and prop it against the wall, but in the process, she stumbled over the glass of lemonade she had set on the carpet. A wet stain spread out in all directions. Bother! She quickly stowed the glass behind the hem of the curtains and took up her position in front of the bay window.

That, too, she had planned. With the light coming in from behind her, she would be able to see him clearly while her own face remained in the shadows. A small advantage, to be sure, but a useful tactic she had learned from her father.

Someone spoke in the passageway, and a moment later, she heard a light rap on the door. Gulping a deep breath, she smoothed her skirts and ordered her arms and hands to be still at her sides.

"Lord Dragoner, milady," said the butler, who withdrew immediately and closed the door behind him.

Dragoner—she had never been able to think of him as Charles—looked very much at ease as he came a little way into the room and halted, his head tilted to one side, his lips curved at the corners. It wasn't a smile.

When he bowed and addressed her, his voice was laced with amusement. " 'Divinest creature, Astraea's daughter,' " he said. " 'How shall I honor thee?' "

And she knew, then, from the nature of his greeting, why he had come. It had been her greatest fear.

Deep inside, where she trusted he could not hear it, her heart was breaking apart like river ice at the end of winter. But for this, too, she had prepared herself. "I beg your pardon?" she said courteously. "Is that a line from a poem?"

"Something of the kind. You must disregard my inclination to misappropriate other people's words. It is one of many frightful habits I picked up in France."

"I see." She remembered to curtsy. "You are most welcome home, sir. I hope you had a pleasant journey. Would you care for tea, or perhaps a glass of wine?"

"Oh dear." His smile was almost genuine. "How singularly awkward this is. Will it help, do you think, if we begin with a polite conversation about the weather, or the inordinate cost of hiring a boat during the Victory Celebrations?"

"I don't imagine it would, actually. But you really ought to try the wine." She gestured to the sideboard. "It cost more, even, than *buying* a boat."

"In that case," he said, crossing to the decanter and glasses, "it must be French."

While his back was to her, she settled herself on a chair she had placed near the window and apart from the other furniture. For the conversation that was sure to follow, she did not want him seated close to her. Nor would her shaky legs permit her to stand, as she'd have greatly preferred to do. Although he was not above average height, and his physique was that of a fencer, he seemed to occupy a great deal of space.

"Do you prefer wine," he asked, glancing at her over his shoulder, "or would you rather some of that yellow concoction in the pitcher?"

"Nothing, thank you." She smoothed her damp skirts, which had an alarming tendency to cling to her thighs. "What has become of the gentleman who accompanied you in the boat?"

"My valet? I have no idea, but more than likely he has gone to practice his Gallic charm on your housemaids. I trust they are virtuous and resolute." Dragoner turned and propped his hips against the mahogany sideboard, his legs stretched out and his feet crossed at the ankles. "If it is not impertinent to ask," he said after tasting the wine, "how came it that a rude fellow calling himself Lord Tewksbury has taken up residence in my London town house, claiming to be the owner?"

"Well, I suppose that's only natural, under the circumstances. But you may be sure that he paid well above its worth, considering the—"

"Good God, madam!" He uncrossed his feet and leaned forward. "Am I to understand that you sold my *house?*"

"Nearly four years ago. But this cannot be news to you, sir. Or did you not receive my letters?"

His gaze shifted to the window. "I may have done. Edoard will tell you that I am notoriously careless about—"

"You fed the fire with them, I daresay. It was to be expected. But there are copies with my solicitors, should you care to examine them. Unfortunately, your letter reached me only this morning. Otherwise I'd have arranged for any business documents of significance to be sent here for your inspection."

"I'll want to see them, of course." He twisted the stem of the wineglass between his thumb and forefinger. "And I did read your letters. Some of them, anyway. The ones that arrived within a few months of the wedding. Naturally, I wished to discover if there had been . . . consequences."

"A child, you mean." She steadied her voice. "Unhappily, no. I was disappointed."

After a moment he drained his glass and put it aside. She understood that, with the gesture, he was dismissing the subject of children as well. "The point is," he said, "how could you have sold the house without my authorization?"

"I didn't like to, but *something* had to be done. After two-score years of neglect, it was practically rotting away. I could not lease it at a decent rate, and at the time, we hadn't sufficient funds to restore it."

He opened his mouth, but she went on before he could speak. "Then Lord Tewksbury took a fancy to live at Grosvenor Square, and with yours the only property on the market, he unwisely paid more than he should have done to have it. Most of the funds were invested in your business interests, but some were directed to the purchase of Drag . . . this residence."

"You mistook my question, madam. I fail to see how you could legally transact the sale of *anything* I own. Owned," he corrected grimly. "Is not my permission required? At the very least, my signature?"

"Actually, no. Do you not remember? I was given full power of attorney, to be used in the event of your death or at times when you were unable to deal with your affairs. You signed papers to that effect. Mind you, I had not considered that you would be *unwilling* to deal with your affairs, but the provision seemed to apply. My solicitors agreed."

"I handed you power of attorney?" He shook his head in disbelief. " 'And she has all the rule of her husband's purse.' Did I perchance grant you any other powers I am unaware of?"

"Rather a great many, I'm afraid. But the papers were there for you to read, had you troubled to do so before signing them. I apprehend that you did not."

"You apprehend correctly." And then, to her astonishment, he threw back his head and laughed. "At least you cannot have sold the ancestral pile from under me. It is, I am fairly sure, entailed."

"Yes. I have been hoping to discuss that with you." This wasn't the time, of course, but with her confidence seeping away, business was the only refuge that she knew. In matters of business, she was always self-assured. "As you are doubtless aware, sir, an entail endures for two generations. And because your father failed to renew it, the entail of Dragon's Hill will cease with your death. To secure the property for your immediate heir, and for his, you are required to sign a few more papers. They have already been drawn up, and—"

"No more, I beg you!" Still laughing, he refilled his wineglass. "I was aware, certainly, that I was marrying a merchant's daughter, but I had no idea your family would turn pickpocket in my absence. Indeed, I should have thought my insignificant assets beneath their notice."

"My family has nothing to do with this, sir. It's true that my father negotiated the terms of the marriage, but every transaction completed since the death of your parents has been entirely my responsibility."

"And to continue your theme," he said, "I hereby accept full responsibility for neglecting my own duties." He began to wander, with calculated aimlessness, she thought, in her direction. "Never mind all this buying and selling and trading, my dear. I'm mostly indifferent, you know. Only a bit surprised. It will get sorted out at the appropriate time."

He had stopped directly in front of her, regarding her from impenetrable gray eyes, and she gazed back at him, her face schooled to the pleasantly interested expression of a merchant at the negotiating table. All her muscles ached from holding still, but she had trained herself not to squirm, which was her body's natural inclination. As for her heart, she quite simply refused to acknowledge its existence. She could not afford to feel the slightest emotion now. He was reaching out to places she could not let either of them go.

To preserve her self-command, she concentrated on his appearance, noting the tiny lines at the corners of his eyes and his lips. His face was harder now, his cheekbones and jaw more firmly defined. He looked, to her, more worldly than any young man ought to be. Far too cynical. And weary, too, but she could put that down to his journey.

"Do you know," he said with the affable disinterest she had already come to loathe, "that when first I saw you walking down the aisle of the church, I could not credit that you were of an age to marry. Your brother—I think it was your brother—was standing next to me, and when I asked, he confirmed that you were. But you look not a day older now than you did then. Have you struck a deal with God, or perhaps with Lord Lucifer, for eternal youth?"

"To the contrary, sir, although I have sometimes prayed for a few inconsequential miracles. But I still have all the freckles I was born with, and the dimples as well. My hair has failed to change color, and it continues to defy gravity. I should like to grow another inch or two. There are some occasions, I admit, when my appearance is useful, because people assume they can take advantage of me. And, of course, I happily exploit their misapprehension. But in fact, sir, as you appear unaware of it, I am nine-and-twenty. To be precise, one year and three months older than you."

"The devil you say!" He made a circuit of the chair, looking her over from every angle. "No. It's preposterous. You are a little girl dressed up in her mother's clothes."

"Thank you very much, I'm sure." He had scratched at an old wound and painfully reopened it. "I may look like a child, sir. I know that I do. But I am not the one who has *behaved* like a child."

His head jerked to one side as if she had slapped him, which in fact she had wanted to do. She had not realized that she could be so angry with him. She was used to excusing him. Salvaging his fortune. Pretending he was what she wanted him to be.

"Forgive me," she said, her tone unnaturally brittle. "I had no right to say such a thing."

"We both know better," he replied after a moment. "I have dishonored you from the beginning, and I am sorry for it. But you must know equally well that I never wanted this marriage, no more than did you. We found ourselves on the same auction block, is all—I being sold to pay my father's debts, and you on offer because your family aspired to the Dragoner title. Neither of us was given a choice."

"In fact, my lord, that is not altogether true. I was in no way compelled to marry you. But I have always wondered why you agreed to the arrangement. You might have defied your parents. You could have said no. Why didn't you?"

"Ah." The mocking glint had returned to his eyes. "We are to have plain speaking. A round tale, full of jocularity and wry wit. But I will be brief. It is one thing to deplore a father's intemperance, my dear, and quite another to refrain from tossing him a rope when he is neck-deep in quicksand. The other end of that rope was wrapped around my neck, but what could I do? Watch him be hauled off to a debtors' cell at Marshalsea?"

That wouldn't have come about, certainly, but Dragoner was apparently unaware that peers could not be imprisoned for debt. Would he have married her, she wondered, if he had known?

He went to a chair on the other side of the room and sank onto it, his head thrown back against the padded bolster. "I did take care, beforehand, to exact a promise from him. The largest part of the marriage settlement was to be directed toward the restoration of Dragon's Hill. And he readily agreed, as you might imagine, declaring it had been his intention from the beginning. He even looked me in the eye when he swore the oath. It is hard for me to imagine now, but I believed him. The triumph of blind, befuddled faith over a lifetime of experience. It is not a mistake I shall ever repeat."

She understood all too well the choice he had made. Blind faith was her specialty. "But surely it's better to have faith and be sometimes disappointed," she said, "than never to believe in anyone at all?"

"If you think that, my dear, then you truly are a child. Did you never wonder why my parents failed to appear at the wedding?"

She had, of course. Her father had been furious. "At the time," she said gingerly, "we assumed they did not care to rub shoulders with tradesfolk. Father had invited scores of his friends to the church, and even more to the wedding breakfast."

"It was as well, then, that Lord and Lady Dragoner chose to be elsewhere. I have no doubt they would have been insufferably rude to the other guests. But their plans had been in place, it seems, for a considerable time. They had arranged to scarper when it would least be expected, on the night before the ceremony. I got the news, along with my shaving water, from a servant. Then I got drunk."

"We could not help but notice," she said, keeping her tone level, as his had been. Most of what he had told her, she had already known. But not the timing of it. Not the sudden blow he'd taken, even as he was preparing himself to honor the contract he had made. It was the pain of his parents' betrayal, she now understood, not the marriage, that had sent him reeling into the church only a few hours later. Dear Lord.

But there was a long afternoon to be got through, and she was fairly sure how he meant for it to end. For both their sakes, she must keep guard on her fraying emotions. He, of course, had come in wearing a full suit of armor. "Instead of applying yourself to the brandy bottle," she said, "you'd have done better to call off the wedding. No one would have blamed you for it."

"Would they not? But my parents already had the money, you see. Perhaps your father refrained from telling you, having been bested in the transaction, but he was compelled to pay the marriage settlement in advance. Mummy and Daddy boasted of it at supper, and promised to give me the funds for Dragon's Hill directly after the ceremony. I recall that they made a toast to our happiness. And all the while, their luggage was being loaded at Southampton."

Bitterness had crept into his voice. "They took every penny with them to Italy, leaving their debts unpaid and their creditors to hound me."

To hound *her,* as it had turned out. But he needn't learn about that today. "My father would not have expected you to go through with the marriage," she said. "Nor would I."

"Perhaps. I never considered it. You will understand that I was not thinking clearly."

"You did not appear to be. But you were sufficiently alert to draw my father into the vestry before the ceremony and extract nearly three thousand pounds from him. To pay your own gaming debts, I believe you told him. You wished to be free of them before marrying his daughter."

He flushed. "That was a lie, of course. I find it irksome to pay gaming debts, and for that reason I generally contrive to win. By now you will have realized that the money was to purchase my commission, along with the necessary equipment, horses, and uniforms. Ironic, is it not? Your father, so kindly doing me a service, provided the means of my escape."

"And then," she said, ending the tale in a friendly voice, "the fair maiden, who was neither fair nor any longer a maiden, watched from her castle window as all the dragons ran away."

"And well rid of them, too, she was. Father, mother, and son. Three of a kind." He sat forward, elbows on his knees, his hands tented under his chin. "I didn't think you'd mind, you know. Not after the way I had behaved at the wedding. And later." He gave a barely perceptible shudder.

She had no intention of revisiting her wedding night. What little she could recall of it had been confusing, unhappy, and brief. It was a blur to her now, and best forgot by the both of them.

"Father was well aware of your intentions when he loaned you the money, sir, although he hoped you would change your mind. If not, the army was like to do you good. Two of my brothers also served on the Peninsula, and they came home the better for it. But of course, he never imagined that you would sever all ties with England. And with your wife."

"He should have guessed. The Dragoners are notorious for breaking promises. And what was there to hold us together, after all? Money changed hands. We spoke vows without meaning them and scrawled our names on a parish register. You knew no more about me than I knew of you. Before that sham of a wedding ceremony, we had never so much as set eyes on each other."

Ought she to tell him? He had dropped his hands, which were now loosely clasped between his knees, and his head was lowered. A shock of black hair had fallen forward, concealing his forehead and his eyes. He looked like a man deep in thought, or a man trying not to think. In either case, he seemed to her more remote than the stars.

The truth, then. What had she to lose by it?

"Not everyone," she said, "is willing to take a spouse sight unseen. I often wondered that you did so. I certainly did not."

He raised his head, an arrested expression on his face. "You saw me beforehand? But I had no part in the negotiations. Where did you see me?"

She understood the question behind his questions. They didn't move in the same circles. How *could* she have seen him? "Oh," she said airily, "I was in your vicinity on any number of occasions. Not at fashionable routs or society balls, to be sure, but even a merchant's daughter is permitted to move freely through most parts of London."

"And she could spend a dozen years roaming the streets and shops," he said, "without once encountering me."

"But she—that is, *I*—knew where to look for you. Did you imagine, sir, that you had been selected at random? When I set out to marry above my class, Father determined which among the crop of fortune-hunting gentlemen were agreeable to marrying beneath theirs. The list was then narrowed to include only those of reasonable age, apparent good health, and lack of egregiously bad habits. After examining the reports, I selected three candidates for further study."

"Study?" He slapped his hands against the armrests of his chair. "What were we, then? Three bugs pinned to a blotter?"

"Akin to that, I suppose, although I never thought of you in such a way. Your family history was traced, with particular attention given to your parents and your own upbringing. That proved somewhat difficult, as they were generally traveling abroad, and you with them. Under the circumstances, I was naturally concerned about your education, which appears to have been a trifle haphazard."

"Ought I to have sat an examination before the wedding?" he inquired too sweetly. An instant later he was on his feet and circling the room like a man who wanted only to escape it. One of his hands caught a porcelain figure on a side table and sent it rolling across the carpet, but he didn't appear to notice.

She welcomed his temper. He had broken first. And just in time, because she had few defenses against him. His sarcasm had long since twisted her stomach into knots. Since he had come into the room, she could scarcely draw breath. And the worst was yet to come.

"Well, do go on," he said. "Am I to assume that you questioned my friends? Interrogated my mistresses?"

"Good heavens, no. Our investigations, while thorough, were unobtrusive. But when the written reports ceased to be useful, it became necessary, or so I believed, to see you for myself. We knew, of course, the places you frequented—your club, the theater, a gaming establishment known as Dicing with the Devil, and another establishment called Madame Benton's House of Delights, which—"

"Don't tell me you went *there*!"

"To a brothel? No, indeed." She gathered her calm from the remnants of his. "I first saw you at the theater," she said. "It was Jonathan Dembrow playing King Lear, badly, and it occurred to me that you were the only one in the audience who attended to the play. On rainy days you were often to be found at Hatchard's Book Shop, reading newspapers and magazines in front of the fire. Once, by sheerest coincidence, we were both at Gunter's. You devoured two dishes of ice cream and a wedge of lemon cake."

The expression of stunned horror on his face nearly made her smile. "Three afternoons a week," she said, "you fenced at Antonio's. Whenever possible, I was watching from across the street, and sometimes I trailed behind you when you left. One day, when you were walking in Hyde Park, some rowdy boys knocked the parcels from a lady's hands. You stopped to pick them up."

She paused then, selecting her next words with care. "I was by that time fairly sure of my intentions, but I believe that was the precise moment I decided to marry you."

"Good God!" He threw up his hands. "Because I performed a trivial service for a female walking unchaperoned in the park? I have no recollection of the event, you will understand, but more than likely my attentions were prelude to a seduction."

"Possibly. I never considered that. In any case, you carried her parcels to Park Lane, where you hailed a hackney coach and handed her into it. I saw you pay the jarvey from your own pocket. You did not accompany the lady, but I presume that was on account of her age. She must have been rising seventy."

"Was she?" he inquired with a look of faint astonishment. "Well, no wonder I fail to remember her. And what you saw, my dear, was me acting on a whim. Did you know that good deeds are reputed to bring luck at the gaming tables? Ah, I thought not." His expression hardened. "It seems that for all your *studying*, madam, you have greatly misjudged my character."

She took a few moments to consider her reply. "I don't agree, sir," she said finally. "But it is true that I was able to observe you only from a distance."

"Observe!"

When he advanced on her, it was all she could do to keep from flinching.

"Let's call it what it was, shall we? You shadowed me. You tracked me through the streets. You bloody well *spied* on me!"

It must have been a trick of the light, which streamed directly onto his face when he planted himself in front of her, but his gray eyes had gone a stormy green. Distracted by the transformation, she could not look away from them.

He was waiting for her to respond, looming over her with his arms splayed like the wings of an outraged dragon. She had gone too far. Told him too much. It no longer seemed a good idea, summoning the dragon from his cave.

"One might call it spying, I suppose," she said tentatively. "I considered it more in the nature of . . . well, of an inspection."

His eyes, now hard as two cabochon emeralds, blazed at her. And then he did the last thing she could have expected. Dropping cross-legged to the carpet at her feet, he doubled over. All she could see was the back of his head and his wide shoulders, shaking as he laughed.

This was not a reaction she was prepared to deal with. Seconds ago he had been angry enough to strike her, not that he would do such a thing, and now he was laughing like a field hand who had just heard a smutty joke. More than anything he had said or done that afternoon, it disturbed her.

After what seemed an eternity, he lifted his head. " 'I see our wars will turn into a peaceful comic sport'," he said, " 'when ladies come to be encount'red with'."

And she knew that, laughing, he had firmly re-erected the barriers that had always lain between them. And added new ones, she feared, even more impenetrable. She would not breach his defenses again without a long and painful siege.

For now, all that remained was for him to tell her the last thing she wanted to hear. And he was finding it difficult, as well he should. She was wickedly tempted to wait, forcing him to muster the courage and the words, but she could not. Her own courage had worn too thin.

"I will spare us both a long afternoon of fencing," she said quietly. "You have come to ask me for a divorce."

The word, suspended in the still air between them, took shape like a living thing.

It was beyond her strength to look at him. She heard him draw a harsh breath, and then another. She heard the chatter of magpies outside the window, and the call of rooks in the elm grove. It seemed as if she could hear the river, too, pulsing like blood as it flowed past the house.

Finally the muffled brush of boot leather against silk carpet told her that he had come to his feet. He paused for a moment, perhaps calculating the precise distance to put between them, but at length he drew up a straight-backed chair and sat in front of her, so close that their knees were almost touching.

"Is there any other answer," he said gently, "for either of us? You must realize that we cannot go on as we are."

She wished he had taken himself to the other side of the room. So near as he was, he stole the breath from her lungs and the thoughts from her head. "How can I conclude such a thing," she replied, "when we haven't gone on at all?"

"But that is the point, surely. There are no bonds between us, save for a few legalities, and those are easily severed."

"Do you think so?" She lifted her gaze to his face. "I believe you will find it otherwise."

Two lines formed between his eyes. "You mean to contest the divorce, then?"

"Not at all. If you insist on proceeding, I've sufficient pride to stand out of your way. I shall even cooperate, within reasonable limits. You would not expect me, I am sure, to swear falsely in a court of law."

"Why should you need to? By any standards, my behavior has been intolerable. Every rational judge in England would leap to set you free of me."

"I expect they would want to," she conceded, nearing firm ground once again. "And I promise not to say that I have no wish to be free of you."

"Ah." He rubbed the bridge of his nose. "We are not in true agreement, then. I am sorry for it. Deeply so, although I don't expect you will believe that. But until this afternoon, I never imagined that you wished for my company, or had gone to such trouble to procur me as your husband. I regret that I have proved entirely unsuitable. One day, perhaps, you will understand that I never meant to hurt you."

"I understand it now," she said. "You gave me no thought at all. But I bear you no ill will for that. We were young, and we both made mistakes. You ought to have stood up to your parents, and I—" She managed a weak smile. "Well, I diced with the Dragon. And I appear to have lost."

After a moment, he buried his face in his hands. "I'm sure I deserve it," he murmured. "But you aren't making this easy."

No, she wasn't. And she disliked herself for it. He hadn't expected her to feel as she did about him. She ought not put the burden of her unwanted love upon him, and was trying not to. But it kept slithering in, venoming her words and turning her away from the immediate goal.

His intentions and her feelings were all but irrelevant now. The question of divorce had come down to business and the law, which she understood and he did not. But all the same, she could not be the one to enlighten him. Nothing more would be settled today.

"It is growing late," she said, rising and moving past him to the bell rope. "Do you wish to stay the night? A bedchamber has been made ready, and we can accommodate your valet in the adjoining room."

When he lowered his hands and looked over at her, his eyes were bleak. "Thank you, but no. The oarsmen are waiting to take us back to London." He stood, hands fisted at his sides. "How terribly civilized we are being. I suppose that's as well. But what is to happen next, Delilah?"

It was the only time he had spoken her name since the wedding ceremony, when he was forced to speak it. "I, Charles, take you, Delilah, as my wedded wife."

She turned away, blinking against a wash of hot tears, and crossed to a writing table. In the drawer, already prepared for him, was a card inscribed with the direction of Higgins and Finch, Counselors at Law.

"We should meet with our solicitors, I expect." She turned, smiling, and held out the card. "Will Friday afternoon at one o'clock be acceptable?"

Chapter 3

"Deadly divorce step between me and you!"

All's Well That Ends Well
Act 5, Scene 3

On Friday morning, which had dawned clear and warm, the Victory Celebrations were in full cry. Crowds of people, eating oranges and drinking ale supplied by roving vendors, thronged the streets and lined the pavements, hoping for a glimpse of a Russian tsar or a Prussian general or a troop of mustachioed cossacks. Abandoning his efforts to locate a hackney, Dragoner set out on foot from the posthouse on the outskirts of the city, which was the only accommodation he had been able to find.

It suited him well enough, since he had little desire to encounter anyone who might recognize him. Edoard, with no such apprehensions, had gone off shortly after breakfast to watch a balloon ascent and would doubtless return in the wee hours, as he had done since they came to London, full of ale and good cheer.

At least his valet was enjoying himself. Dragoner had spent all of Thursday closeted in his shabby room with a book and the innkeeper's flea-ridden mongrel, trying not to think about Delilah.

Dodging passersby, he wove his way toward Chancery Lane and arrived twenty minutes after the appointed time at the offices of Higgins and Finch. Until he spotted the discreet brass plate with their names inscribed, he had been convinced he'd come to the wrong place. The entrance to the tall building was fronted by marble pillars supporting an elegant portico. The gleaming windows and polished oak doors could as well have graced a duke's town house.

These were, he realized, very expensive attorneys. They would mow him down like a weed.

He felt surprisingly nervous, considering that the hard part was over and done with. He had—well, *she* had addressed the subject of divorce and had given her consent. Or something of the kind. She did not intend to oppose him, at any rate, which was as it should be. At the end of the day, he was doing this entirely for her sake. And if her attorneys plucked him for everything he owned, she would acquire only his clothing, an unreliable pocket watch, and the black pearl stickpin his mother had given him on his eighteenth birthday.

A businesslike young clerk greeted him at the door and summoned Mr. Josiah Higgins, who turned out to be a thin and blessedly unremarkable man of middle age. His pale blue eyes appeared overlarge behind the thick gold-rimmed spectacles perched on his nose. "You are most welcome, my lord," he said politely. "Will you follow me, please?"

" 'I have no superfluous leisure,' " Dragoner replied, " 'but I will attend you a while.' "

Looking confused, Higgins turned and led him up a side staircase and down a long passageway. The murmur of voices told Dragoner that business was being conducted behind the many doors they went by. When they reached the end of the passageway, he was ushered into a large conference room furnished with an enormous rectangular table and a dozen highbacked, intricately carved wooden chairs, putting him in mind of a Medici dining room he had once seen in a Florentine palace.

His soon-to-be-former wife, seated alone at the far end of the table, glanced over at him with a faint smile on her lips. He almost failed to recognize her. She had done something different with her hair, which was twisted into a braided crown on top of her head. He preferred it down around her shoulders, the way it had been two days ago, and profoundly disliked her plain, mud-colored dress with its high stiff collar and long, fitted sleeves.

She had made an attempt to look her age, he supposed. To little avail.

Higgins directed him to the chair directly across from Delilah and then sat to her right, leaving the chair at the head of the table empty. There was a folder for each of them, along with an especially thick one for the vacant chair, and a supply of pens and ink pots within easy reach.

"Are we waiting for someone?" Dragoner asked. "I have several other appointments this afternoon."

"Then by all means," said Delilah, "let us proceed. I thought it advisable, sir, to begin with a comprehensive review of your financial situation. But as your time is limited, perhaps Mr. Higgins will confine himself to a brief overview."

"It could scarcely be other than brief," Dragoner said, "since I am devoid of finances, situational or otherwise. Or does he mean to list the debts you have accumulated in my absence? I cannot pay them, you know."

She folded her hands on the table. "Mr. Higgins?"

"There are no debts, Lord Dragoner. Quite to the contrary." The solicitor opened his folder and adjusted his spectacles. "I suggest you take a few moments to examine the first two pages of my report, where I have listed your primary assets and investments along with their current value. Then I shall be glad to answer any questions you may have."

Assets? *Investments?* What the devil was there to invest? He knew about the house on the river, which Delilah had bought with the proceeds from the sale of his town house. But if there had been money left over, she would certainly have required it for living expenses.

He opened the Moroccan leather cover and scanned the neatly inscribed page with its record of mystifying purchases followed by numbers. Very *large* numbers. His hand was shaking when he moved the first sheet aside to read the second page. By the time he reached the figure at the very bottom, the sum total of the numbers that had gone before, his heart was thumping like a battle drum.

"I don't understand," he said. "That is, I see what's been done. But how did it all get started? Where the deuce did you come by the money to"—he flipped back to the first page—"to buy a *ship*?"

"Only part of a ship," Delilah corrected. "You are one of three partners. And although it is not listed in the summary account, the company has recently purchased a second vessel, which is currently in drydock for refitting."

"The money came from your family, then."

"In a manner of speaking. The early investments were funded from the marriage settlement, which was, of course, paid by my father."

"But my parents—"

"You have been under the misapprehension, sir, that they took with them all that was to be had. That is not the case. But Mr. Higgins can better explain than I, since he negotiated the contract."

"The settlement," Mr. Higgins said, "being exceptionally generous, was naturally tied up in every way possible to benefit you and Lady Dragoner. It was a rather tidy piece of work, I am pleased to say, with a great many clauses and subclauses. Any one of them—nay, virtually all of them—would have been detected and overturned by a reasonably competent solicitor. But the previous Lord and Lady Dragoner employed a man of little skill and no apparent intelligence. If he read the contract at all, I should be very much surprised."

His parents certainly wouldn't have bothered, Dragoner thought, no more than he had troubled to read Delilah's letters. But surely they would have noticed that the bank draft they made off with fell far short of the sum they had been expecting. He said so to Higgins, who returned a polite shrug.

"That was my father's doing," Delilah said. "After providing Lord Dragoner with a draft for two thousand pounds, he offered a letter of credit to his bank in Geneva for the remainder of the settlement, which he said would fluctuate slightly with currency exchanges and the like. Lord Dragoner never questioned the value of that letter until he arrived in Geneva and presented it."

"And it was worth precisely nothing?"

"Ten pounds, more or less. There was quite a scene at the bank, we were later informed, and my father received a fairly vitriolic letter from your father, to which he replied with a letter of explanation and a copy of the marriage contract. After that, we heard nothing more."

"I see." He had been born into a pack of rats and married, it seemed, into a nest of scorpions. Dragoner suppressed an acute impulse to laugh. His devious little wife had made him a wealthy man. Clever girl. But he had no intention of remaining shackled to her, even with chains of gold.

The solicitor continued speaking, his voice like the drone of bees, until Delilah put a hand on his arm. "I believe Lord Dragoner would prefer to examine the documents at a later time," she said gently. "Perhaps you should ask Mr. Finch to join us now."

When Higgins was gone, Dragoner raised his eyes to look directly at her. "I am impressed," he said. "Which you intended me to be. But it makes no difference."

"I didn't expect that it would. But I thought you ought to know."

"And now I do. Nevertheless, the money is entirely immaterial. You will keep it all, of course, and buy more ships and houses. Whatever takes your fancy. Write the divorce contract to suit yourself, with as many clauses and subclauses as your solicitors can devise. I mean to take no more from this marriage than I brought to it."

Her expression remained serene. "Your generosity is noted, sir, but the courts would never permit a settlement so greatly in my favor. To propose such an arrangement would imply collusion, which is a primary obstacle to securing a divorce. An outraged husband does not turn over his entire fortune to a cast-off wife."

"But I'm not in the least outraged," he pointed out.

"Well, if you wish to be shed of me, sir, you will have to pretend to be." She glanced over at the door. "But here is Mr. Finch. I'm sure he will explain everything to your satisfaction."

Finch, tall, obese, and bald as an egg, made his way ponderously to the head of the table and lowered himself onto the chair with a grunt. His several chins jiggled like aspic. "You will forgive me, my lord, for keeping you waiting. Bad fish for lunch. Bad fish. But let us get to it. My associate informs me that you are not represented by a solicitor. I advise you to secure one. Indeed, I shall provide you a list of my most formidable rivals, should this matter proceed beyond today's conference. I cannot imagine that it will."

Dragoner wrenched his gaze from the bizarre solicitor to his wife's tranquil face. "You have changed your mind, then? You mean to fight the divorce?"

"Not at all," she replied. "There is no need."

"And what the devil does *that* mean?" He looked down with surprise at his fist, which had just pounded itself on the table.

"I suspect," Finch said, "that Lady Dragoner has jumped one or two steps ahead of where we ought to be." He gave her a fatherly smile before turning back to Dragoner, his small eyes like lumps of amber set in a mound of rising bread. "Shall we begin at the beginning, my lord? I am told that you have spent very little time in England, and may therefore be unfamiliar with the present state of the law regarding dissolution of a marriage. Lady Dragoner believes you will find it helpful if I begin by reviewing the conditions required to sue for divorce and the procedures that must necessarily follow."

"Fine." Dragoner leaned back and folded his arms. "But I don't want to hear a lot of legal blather. We have already agreed to seek a divorce. Skip the details and tell me how to go about it."

"The devil is in the details, naturally, but we needn't consider them now. You are, I understand, concerned with securing a full divorce, one that permits the both of you to remarry?"

"Certainly." Was there any other kind?

"In that case, I shall limit myself to the pertinent requirements." Finch settled back on his chair, hands clasped over his bulging stomach. "It will first be necessary to secure from the ecclesiastical courts a writ of judicial separation. If uncontested, the procedure is generally completed within six months. You have agreed on the grounds for such a separation?"

"We haven't discussed specifics," Dragoner said. "Would desertion suffice? Until two days ago, I had not seen my wife for six years."

"Any number of soldiers could say the same thing," Finch observed. He had taken up his pen and begun to pick his teeth with it. "We must also rule out extreme cruelty—meaning a clear threat to life itself—which leaves us with the only practical alternative. Adultery."

Familiar ground, Dragoner thought with some relief. "Then by all means, adultery. That's simple enough. I readily admit to it."

"But you, my lord, would unavoidably be the plaintiff. It is the *wife's* adultery that must be proven."

Dragoner's gaze shot to Delilah. "That's preposterous. Why can't she sue me? She damn well ought to. I'll provide all the evidence and witnesses she needs."

"But who would listen to them?" Finch inquired. "No court in England, I assure you. Oh, it's true that an adulterous husband is not permitted to sue his wife on grounds of adultery, but that condition is observed only in theory. In practice, save for cases of incest, the courts have tended to disregard evidence of a husband's infidelity. It seems rather to be expected that he will stray."

"Good God." Dragoner splayed his hands on the table. "Where's the justice in that?"

"There is very little justice, I'm afraid, in the divorce laws as they stand. Perhaps one day you will speak in the Lords on behalf of reform. But in the meantime, I fear, you must deal with current procedures. Shall I continue to advise you of them?"

Dragoner longed to plant a fist into Finch's doughy face. "Go ahead," he said between his teeth, suspecting that the news was about to get even worse.

With alarming speed, it did.

"Assuming that you have proven Lady Dragoner an adulteress," Finch said, "and received a judicial separation from bed and board, the next step involves a civil action against her lover for criminal conversation. The proceedings now move to King's Bench, where a jury hears testimony from both sides before awarding appropriate damages to the offended husband."

"Let us be clear, Mr. Finch. The law be damned, *I* am the offender. I want no damages, and I've no intention of profiting from a debacle of my own making."

"Nonetheless, your case for a divorce is improved if you receive a large settlement from the co-respondent. Indeed, until you have been successful in a common law action, your application will not be considered by Parliament."

"Parliament? What in blazes has *Parliament* to do with it?"

"Why, everything, my lord. Only a bill of divorcement, passed into law by both houses, secures absolute dissolution of a marriage. As you might imagine, it is a long, arduous, and expensive procedure. I would estimate that in the last century, no more than sixty or seventy divorces have been granted."

This had to be a nightmare. Dragoner, his brain whirling, tried to order his thoughts. "In France," he said, "divorces are easily come by. Or relatively so. I made a small study of it."

"Yes, indeed," Finch said. "I, too, have examined the civil procedures in France and quite approve of them. But they are nothing to the point. Our own countrymen—the ones that make the laws, at any rate—fear the revolutionary spirit that lost the American colonies and toppled the French aristocracy. In response, they have dedicated themselves to preserving the status quo. You must resign yourself, my lord, to the present state of British law."

"I see." Or rather, he didn't want to hear any more. Teeth grinding with his frustration, Dragoner turned to his wife. "Are you agreeable to a private conversation, madam, without your solicitors to advise you?"

"If you like." She smiled at Higgins and patted Finch's pudgy hand. "Thank you both. We shall send for you if Lord Dragoner has further business to discuss."

When the door closed behind them, Dragoner erupted from his chair and made a complete circuit of the table. "You might have told me," he said as he passed behind Delilah.

"But would you have believed me?" she asked reasonably.

"I don't know. Probably not." He came to where he'd started and put his hands on the back of his chair. "The laws are barbaric. I had no idea. When I asked for a divorce, I never imagined what it would entail."

"I quite understand. You presumed it would be as it is in France. And if you had in mind to ask, let me assure you that we cannot obtain a divorce by applying there. Naturally, you are free to verify that."

"I will," he lied, knowing it would be a waste of time.

Delilah Dragoner, he had come to realize, could probably teach her solicitors a few things about the law. What a remarkable woman she was. He could not help but admire her. To be perfectly honest, he was more than a little in awe of her. Which changed nothing, of course. He still intended to make her free of him. And an idea—a pernicious and humiliating idea—had popped into his head.

"I don't suppose," he said, "that you . . . I mean—" His voice cracked, as it hadn't done since he was thirteen years old.

"That I am an adulteress?" she finished brightly. "I'm afraid not. Would it make a difference?"

His hands dropped to his sides. "No. That wasn't what I meant to ask you. But since a divorce appears to be out of the question, I only wondered if we might seek an annulment." There. He'd said it.

She looked as if she had been expecting the suggestion. "On what grounds?" she asked unhelpfully.

She knew bloody well what he meant. He could see it in her eyes. But she was going to make *him* say it. "Failure to consummate the marriage," he blurted, fairly sure his hair had gone on fire from embarrassment. "We did, of course, in a perfunctory sort of way. But I was sotted before, during, and after. Any number of witnesses could testify to that. Well, excepting for the extremely short time we were alone together. Would you mind telling whatever court hears pleas for nullity that my husbandly duty was left undone?"

By the end of the speech, perspiration was streaming into his collar. "I know you do not wish to lie in a court of law," he added in a muffled voice. "You have already told me so. And before today, it never occurred to me that it might be necessary. But what other choice is left to us?"

She brought her clasped hands to her chin. "Although I have a profound distaste for lies," she said finally, "I expect that I am capable of dishonesty. But in this case, nothing would be accomplished by it. Failure to consummate the marriage, sir, is immaterial. What must be demonstrated is your *inability* to do so—then, and now, and in the future. I'm not quite sure how that is proven, of course."

"Well, I'm damned if I'll *testify* to it!" For that matter, a score of Frenchwomen could accurately swear that he was more than capable, thank you very much. After a long silence, he dropped onto his chair. "What are we to do, then? You seem to have all the answers. Is there no way out of this quagmire?"

Had he not been watching her so closely, he would have missed the small, traitorous break in her composure. A tinge of color rose to her cheeks, and her folded hands tightened, showing white at the knuckles. But she continued to regard him with those calm, pellucid eyes that saw, he was very much afraid, far more than he wished to reveal.

"There might be," she said quietly. "A private separation is not out of the question, although it would leave neither of us free to marry again."

"I've no intention of doing so," he said immediately. "And as matters stand, we couldn't anyway. Right? So what are the advantages?"

"They are primarily concerned with finances, and Mr. Finch has outlined them for you in detail." She pointed to the folder. "Pay special attention to the provisions concerning any child I might bear in the future. Unless you can prove otherwise, it will be regarded as yours. A son would inherit your title and property."

The thought of Delilah carrying another man's child was startlingly repellent. But he could scarcely object. She deserved children, if she wanted them. In fact, he wouldn't mind giving her—

He shut off the idea before it took hold of him. No sane man imagined making love to a wife he was trying to be rid of. "So be it, then," he said, electing the less satisfactory role of martyr. "I am willing to acknowledge any heir you chance to produce."

"That is most kind, sir, but may come a time when you feel differently. In any case, the situation is unlikely to arise."

She had gone pale, he saw. After a moment she rose and crossed to the window directly behind him, putting herself beyond his scrutiny unless he stood as well and turned to face her. He decided to stay where he was.

"Even a divorce might be secured," she said. "Not without considerable difficulty, to be sure, and it would require some quite illegal maneuvering on both our parts. At the present time,

I do not consider it an option. And even a private separation, should you desire one, cannot be obtained unless I choose to cooperate."

He recognized the sound of a gauntlet hitting the floor. She wanted something from him. And because she could not bring herself to look him in the eyes when she told him what it was, he knew that he wasn't going to like it. Unless she wanted a child. He was perfectly willing to bed her again, if only to get it right this time. Several times. As many times as she wished.

He wiped his forehead with his sleeve. The room had gone devilish hot of a sudden, and he was having difficulty drawing breath. Pride brought him to his feet and carried him to where she was standing, arms at her sides, waiting for him. She had known that he would answer her summons.

It made him angry, her quiet self-confidence and the fact that he'd gone to her like a compliant spaniel. "I take it," he said coldly, "that there is a price for your cooperation. But as you have ruled out a divorce, and because I see little to be gained by the alternative, I can think of no reason to pay it."

She smiled. Or her lips did. Her eyes were somber and touchingly resigned. "Then I expect we have nothing more to say to each other, sir. It seems we are to go on as we have done. But I encourage you to employ a solicitor and keep open the lines of communication between us, if only so that you can draw upon the money that is legally yours. And you may wish to withdraw my power of attorney. The actions I have taken on your behalf appear to disturb you. Naturally I hope you will not leave me destitute, and you may be sure that I shall enforce the terms of our marriage contract to make certain that you do not."

He caught up with her just before she reached the door, unsure why he had followed her, or why he was unwilling to let her go without knowing what she'd had in mind. "What were you going to ask of me?" he asked more harshly than he intended.

She turned, her brows lifted in surprise. "Only that you come to Sunday dinner with my family. Well, perhaps a little more than that," she confessed with another smile that failed to reach her eyes. "But I meant to see you well fed beforehand."

"What time on Sunday?" he heard himself ask. Some daemon must have taken possession of him. He didn't want to spend a single instant with Delilah's family. Not unnaturally, they held him in contempt.

"Oh, two o'clock or thereabouts. Unless you wish to come to church with us. Services are at eleven."

"Two o'clock then," said the daemon. "Maybe. I'm not making any promises."

This time, Delilah's smile was genuine. "Just as well that you don't, sir. Thus far, you haven't kept to the ones you already made."

Chapter 4

"Breaking his oath and resolution like a twist of rotten silk."

Coriolanus
Act 5, Scene 6

On his way to the Bening house and what portended to be a gruesome afternoon, Dragoner found himself thinking about his wedding night.

What little of it he could remember, at any rate. Images flickered across his mind—a large room at an hotel and a painting of a pheasant over the mantelpiece. A brace of candles on a table, their mellow light failing to reach the bed. A mound in the center of it, and masses of hair on a pillow.

Sometime later—he could not recall how he arrived there—he was naked in the bed. Had he spoken? Had she? A silken night rail, and his hands raising it to her waist. A faint scent of lilacs. Soft flesh and a muffled cry.

He awoke in another room, wearing his breeches and nothing else. There was an empty bottle of brandy on the floor next to his hand, and rain spat against the windowpanes. He raised the casement and cast up his accounts on the street below.

Head pounding, he had pulled on the rest of his clothes, which were scattered about him on the floor, and made his way home through the rain, where he fell into bed and slept the day away. Late that afternoon, a servant arrived with a bank draft for three thousand pounds and a note from Mr. Bening. His daughter would be staying with her family, it said, until her husband sent for her.

He had no intention of sending for her, of course. The next

morning he presented himself at Horse Guards, and within the week he was aboard the HMS *Conqueror*, bound for Mondego Bay and Lieutenant-General Arthur Wellesley's expeditionary force in Portugal. From there he wrote to his father-in-law, informing him what he had done. And as he sealed the letter, he resolved to seal his mind as well from thoughts of his marriage and the stranger he had wed, bedded, and deserted.

At the time he had felt nothing but a searing anger, which he directed toward any luckless French soldier who came within reach of his sabre. The war became his passion. And when the rage finally burned out, it left him so cold that he felt nothing at all.

Later, his duties in Paris had restored a few emotions he'd have been better off without—shame, for one, and remorse. Self-disgust. But they had nothing to do with his wife, except to make it the more evident that she was well rid of him.

He still thought so. No, he was bloody well sure of it. If she knew the least thing about what he was and the sins inscribed by his name in heaven's ledger, she would put him from her mind as completely as he had put her from his own.

But he had no intention of opening his dark soul for Delilah's scrutiny, nor did he care to visit there himself. Most likely the details of his wedding night were stored in some ragged corner alongside a hundred other recollections that could not bear up to the light.

Following the directions she had given him, he made the turn from Kings-Gate Street onto an airy square rimmed with tall, attractive houses. At the center, circled by a delicate wrought-iron fence, was a park where children, laughing and squealing, romped on the grass. There was an organ grinder with a monkey fitted out in a jaunty red waistcoat and cap, a juggler tossing colorful balls in the air, and peddlers flogging apples, gingerbread, and honey cakes. Smiling people sat on benches in the park or strolled along the pavement, chatting and enjoying the sunny afternoon.

The Bening house was located at the other side of the square, an exceptionally large building in the Grecian style with two smaller houses pressed against its sides like bookends. A semicircle of marble stairs led up to a small landing and a set of carved ebony-wood doors.

He mounted the steps, dread congealing inside him, and reluctantly lifted his hand to the knocker. But before he reached it, something struck him squarely on the back.

"Sorry, sir," said a piping voice, which came from the vicinity of his waist.

A small hand reached around to open the door, and three boys pelted by him into the house, their leader holding his arms straight out with one hand cupped over the other. The boys dodged a servant coming down the passageway and veered to the right of a graceful staircase before disappearing. The servant glanced up at him, bowed, and followed the children.

Bemused, Dragoner stepped into the entrance hall and looked around. The black-and-white marble checked floor shone in the light pouring from windows in a cupola directly overhead. Niches were set in the walls on either side of the hall, some holding marble statues and others containing flower-filled vases. The house bespoke the wealth of a successful merchant and the exquisite taste of the Earl of Rayford's daughter, whom he had taken to wife.

Dragoner had forgot that he was not the first aristocrat purchased into the family by Samson Bening, who appeared to collect them like some people collected Egyptian antiquities.

He removed his hat, peeled off his gloves, and set them on a graceful marquetry table before he succumbed to an awful temptation to put them on again and take his leave. He could have done. From the sound of voices and laughter, the house was thronged with people, but not a one of them had taken note of his arrival. He heard the cry of an infant from somewhere upstairs, and male voices arguing in a room to his left. From the direction the boys had taken came a shriek.

Since he was apparently meant to barge in on his own, that struck him as the likeliest destination. He was halfway down the passageway when Delilah emerged from a noisy room near the back of the house.

She had been laughing, he could tell. The freckles on her rather pretty nose looked like a dusting of copper on a field of pale pink, and her teeth were white as salt behind lips that curved upward at the corners. She wore a simple muslin dress, wheat-colored with small puffed sleeves and ruffles at the hem. Her hair was swept back from her temples and barely contained by two tortoise-shell combs before cascading in a riot of curls down her back.

His heart skipped several beats and settled again.

When the servant he had seen earlier came out of the room as well, Dragoner assumed that Delilah had been informed of his arrival. Without pleasure he watched the open, happy expression on her face form into the calm expression he remembered from the solicitor's office.

Although he changed masks the way most people changed their smallclothes, he did not like it that Delilah had masks of her own. This time he'd caught the transformation, but knowing that she had put on a false face did not help him to see beyond it.

"I had decided you did not mean to come," she said, stopping two arms' length away and dipping a curtsy.

"I'm always late," he replied, carefully matching her tone of voice. "My pocket watch keeps time somewhat less precisely than a sundial. And, too, I decided to walk."

"Joshua found a lizard," she said. "In the park. That's what all the commotion was about, when the boys nearly trampled you. Grayson"—she gestured behind her, apparently not realizing that the servant had gone—"told me about it. Naturally the boys had to show off their lizard, but I'm afraid it has escaped. If you step upon something unexpectedly, it will be a lizard. But do come into the drawing room, sir. My mother is most anxious to reacquaint herself with you."

He had no recollection of ever meeting his wife's mother, although he supposed he must have done. She would have been at the wedding. As Delilah escorted him into a parlor the size of a ballroom, he felt like a man on his way to a firing squad.

Oddly, none of the thirty or so people clustered in small groups around islands of chairs and tables paid him much notice. He saw eyes shift in his direction, which meant they were aware of him, but all gazes swiftly turned away. The several conversations went on as if he wasn't there. Four little girls were playing with dolls in one corner, and three boys, their rumps upturned, were crawling amongst the furniture.

In search of the lizard, he supposed, following Delilah to a sofa where a beautiful woman about fifty years of age smiled up at him. He detected a dimple on her right cheek and a scatter of freckles across her nose. Her light brown hair, streaked with gold and gray, was drawn softly into a chignon at the back of her head.

He cast about in his mind for her name and found it just as he emerged from his bow. "Lady Barbara," he said with all the charm he could muster. "It was kind of you to invite me. I am honored to make your acquaintance again."

"Oh, piffle," she said, lifting her brows. "Go away, Delilah, while I have a few words with the gentleman who is about to sit here next to me."

Confronted with the horror of a private conversation with her mother, he for once had no wish to be shed of his wife. But she had already turned and was crossing to the door, so he lowered himself onto the sofa and put his hands on his knees, willing them not to shake.

"You needn't be uneasy," she said. "I told my husband to lock away all the guns."

Startled, he looked over at her. There was only kindness in her eyes, and an expression of gentle amusement on her face.

"It was rather brave of you to come here, under the circumstances. We are aware, of course, that you do not mean to stay in England. No, Delilah has said nothing. But she would have done, I am sure, if you had given her any reason to believe you wished to take up your marriage where you left it off."

Lady Barbara had no need of a gun. She fired words like bullets. "I greatly regret that I have caused her distress," he said. "It was never my intention."

"Oh, I quite understand, although most of the family will not. They haven't the sort of experience you and I have shared. We know how it is to be obliged to accept a marriage of convenience that was orchestrated solely for the convenience of others."

"Obliged? Delilah maintains that I ought to have flatly declined. I expect she is right. It would have spared everyone a great deal of trouble."

"But at the time you felt it impossible to do so, and I'm sure that it was. Save that his financial losses were not taken at the gaming tables, my father's situation was not so different from that of Lord Dragoner. It resulted from poor management of his estate and bad investments, which left him with three daughters who could not be dowered and two sons without prospects for the future. One of his children had to be sacrificed for the sake of the others, and it happened that I was the only one of marriageable age."

Why was she telling him this? "Perhaps our circumstances were similar to begin with," he acknowledged, recognizing that it was his turn to speak. "But unlike me, you accepted the obligation thrust upon you and entered your marriage with dignity and good grace."

"Oh, indeed I did not!" she said with a laugh. "When Father informed me I was to wed a man nearly twice my age, a man who engaged in *trade*, for pity's sake, I launched a tantrum that set dogs barking from London to King's Lynn. And after the wedding I spent an entire year in the mopes, nursing my grievances and mourning the demise of all my girlish dreams. I had planned to snag a handsome marquess, you see, and reign as the toast of London society. Instead, I found myself dwindling away in an unfashionable neighborhood with tradesmen's wives for company and an old stick of a man in my bed. How Samson endured my horrid behavior I cannot fathom, save that he is blessed with an infinite store of patience."

Dragoner, embarrassed at receiving these confidences, examined his hands, which had begun to maul his knees. "I believe that I am missing your point, Lady Barbara."

"Because I am circling it, or rabbiting on, as Samson would say. I am trying to tell you, and doing it badly, that I came to my marriage in much the state of mind as you came into yours. The only difference is that—being a woman—I had no choice but to stay and make the best of things."

Newly acquainted with England's marriage laws, which rendered a woman virtually powerless, he could well imagine her dismay. Only yesterday he had kept an appointment with one of the solicitors on Finch's list, a ghoul who outlined several perfectly legal methods by which Lord Dragoner might compel his wife to accept a private separation at terms favorable to himself. He was apparently permitted to beat her, strip her of all possessions save for a few necessities, and confine her in an unpleasant out-of-the-way place.

And while it was not quite legal, he could probably get away with hiring a man to be discovered with her in a compromising situation, along with witnesses to vouch at a trial that she was an adulteress. A cunning man could successfully divorce a perfectly innocent wife and leave her near to penniless, especially if he chanced to be an aristocrat and she a common merchant's daughter. Should it please Lord Dragoner, Silas Wickup would be delighted to arrange everything.

"I had thought," Lady Barbara was saying, "that Samson married me in order to nudge his way into society. I was certain that he meant to exploit my family and use me as a lever. But as the months went by, it became obvious that he had no such intention. And while he was too reticent to say so, believing I would assume it to be a middle-aged man's infatuation with a young beauty, he had fallen in love with me."

Her voice softened. "Over time I came to recognize his love by the way that he treated me, and the devotion he gave me, and by the light in his eyes when he gazed on me. And—dare I say it?—he was, and is, a wonderful lover. I cannot remember the exact moment when I realized that I was as deeply in love with my husband as he with his foolish, obstinate wife. It came upon me slowly, and grew with each passing day, and continues to grow. We have been happy together for three-and-thirty years, and all because I could not leave him before discovering what a treasure had been given me."

She laughed. "And that, my dear, is the end of my sermon. You were due to hear one, this being the Sabbath and you failing to accompany us to services. You should have done. The rector spoke on the subject of giving generously to rebuild the bell tower, which wouldn't have applied to you at all."

He released a breath he had been holding all through her speech. Her sermon. "I'm not sure that what you have said applies to any greater degree, Lady Barbara. The fact remains that

I am no fit husband for your daughter. On that you must take my word."

"Ah, but I have nothing to do with it. Beyond seizing this chance to read you a cautionary tale about missed opportunities and the possibility of a happy ending to a business badly begun, I'll not interfere in any way. Nor will my husband, nor any member of the family. Delilah is resourceful, and possibly more clever even than her father. She is also impulsive, I'm afraid, and given to flights of fancy. Why else did she marry you? But if you are determined to cast her off, I trust that in time she will come to her senses and seek elsewhere for happiness."

Wherever that hapless lizard had concealed itself, Dragoner desperately wished he could join it. "I believe, ma'am," he said, "that I would have preferred you to arm all your sons with pistols and stand me up against the garden wall."

"Don't imagine I didn't think of it. When a mother pauses outside a door and hears her child weeping, a firing squad is the least of the tortures she wishes to devise for the man who elicited those tears."

She looked toward the door. "But here is Delilah, come back to see if you are in need of rescue. Run along, young man. She will introduce you to her brothers and sisters, and their wives and husbands, and all your nieces and nephews that haven't gone down for their naps. If anyone looks terribly threatening, you may assure them that I have granted you amnesty until sundown."

I am vanquished. These haughty words of hers have battered me like roaring cannon-shot.

Bowing his leave, he was surprisingly glad to retreat in the direction of his wife. She was waiting for him across the room, gazing at her mother as if trying to read from Lady Barbara's expression what had taken place. But before he could get to Delilah, a knee-high obstacle planted itself in his path and raised two fat, fisted hands.

"Up!"

Dragoner, stopped in his tracks, looked down at a small boy with curly black hair and a mulish expression on his round face. He was clad in a blue mariner's suit with pipings of white on the square collar.

"Up, up, *up*!" shrieked the child, pounding on Dragoner's thigh with each word.

"He wants you to pick him up," Delilah said, approaching him with a suspiciously guileless smile on her face. "I advise you to do so. Otherwise he'll throw a fit, and there will be no end to it until he gets his way."

Were *all* the Benings out to terrorize him? At least this one had a limited vocabulary, if abysmal taste in his choice of companions. Bending down, he scooped the boy in his arms and endured a full minute of kicking and squirming while the fretful parcel settled himself with one hand clutching Dragoner's hair and the thumb of his other hand stuffed in his mouth. He looked reasonably content, at least for the moment.

"How long must I hold him?" Dragoner asked his grinning wife.

"Until he says 'Down' or soils his nappy, whichever comes first." The grin widened. "I hope you didn't pay too much for the coat you are wearing. This is Felix, by the way. He is two years old and a tyrant. His mother is upstairs in the nursery, feeding his younger brother, and his father is playing billiards. Perhaps when we arrive at the billiard room, you will be able to foist him off. Meantime, shall I introduce you to your other unwanted relations?"

The knife of her last sentence slipped between his ribs, where it remained while she presented him to a bewildering array of Benings. There were four brothers and three sisters, all but two of them married, along with a dozen children, a handful of aunts and uncles, and a large assortment of cousins. Their brief, stilted conversations were confined to introductions and comments about the weather or the Victory Celebrations.

He felt as if Delilah were passing him from one physician to another for an examination, and from the looks in their eyes, he had been diagnosed with rabies.

It wasn't difficult to recognize, by their stiff expressions, the two brothers who had served in the army. They knew his reputation. He wondered if they had heard the worst of the stories, and if they'd told the others.

He's a sworn rioter. His days are foul and his drink dangerous.

He wondered why he gave a rat's arse what they thought, and decided that he did not.

It seemed inappropriate to smile, even if he were capable of doing so. Contriving to look pleasantly interested, he followed Delilah from room to room and group to group. An elderly lady asked him if the fireworks had been to his liking. With no idea what she was talking about, he said that he had found them spectacular. A young man wondered if he had met Bonaparte in Paris. He hadn't. A young woman wondered if he had met Josephine. He had. He'd also attended her funeral not very long ago, but he didn't say so.

All the while, Felix drummed at various portions of his anatomy with a pair of small feet, and Dragoner shifted him higher before the boy made contact with his privates.

The party of three was on the way to the billiard room when a bell sounded near the rear of the house. "Dinner," said Delilah, drawing him up the staircase a short way as people began to emerge into the passageway. "Wait here a moment while I find someone to take Felix."

Hearing his name, Felix gave a powerful tug at Dragoner's hair. "Down!" he demanded.

"Not now," Dragoner said. He couldn't very well loose the child into a stampede. "Shall I tell you a story?"

"No!" He kicked with both feet at Dragoner's stomach. "Down!"

Just as well. Dragoner didn't know any stories. He took hold of Felix under the arms and held him so that their noses were practically touching. "Listen to me, you pestilential brat. You will do as you are told. Keep still and behave yourself. Understood?"

A pair of wide blue eyes gazed into his. Felix looked stunned. Then he giggled. "Lizard," he said clearly.

The Benings were quick to take his measure. "Yes, I am. And don't you forget it."

Dragoner gathered the laughing child into his arms again. The boy had gone as boneless as a sleeping cat. He was hugging the small body to his chest, a not unpleasant sensation, when a young maid materialized at his side.

"I'll take him now, sir," she said.

"And I am Julia," said a voice at his other side as he gave Felix to the maid. "If you hadn't come along and married my sister, I'd be known as the black sheep of the family. Thank you for sparing me that distinction. And for your sins, you are to be my dinner partner. We'd better hurry or all the good places will be taken."

Slipping her arm around his elbow, she towed him down the stairs and bullied them through the crowd. Children, protesting loudly, were being led in the opposite direction, and he saw the boy who had run past him with the lizard in his hands. He appeared to have recaptured it.

Dragoner knew how that lizard was feeling right about now. Once a Bening had hold of you, there was no escape.

Julia hauled him relentlessly through a pair of open double doors into the dining room. He saw an enormous table laid out with an embroidered tablecloth and topped with gold-edged dishes, gleaming silver, and sparkling crystal. At the head of the table, standing behind his chair, was the one man he remembered meeting at the wedding.

Samson Bening, broad-shouldered, powerfully built, and taller than his son-in-law by several inches, had a headful of thick gray hair over a face remarkably unlined for a man who must be rising seventy. He gave Dragoner an impersonal nod and returned his attention to the family streaming through the doors and taking their places.

Fearing that he would be expected to sit next to Mr. Bening, he was relieved when Julia drew him to the middle of the table and a chair next to one occupied by an elderly gentleman. "That's Uncle Barnabas," she said. "He's deaf in his right ear, so you won't have to talk to him. We all sit wherever we like, you see, except for Mama and Papa."

When everyone was gathered, a hush fell over the room.

"Dearest Lord," Mr. Bening said, "we thank You for bringing us together in good health and joy of heart as we celebrate Your holy day."

Looking around, Dragoner realized he was the only one who had not bowed his head. He quickly lowered it, fixing his gaze on his soup bowl.

"We thank You for peace, and ask Your blessings on those

who have suffered in the war, especially the children. Give our leaders the wisdom to guide us safely through the difficult times ahead. For all Your kindness to our family, we humbly express our gratitude and renew our promise to share with others the bounty You have bestowed upon us. May we walk honorably through this life, guided by Your Commandments and the light of Your love. Amen."

"Amen," came the echo from thirty voices, including his. It occurred to Dragoner that the lone word, mumbled under his breath, was as close as he had ever come to praying.

A moment later everyone began to talk at once. Except for himself, of course, and Uncle Barnabas, who was busy tying his napkin around his neck. Servants, a horde of them, were pouring wine and ladling soup from tureens. Dragoner unfolded his napkin and located Delilah, who was seated next to her father. Then his gaze met a pair of hostile blue eyes directly across from him.

"That's Aunt Heppy," Julia said. "She's Delia's companion. She doesn't like you."

"I had noticed. *Delia?*"

"Most of us call her Delia. She hates her real name. And besides, the children have a hard time saying Delilah. What do *you* call her?"

He reached for his glass of wine, thought better of it, and took up his soup spoon instead.

"Well, I suppose you haven't had much chance to call her anything," Julia said, not in the least discouraged by his failure to reply. "I am the youngest sister, by the way, in case no one has mentioned me. People generally don't, if they can avoid it. I am thought to be incorruptible."

Her dark brows drew together in a frown. "No, that's not right. Incontinent? Drat. I hear it so often, you'd think I would have it by heart. Inconvenient? Well, that's close enough, I suppose, but—"

"Incorrigible?" he supplied, amused in spite of himself.

"Oh, precisely!" She beamed at him. "I just knew we'd get along. That's why I made sure to snag you so that we could sit together. Well, it's one of the reasons. The others all roll their eyes and sigh when I sit next to them at table, which is not at all conducive to amiable discourse, let alone proper digestion. I have an excellent vocabulary, don't you think? I memorize ten new words every day."

"An excellent idea," he said, "and I am delighted to be your dinner companion. Would you think me rude to inquire how old you are?"

"Ten-and-three, come September. I was at your wedding, but you probably don't remember me. And you didn't join us at the breakfast afterward. Why not?"

Sitting next to young Julia was a mixed blessing, he decided, barely stopping himself from rolling his eyes. "I don't recall," he said, pointedly applying himself to his soup. His stomach clenched, he was so tense, and he wondered if he dared eat anything.

"Jeremiah—that's my oldest brother—said you were too foxed to make an appearance. I think that means you had been drinking spirits, but no one explains anything to me. What has drinking spirits to do with a fox? Anyway, I was vastly disappointed. You were quite the handsomest man I had ever seen, and I wanted to see you again. You still are, actually, the handsomest, not that I am permitted to see very many men. Almost none who are not related to me, in fact. But I quite understand why Delia fell in love with you."

"Do you?" Cold sweat was gathering under his collar. Love. Ha! Delia—Delilah—might well have been infatuated. But *love*? No. He refused to consider the possibility. How could she have fallen in love with a scoundrel she had seen, by her own admission, only at a distance? Young females must have decidedly odd notions about the business. Not that he knew the least thing about it either, but then, he had never imagined himself in love with anyone.

"Certainly," Julia declared. "I have remarkable insight and unfailing instincts." Somehow, despite the fact she never seemed to stop talking, she had finished her soup. "Everyone else thought she wanted you because you would be a viscount—and sure enough, now you are—but I knew the moment I saw you that she wanted you because you are beautiful. And lonely. She must have seen that in your eyes, the way I did."

He blinked. "If either of you came to that conclusion, you

were mistaken," he said in a voice that sounded false even to himself. "Look, here's roast chicken."

For a short time, as the servants filled their plates with meats and vegetables, Julia kept herself busy choosing from the wide assortment of dishes offered her. He looked over at Aunt Heppy and saw the blue eyes boring into him like a miner's drill.

He should never have come here. For Delilah's sake, or more accurately, to prove he wasn't totally unfeeling, he had landed himself in a country wholly foreign to him. The natives pretended to be friendly, but nearly everyone in this room would be pleased to see him turning on a spit.

The lady seated to Julia's right kindly engaged her in conversation for several minutes, freeing him to toy with his food in silence. He stole a glance at Delilah. She was looking back at him, but her gaze quickly slid away. He thought the meal would never end.

And it did not, for the longest hour he had ever spent. Julia devoted herself to plying him with questions about London society—particularly those aspects relating to a young woman making her come-out—which he fended off as best he could. If she was angling for him to see her presented, she'd gone fishing in the wrong waters. A social outcast, even one with a title, could be of no use to her.

At last the covers were removed and an assortment of cakes, puddings, cheeses and nuts laid out. Uncle Barnabas dropped a glass of wine on his lap and was led away by a footman to change his trousers. Aunt Heppy cracked walnuts with a silver mallet, *thump thump thump*, glaring all the while at him. He knew precisely what she wanted to do with that mallet.

"They'll make me leave soon," Julia said with a pout. "Why is it that females must withdraw after dinner when some of us would much rather stay with the gentlemen? Do you think that if you were to ask Papa, he might permit me to remain?"

"I am a guest here, Julia. It would be impolite for me to make such a request."

"But you're *not* a guest. You are family. Besides, Delia gets to stay if the gentlemen are planning to discuss matters of business, so why shouldn't I?"

He was spared answering when Lady Barbara stood and

pointedly gazed at Julia as she invited the ladies to join her in the drawing room. Casting him a wounded look, Julia slumped out after the others, and Dragoner was left sitting in relative isolation at the center of the table, surrounded by empty chairs. He wished he had made the effort to keep Julia at his side.

As the butler began to serve port wine from a crystal decanter, Samson Bening abruptly came to his feet. "I beg you to excuse me, gentlemen. It's time for my Sunday cigar. Lord Dragoner, would you care to join me in the study?"

No one seemed particularly surprised when they left, which struck Dragoner as an ominous sign. Any hope he had cherished of escaping the house without a stern lecture from Delilah's father melted away as he followed Mr. Bening up the stairs and into a middle-sized room. It was fitted out with an enormous desk, a sideboard piled high with ledgers, and two wingback chairs angled in front of a fireplace with a table set between them. On it was a tooled leather box, from which Bening withdrew a pair of cigars.

When Dragoner shook his head, he put one back. "Smelly things, I know, and bad for the throat. Barbara permits me one cigar a week, but only if I take it outside. That's why I chose this room for my office. It has a balcony."

After Bening had clipped the end of his cigar and used a tinderbox to light it, they proceeded through the French windows onto a tiled balcony overlooking the kitchen garden. "You may relax, young man," he said. "I brought you here because the others expect me to have words with you, and it's best if we let them think I am doing so. But in fact I have nothing to say, although there are one or two questions I should like to ask. You are under no compulsion to answer."

"In that case, why not spare me the questions? I expect I won't like them."

"Oh, they are nothing to do with my daughter. I have no intention of being an interfering father-in-law. It was bad enough of me to support the marriage in the first place, and I have learned from my mistake. Delilah was very young when she decided that she must have you, and foolish in the matters of the heart. I ought to have put a stop to it."

He puffed on his cigar. "But she has always been able to

wrap me around her finger, you know. I could not bring myself to disappoint her, and now she must live with the consequences of a marriage that ought never to have taken place. As must you, of course."

Dragoner leaned his hips on the marble railing. "You had questions?"

"Want to change the subject, do you? Very well, then. I have been puzzled by the circumstances surrounding your capture by the French. After learning you had been taken, I went immediately to Horse Guards with the intention of posting a ransom. But the officer spoke with me in the way of—how shall I say it?—a businessman attempting to conceal an illicit transaction. No ransom was possible, I was told. Perhaps you would be exchanged for a French prisoner, and perhaps not. I was directed to make no further inquiries. Can you explain this to me?"

"Easily." By now, Dragoner had his story by rote. "I was a terrible soldier. Insolent, indolent, and drunk three-quarters of the time. They didn't want me back."

Color drained from Bening's face. "I hadn't wanted to believe it. Are you telling me the rumors I have heard concerning your behavior in Paris are to be believed?"

"Oh, yes, if they include gaming, whoring, and making a general nuisance of myself. And you will hear worse of me in future, when officers with whom I served return to England carrying tales. If it matters, I regret that my indiscretions will reflect on your family, but you were not in my thoughts at the time. And I'd have done the same in any case, I expect. My marriage began and ended the day it took place. After that, it was of no consequence to me."

"I quite understand," Bening said, chewing on the tip of his cigar. "And yet—put it down to a tradesman's instincts—something in what you say rings false. But I'll not pursue the matter. By now my daughter is waiting in the passageway, wishing to speak with you privately. Unless you have some objection?"

"None at all," Dragoner assured him, giving serious thought to taking a dive over the balcony. Compared to dealing with his in-laws and his wife, war had been a picnic and spying under Boney's nose a piece of cake.

Far too soon Delilah was standing opposite him on the balcony, serene as a Raphael Madonna. She meant to offer him a deal of some kind, he supposed, preparing himself to reject it.

"Julia wants to marry you," she said. "Of course, that will require me to turn up my toes when she comes of age. Should I oblige her, do you think?"

"Not unless you are hell-bent to punish me," he said cautiously, unable to read her mood. "Your father said that you wished to speak with me."

"Yes. But I'm finding it difficult. There is so much I want to say, and I'm sure that you don't want to hear a word of it. Already you are wondering how quickly you can make your escape."

Heat rose up his neck. "In fact, I was wondering why you thought it a good idea to troll me past your family. Have you failed to notice that they wish me to the devil?"

"Only because they imagine you have hurt me. And they are *your* family as well, sir. I wanted you to know that, and to meet them."

"I have had a family," he said darkly. "I have no wish for another."

After a moment, she released a small sigh. "It's too late, I'm afraid. For good or ill, you are one of us now. And should you come to us at any time, for any reason, you'll not be turned away."

" 'That's somewhat madly spoken'," he observed, wildly uncomfortable as her net began to enclose him. "What if I want to borrow money?"

She retreated a pace. "The Benings are canny tradesfolk, sir. You are not a good risk for a loan."

"In that case," he said, "your family will be spared my company. Tell them so. They will be greatly relieved to hear it. Was there anything else?"

For a time he thought she did not mean to answer. He leaned heavily against the balcony railing, his hands curled around the sun-warmed marble, wishing she were not standing between him and the door. He had tried to push her away with words, but she would not go. White-faced and silent, she gazed past him into the garden.

Then she appeared to brace herself. "I have two things to ask of you," she said. "I practiced how best to do it, but now I cannot remember my speech. It wasn't very good. There is no good way to say any of this. But while I am stumbling around, please, sir, just this one time . . . do not mock me."

Dear God. His fingers clamped on the railing so hard that the sharp marble edge drew blood. He could smell it, mingled with the fragrance of rosemary and lavender floating up from the garden. "No," he said when he could breathe again, his voice the barest rattle in his throat. "I won't."

A faint smile ghosted across her lips. "I'm sure you'll want to," she said. "What I am proposing will not meet with your approval. But don't refuse me immediately. While you may not think so straightaway, my plan has some merit to it. Enough for you to give it serious consideration, at any rate, and all you stand to lose by accepting it is a little of your time. Will you agree to think it over before giving me your reply?"

He nodded, smothering a rude demand that she get to the point. Although the sun was warm on his back, he had begun to shiver. Delilah with a plan scared him senseless.

Chapter 5

"Oh my dear lord, I crave no other, nor no better man."

Measure for Measure
Act 5, Scene 1

Delilah saw her husband shudder and was astonished at it.
Otherwise, although rather subdued, he appeared perfectly at ease. He continued to lean against the balcony railing, his legs stretched out and crossed at the ankles, as if he'd nothing more on his mind than enjoying the late-afternoon sunshine. The light glinted off his dark hair and snowy neckcloth. His gaze drifted to the tiles at his feet. He was enduring this encounter with little interest, she could tell, and waiting dispassionately for it to be concluded.

Her heart sank. She had paced her room all night, considering what to say to him, and now the lack of sleep had befuddled her brain. Still, there was nothing for it but to plunge ahead and trust she would land safely.

"However much you may regret it," she said, "the fact remains, sir, that we are married. And we shall continue to be until death do us part. Unless, that is, we join in a conspiracy to obtain a divorce."

He looked up, his eyes suddenly alight. "Is that possible? You mentioned something of the sort at the solicitor's office, but I didn't think you were serious."

"The rest of my life is at stake, sir. You may be sure I take everything that happens between us quite seriously. That includes the vows I made you on our wedding day, of course, which makes what I will say next all the more difficult for me. Our chances of securing a divorce are slim—you should know that from the outset—but I am willing to do whatever I must to help you."

She took a deep breath. "Naturally, I expect something in return. Well, to be more precise, in *advance*."

He looked alarmed, which she had expected, but keeping to his word, he made none of the sarcastic comments that must be burning on his tongue. This was difficult for him, too, she had to remember. He had no love for her. None of the desperate hope that fired her to continue.

"I cannot blame you in the least," she said, "for leaving me when you did. Oh, I blamed you at first, to be sure, but now you have explained that you were coerced by your parents, and told me how they betrayed you. But that is the trouble, don't you see? Until a few days ago, we had never even spoken to each other. We made a contract for life without the slightest regard to the consequences. I believe, sir, that our marriage ought not to be cast aside as carelessly as we entered it."

"But I thought you had set your cap for me," he said, confusion in his tone. "You told me so. I thought you wanted the marriage."

"I did. I still do. At the least, I want us both to give it a chance to succeed. And that is what I am proposing to you, sir. One year is all I ask. One year of living together and making a genuine effort to discover if we wish to remain together, or if we would do better to agree to a private separation. If you insist, a divorce. Either way I promise to cooperate, so long as you first grant me this little space of time to find out which of us has been mistaken—me for wanting you, or you for not wanting me."

His eyes, a cloudy gray, met hers directly. "That's not how it is, Delilah. It has never been a question of whether or not you would be a good wife. It all comes down to the inescapable fact that I would be a terrible husband. You needn't waste a year finding that out for yourself."

"But as things are, what have I to lose? And if we are to speak honestly, I believe that you can spare a few months right now. The war is ended, and you are no longer a prisoner. If you are unwilling to return to England, then I shall gladly join you in France or wherever else you wish to go."

Hot with embarrassment, she clasped her hands together and looked down at them. "I don't mean that you must take me to your bed, sir, if it displeases you. That would not be part of our agreement. We can live together as friends, or as two people who might become friends—"

When her voice broke on the last word, she gave up trying to explain herself. By this time, surely he understood her intentions. Her original speech, the one she had prepared and forgot, had made mention of her desire for children and his need of an heir. But at the end, she could not bring herself to weave a child into their tangled relationship.

"Will you consider what I have said?" she asked.

His expression was somber. "Yes," he said at length. "I shall consider it, and write you when I have come to a decision."

She did not think he was lying. "There is one thing more, sir. I believe that while you are in England, you ought to pay a visit to Dragon's Hill."

"I should like that, of course, but it won't be possible. I've pressing business that requires my immediate return to Paris. Passage has already been secured. I leave tomorrow for Dover and sail on Tuesday's tide."

"That is unfortunate," she said, tucking a loose strand of hair behind her ear. "Did you not tell me that you consented to the marriage in great part because your father had promised to restore the estate? You paid a high price for Dragon's Hill, my lord. I think you should see what you got in exchange for your freedom."

Lines had formed at the corners of his mouth. He was looking past her, at the open French windows. "I cannot," he said.

"Well, then, perhaps another time," she said briskly. He hadn't moved, but she knew he would not be held here a moment longer. "I expect you do not wish to run the gauntlet on your way out, sir. A footman is waiting in the passageway with your hat and gloves. He will take you down the back stairs, and there is a hackney just around the corner. Please dismiss the driver if you decide to walk instead."

Relief swept over his face. "Thank you," he said, waiting

until she had gone into the study before leaving his position by the railing to follow her. "Will you give my regards to your parents and convey my appreciation for their hospitality?"

It was chilling to watch him preserve a careful distance as they came to the door, his hands clasped firmly behind his back. He did not mean to touch her. He was making sure that he would not.

"Have you a message for Julia?" she asked, unable to bear that he would go without one small gesture to bridge the chasm he had opened.

· He paused, his hand on the latch, and turned to smile at her. A real smile, this time, with a glint of genuine humor in his eyes. "Tell Miss Julia that she terrifies me," he said. "Or, no, perhaps you had better not, although it's quite true. Tell her that I enjoyed her company at dinner, and make up whatever sort of compliment she would most like to hear. Oh, and you might point out that a widower is not permitted to marry his sister-in-law. I should not like to hear that she has fed you poison to get to me."

For all the ache in her heart that he was leaving with nothing settled between them, she could not help but smile back. "I hadn't thought of that. Besides, I suspect that Julia will hold out for an earl or a marquess. Until she met you, a mere viscount was far beneath her notice."

His face grew solemn again. "I *will* think on what you said, Delilah. But don't hope for too much from me. I have very little to offer, you know, however much I wish it were otherwise. At the very least, any letter you send me will be read, and I shall reply to it. More than that I cannot promise."

And then he was gone, down the passageway in company with the footman, and only God knew when she would see him again.

Brushing a vagrant tear from her cheek, she wandered back to the balcony and lifted her head to the sky. The breeze had picked up, stirring her skirts, and clouds were scudding in from the west, casting shadows over the garden. She was glad she had thought to hire a hackney for Charl . . . for Dragoner. It would rain soon. Within the hour. Why couldn't she bring herself to think of him by his first name?

He called her Delilah. She wished he would call her Delia. But then, she wished for a great many things he was unwilling to give her.

He had been kind, though, this afternoon. Felix had liked him, and Felix had never before allowed a stranger to touch him. Why he had been drawn to Dragoner, why he had wanted to be held by him, was a mystery. Julia, of course, was attracted to him because he was a handsome aristocrat. No mystery there.

From her position across the table and at the other end of it, Delilah had watched the two of them with considerable amusement. If only she were as flagrantly open about her feelings as her sister, who had no fear of rejection. It never occurred to Julia that she could not have whatever she wanted. But then, Delilah had once felt much the same about her own prospects, until Dragoner taught her otherwise.

Her gaze lowered to the balcony railing, where she saw two rust red stains blotting the white marble. They were about two feet apart, defining the place where Dragoner had stood. She moved closer and touched one of them. It was still damp. When she brought her fingertip to her nose, she smelled the coppery scent of blood.

Dear Lord. She ran her fingers across the sharp edge of the railing. She remembered how he had clung to it, and not let her see his hands after he let it go.

What she had taken for unruffled composure had been restrained anger, she was now certain, held in check by a ferocious act of will. What else could it signify, this evidence of self-inflicted pain?

With her handkerchief, she wiped away the traces of blood as best she could. The rain would take care of the rest. Then, reflectively, she made her way up the servants' stairs to her bedchamber.

Heppy had got there before her and was ensconced on the carved wooden chest at the foot of the bed, her arms folded and a militant gleam in her eyes. "I take it he's gone," she said in a withering tone. "And to the devil, unless I am very much mistaken."

"To Dover," Delilah said, sinking onto the chair in front of her dressing table. "And from there, back to Paris. You'll not be able to scratch out his eyes any time soon."

"Then it was all a waste, bringing him here. I told you nothing good would come of it."

"He met the family, and there were no explosions. That must count for something. And really, he conducted himself well, don't you think?"

"Pah! The boy has proper manners, that is all. I was watching him. He looked like a harried fox."

"I expect he felt like one." Delilah gazed at her reflection in the mirror. Freckles splotched her pale cheeks beneath eyes glazed over with uncertainty. Dragoner the fox. And she looked for all the world like a benumbed rabbit. If nothing else, the two of them could help stock a menagerie.

"It cannot have been pleasant for him," she said, "being introduced to our decidedly odd family and aware all the while of what they must be thinking. I was watching him, too, you know. It was my distinct impression that underneath his considerable social polish, he is really rather shy."

Heppy launched herself off the cedar chest and stalked over to the dressing table. "That was *guilt* you saw, my girl, plain and simple guilt. You brought him face-to-face with two score of people who have reason to loathe him. How did you expect him to react? Well, I'll tell you. Just as he did. Was it your intention to punish him? I wish it were so. He deserves to be punished."

She began to remove the combs from Delilah's hair. "The fact is, you have no idea what you meant to accomplish. You are merely scurrying about, trying one thing after another, hoping he'll stumble into one of your traps and stay there. What I cannot fathom is why you want to keep him."

"I'm not sure that I do," Delilah said after a while. Heppy had taken up the silver-backed brush and begun to stroke it through her tangled hair. It felt so very good, to be touched with gentle hands.

And that, she realized of a sudden, was at the center of her turmoil. She had never before added it to her calculations. And when she did, her uncertainty multiplied a thousandfold.

She ached to be touched by other hands. *His* hands. Her

body, which lay every night alone between cold sheets, was starved for passion. She had never experienced it, not in any meaningful way, but she knew what it was from lacking it. She had felt the longing, and the emptiness inside her, and the gnawing of pure female desire that would not let her sleep.

Her mind, so good with numbers, so practical, was of little use to her when her flesh made unreasonable demands of its own. And there was another factor as well, the most demanding of them all. What if she loved him?

In a general sort of way, she had always assumed that she did. Why else would she jump through all the hoops it had required to tie herself to him in marriage?

But how could she love a man she scarcely knew? She had devoted a half-dozen years of her life to a man who had not, during all that time, given a single thought to her.

Heppy must be right. She ought to let go of him. Stop playing Patient Griselda, the simple country lass in Chaucer's story who endured every sort of abuse from the aristocrat she had wed.

And yet . . . And yet . . .

"Why do you hate him so?" she asked.

"Because he has hurt you, of course. Because he is selfish and wanton and without honor."

"We cannot be sure of that. Of all the people involved in bringing about this marriage, he was the least responsible. He entered it for what seemed good reasons at the time. But yes, he has behaved badly ever since. I cannot deny that. Perhaps it means I have wholly mistaken his character. He may be exactly what you think he is."

She turned on her chair to look directly into Heppy's eyes. "You should know that I have asked him to spend a year in my company. It's by way of an experiment, I suppose, a chance to become better acquainted and discover if there is anything to be salvaged from the wreck we have made of our marriage. He has promised to consider my proposal."

"Oh, my dear," Heppy said mournfully. "Consider? But he has gone off to France again. You needn't hope he will agree to anything now. Out of sight, out of mind. Mark my words, he will resume his old life, whatever it was. Without you there to prod him, he has no incentive to change it."

No incentive. Delilah's heart gave a lurch. Could she provide one? Did she dare?

"I need to think," she said. "Will you make my excuses to Mama and Papa? And Lord Dragoner's as well. He asked me to give his apology for leaving without thanking them. I helped him to sneak away, Heppy. It was all my idea, so don't blame him for seizing the opportunity."

"Humph!" was the only reply.

"One more thing," Delilah persisted. "If I were to do something you didn't approve of, something altogether mad, would you stand with me?"

"Oh, I expect I'd have to. You cannot be let to run wild on your own."

Chapter 6

". . . we are high-proof melancholy and would fain have
it beaten away."

Much Ado About Nothing
Act 5, Scene 1

"The duke won't like it," Edoard said, opening the portmanteau he had finished packing only an hour earlier. "He's returned to the Continent, or so I hear. When he sends for you, what am I to tell him?"

"You're a clever chap. Make something up." Dragoner emptied the tankard he had procured from the taproom before coming upstairs. "Now if you have no further objections, may we get on with it? I'll wear the buckskin breeches and the blue riding coat. For the rest, select only what will fit in a saddlepack."

"I know my job, thank you, your lordship. And you don't have a saddlepack. Or when it comes to that, a horse to put it on."

Which was undeniably true, and neither would be easy to come by of a Sunday evening. He meant to try, though. Sleep was out of the question, and if he set off tonight, he would be well out of the city before Monday traffic clogged the roads. "I'll leave enough money to get you from Calais to Paris," he said. "The rest is paid for, and I expect you can sell my berth on the packet."

"You'll have the devil of a time getting another, I warrant. Half the nobs in England are queued up in Dover to cross the Channel."

"So you have said." Dragoner brushed back the swath of hair that had elected, since he was a child, to droop over his forehead. Keeping it in place had been an ongoing battle, rather like this one with his valet.

Relenting, he unpeeled several banknotes and laid them on a table. "I expect to follow within a few days, Eddie. But if I am held up, go about your usual business. Your reports are far more valuable to Wellington than mine."

Edoard gave him a genial grin. "Now don't start turning up sweet on me, your lordship. Makes me nervous. As for the duke, I heard he is making for Brussels, not Paris, but the gossip didn't run to why he'd be going there or how long he'll stay. I suspect he won't be missing you right away."

"I am relieved to hear it." Dragoner, aware how little time and thought the Duke of Wellington spared for his meager efforts, grinned back. "Use the bed tonight instead of the cot, and stack the things you have gathered for me by the door. It may be late when I return to collect them."

A few minutes later, dressed for riding, Dragoner sought the advice of the innkeeper and was directed to a nearby stable. It had no horses available for hire—the pestilential Victory Celebrations again—but an ostler sent him to another stable where his luck was equally bad. It wasn't until the fifth stable that he acquired a mount and a saddlepack, and it was rising dawn before he rode out of London. Edoard, snoring like a drunken sailor, had not awakened when he went to retrieve his gear.

Dragoner spent the next night in a barn, reserving his diminishing supply of money for when it would most be needed. While the opportunity was at hand, he ought to have applied to Delilah for a loan, or being denied, asked instead for a portion of the fortune she had accumulated on his behalf.

It amused him to think of demanding money from her. If ever he should sink that low, perhaps someone would have the kindness to shoot him.

In any case, he didn't expect to be long in England. Another few days at the most, to inspect his estate because Delilah had asked him to, at which time he could depart with his conscience clear and the satisfaction of having proven himself a cooperative sort of fellow.

Well, cooperative within reason. There was nothing remotely reasonable about her other request.

She wanted him for a year, of all things. A *year*! With her. Living with her. Bedding her, or not bedding her—his choice. What kind of a rackety offer was *that*?

But he had promised to consider it. And he would, when his service with Wellington had come to an end. There was no point whatever taking a decision until free to act upon it. Stood to reason. Why twist himself into knots debating the goods and the bads and the wherewithals when he could nicely put it off for another few months?

He crossed at last into Berkshire, and about then it dawned on him that he ought to have asked Delilah for directions.

He had been born at Dragon's Hill, named for the nearby spot where, in legend, St. George had made a name for himself. But the family took to the road when he was five, driven from England by his father's creditors, and Dragon's Hill had been leased to a succession of tenants with the rent money applied to outstanding debts. Perhaps they had been paid off by now. He didn't know for sure.

When his father thought it safe to return to England, they never came to Dragon's Hill. There were no gaming hells in Berkshire. And only two years passed before Lord Dragoner was again neck-deep in River Tick, at which point he sold his son for the money to go traveling again.

This time his parents left him behind, and he was in Paris when news came, months after the coach accident, that they were dead. It never crossed his mind to mourn for them. Instead, in every way the Dragon's son, he promptly set about taking advantage of his new status.

The lowly Captain Dragoner, with no cachet in French society, had been forced to scrounge in the stews of Paris for the information Wellington required of him. But Captain *Lord* Dragoner, however undeserving in the general way of things, was otherwise presentable and soon found that doors previously closed to him were swinging open. Excepting only the entertainments provided by the emperor himself, he was welcomed everywhere.

In no other way was the title of significance to him, and he had never given the slightest thought to passing it on. When he hopped his twig, a distant relation would inherit, or perhaps it would revert to the Crown. He told himself that he was entirely indifferent to the matter, and for the most part, it was quite true. He really *didn't* care, except, perhaps, about Dragon's Hill.

Some part of him—the boy who'd never had a home, he supposed—grew up building one for himself in his imagination. He had married Delilah for the sake of Dragon's Hill, which even at the time had struck him as irrational. But he'd taken the vows anyway, with a small degree of hope that was, as it turned out, immediately demolished. He might legally own the place, but he now accepted that it would never really be his.

A wide-wheeled wagon forced him to the side of the road, where he paused long enough to take note of his surroundings. The gently rolling fields had given way to thick-grassed, sheep-studded hills. He rode on, more alert now, and within a few minutes came upon a sight he recognized.

Above him, blindingly white, the great horse that had been carved out of the turf seemed to have leaped from its bed of chalk to race across the hillside, forelegs extended and tail streaming behind. Although he had seen it only once before, the image had never left him. Playing alone in the nursery, he'd used to fancy that the white horse had come down from its mountain and all the way to his house, purposing to take him up and gallop off with him.

Another wagon, this one piled high with melons, trundled by, and from the driver he secured directions to Dragon's Hill. It lay only a few miles to the northwest of White Horse Vale, and he found his way there without difficulty until the avenue of tall elms came into view. Then his heart began to jump in his chest.

He followed the straight road perhaps half a mile, passing a gatehouse that appeared to be uninhabited, and came to where the road divided to form a circular drive. Directly ahead of him lay the sprawling house.

He wasn't sure what he had expected. A transformation, he supposed, given Delilah's knack for working wonders. But there had been no miracles done here. Most of the windows on the top floor were boarded over, and only a few smoke-stained chimney pots rose above the broken-tiled roof. The ivy that had covered the walls was gone, but he could see traces of where it had clung to the stones. The unkempt shrubs that used to line the wings on either side of the main building were gone as well, but otherwise the house looked as if it had been abandoned for a quarter of a century.

Disappointment burned in his throat. "I think you should see what you got in exchange for your freedom," she had said. Now the words struck him as malicious.

Guiding his mount to the right, he began to hear, over the crunch of hooves on gravel, the rasp of saws and the pounding of hammers. The noises came from the rear, so he left the path and arced around the wing where the nursery had been, glancing up at the window where he used to watch for the White Horse. One of the leaded panes had broken out, and another was cracked from corner to corner.

Harsh smells—lime dust, he thought, and tar—grew stronger when he reached the stable block. Voices could be heard from the courtyard, some laughing, others shouting. There were children, he could tell, and women. The male voices appeared to be coming from the roof at the back of the house. He rode as far as the arched entrance to the stable yard and reined to a halt.

The flagstone courtyard swarmed with people, most of them engaged in tasks he could not interpret. He saw a ring of bricks with a fire built inside and an enormous black cauldron suspended over it from a rigging. There were three large kilns set in a row, smoke streaming from openings at their tops, and empty wooden frames piled up to one side. On the other, frames filled with terra-cotta tiles were laid out next to stacks of tiles that must be ready for use, because giggling children were gathering them up and rushing off with them. A small boy who reminded him of Felix stood over the shattered remains of a tile he had dropped, sobbing until a woman lifted him in her arms.

Dragoner looked beyond the stable block to the back of the house and the rope pulleys that were drawing buckets filled with tiles to the roof. Then the courtyard went suddenly quiet. He swung his head back to see every face turned in his direction. A few moments later the noises from the roof had stilled as well.

Had he turned green, to draw such attention? They couldn't know who he was. Well, not unless Delilah had told them to expect him—*before* advising him to make the journey.

He didn't like the notion, not one bit, that she could predict what he'd do.

A tall, burly man about forty years of age detached himself from the silent crowd and waved them to return to work. "Good afternoon, sir," he said, smiling broadly. There was no glint of recognition in his cornflower-blue eyes. "How may I be of service?"

The gelding, disturbed by the sharp stench of tar, or perhaps by its rider's nervousness, danced sideways. Dragoner brought himself and his horse under control and dismounted, unsure of the best way to introduce himself. After a space, he said simply, "I am Dragoner."

"I rather thought so," said the man. "We had word you were in England and might stop by, although we didn't know when to expect you. Or if you'd come at all, for that matter. My name is Cuchulan Cunningham, m'lord, but folks hereabout call me Paddy. Lady Dragoner hired me on to manage the estate three years past. You already know that, of course. And I'm sorry for blathering, but it's my failing to keep talking unless somebody stops me. Let's see to your horse."

Turning, Paddy beckoned to a boy who hurried over to take the reins. "You'll want a washup," he said, still blathering, to Dragoner's great relief. His own tongue felt dry as a baked tile. "Go on into the house and find m'wife. I'll follow shortly. Work's about done here for the day, but I need to see it closed down proper. Then I expect you'll want to quiz me."

"I don't wish to impose myself," Dragoner said haltingly. "I can come back tomorrow. Is there an inn nearby?"

"None where you can eat Rosie's cooking. Nine-tenths of the house is a shambles, as you can plainly see, but we made a room ready for you. Not what you're used to, I'm sorry to say. The sheets will be clean, though, and everything's been dusted." Paddy lifted a brow. "Do you not want to stay with us, m'lord?"

Yes, he did. Very much so. But he felt like an intruder here, in the home his family had owned for centuries and permitted to crumble—until his wife made it her business to restore it.

He remembered his manners. "Thank you," he said. "Your hospitality is most welcome."

And he was made welcome, in an oddly casual way, in the days that followed. Paddy took time from supervising the workmen to introduce him to Dragon's Hill, brick by nail by board, it seemed, from the musty cellars to the rain-warped floors of the upper rooms. He ducked once into the nursery, now furnished only with cobwebs, and once into the master's bedchamber, which looked uninhabitable and bore no trace of his father. The rest of the house held few memories for him, and none worth exploring.

After the first meal alone in his room, he accepted Rosie Cunningham's invitation to join the family around the large kitchen table. It was a noisy, cheerful crowd that assembled there for breakfast and supper, including the senior artisans and all eight of Paddy's children. And while he found it difficult to participate in the several conversations going on simultaneously, the silent presence of the lord of the manor never appeared to disturb the others.

He learned that the funds sent by Lady Dragoner had been, thus far, directed to clearing the fields for planting, buying livestock—primarily sheep—and draining the marshlands at the east end of the property. The income from last year's harvest was financing the new roof, and Paddy had high hopes for the harvest soon to begin. Dragoner tasted beer brewed from his own hops and barley, ate bread made from his own wheat, and sampled bacon from one of his recently slaughtered pigs.

One afternoon Paddy rode out with him to survey the land. A few workers, those who could be spared from the roof, had already begun to bring in a field of golden wheat. They were shirtless, and singing, and healthy as fine young horses. He longed to pull off his coat and join them. But they would find it awkward to work alongside a viscount, he supposed, and with no idea what to do, he would only get in their way.

At the end of a week, astonishingly reluctant to go, he took his leave of the Cunninghams. Children romped behind him on the path as he rode away, calling good-byes and making bubbles with rings of wire and soapy water. The transparent globes, red and blue and green as the light refracted through them, danced around his head and shoulders like faeries. He felt as if he were departing from Paradise.

No wonder now why Delilah had wanted him to come here. *She works by charms, by spells.* She offered golden apples on a plate. But he dared not permit himself to bite into them, not yet. Probably not ever.

Closing his mind to anything but the necessities of the journey, he made it to Dover in short time, and what he found there snapped him back to earth in a hurry. As predicted by Edoard, passage across the Channel was impossible to come by. Rough weather in the south had halted shipping for several days, and disappointed travelers were shoulder-to-shoulder at every post-house and inn. He took lodging in the nearby village of Guston and rode to Dover every morning, where he searched the docks for any vessel with room for one more passenger.

Five days later he was no closer to France than when he'd arrived at the port. And now he really did wish he had asked Delilah for money, because he'd discovered that only a considerable bribe would buy him so much as deck space on a fishing boat.

He was huddled over a tankard of ale in a dockside tavern, the droopy-brimmed workman's hat he'd bought to conceal his face streaming with rainwater, when his luck changed. Not unexpectedly, it was for the worse. Several uniformed officers, who had apparently been drinking in a room upstairs, stomped through the taproom in high good humor, on their way out until one of them bumped into his table and got a close look at him.

"Dragoner?" The officer's lips curled in a snarl. "By God, it *is* you. Thought I recognized your traitorous face. Come to England to be hung, have you?"

"Mistaken as usual, Gipford." Dragoner knew the man slightly. A bad soldier and a surly drinker, John Gipford. "Prinny wants to give me a medal."

A cannonball-sized fist swung at his chin.

He caught Gipford's wrist just before the blow struck home. Rising slowly, Dragoner wrenched his opponent's arm up and back until Gipford dropped to his knees, his face twisted with pain.

"Now, now, children." The curved steel of a sabre lowered between them. "Do behave."

Dragoner looked over to see the smiling face of Major Lord Jordan Blair, a flamboyant hussar he had met a time or two in the officer's mess. With a shrug, he let go Gipford's wrist and backed away.

"That's better," said Jordy, holding his blade to Gipford's chest. "Come along, old sod. We are to dinner, yes? No point spoiling our appetites in the present company."

And that, Dragoner thought, slouching onto his chair again, was the welcome he could expect if ever he returned to England. Assuming he got *out* of England before a similar confrontation turned bloody and put him six feet under English soil.

He had nearly finished his drink when Jordy Blair appeared again and hunkered beside his chair.

"I can't stay long," Jordy said. "The fellows think I'm taking a piss. So why are you here, Dragoner? Coming or going?"

Surprise put an edge on his voice. "Trying to go, but I can't get passage."

"The fellow that brought us in means to sail back to Calais on the next tide. I think I can arrange something. Wait here a couple of hours and keep your fingers crossed."

"W-why?" Dragoner blurted as Jordy started to move away.

He turned his head. "The stories about you are damning, that's certain. But you've always seemed the right sort to me, and I trust m'instincts. You can pay me for the ticket when next we meet. Meantime, take care. Dover is swarming with Gipfords."

Dragoner waved a farewell to his back. And an hour later, still bewildered and wildly grateful, he passed a coin to the young sailor who came with a stamped ticket in hand to escort him to the boat.

It was sunny and hot when Dragoner arrived in Paris after an uncomfortable ride in an overcrowded coach. His saddlepack slung over his shoulder, he walked the last two miles from the inn where the passengers had been disgorged, looking forward to the pleasures of a lingering bath.

But when he rounded the corner onto the street where his house, the bath, and, without doubt, Edoard and his "I told you so's" awaited him, he was brought up with a start. Stopping in his tracks, he gazed with confusion at the scaffolding arrayed in front of his house and at the fresh white paint that had been applied from the roof to the top of his front door. Two workmen were seated on the bottom shelf of the scaffolding, eating sausages.

He nearly asked what they were doing here and thought better of it. Quite obviously they were painting the house. Striding past them, his temper barely in check, he entered through the open door and came again to a dumbfounded halt.

At his feet, the wooden floor gleamed with polish, matched by the sheen on the ancient balustrade. The bare walls were newly plastered and painted blue, with the wainscotting picked out in white.

Oh, no. It couldn't be. But he greatly feared that it was.

Taking the stairs two at a time, he reached the top floor without seeing anyone. "Edoard!" he called, flinging open his bed-chamber door.

The room was empty. Emptier than usual, he realized a moment later. Half the furniture was gone. His bed was there, but not the frayed tester or the tattered bed curtains that used to hang from it. Not the thin, worn carpet, or the tall armoire with the broken hinge that used to stand against the wall. The floor had been sanded. He went to the dressing room, which looked much as always, and came out again, shouting for Edoard.

His valet appeared in the doorway a few moments later, a decidedly furtive expression on his face. "Welcome home, sir," he said with none of his usual cheekiness. "I had expected you a fortnight ago."

"Never mind that! What's all this?" Dragoner made a sweeping gesture with both arms. "Where's the bloody furniture? And why the devil are you painting the house?"

"Strictly speaking, sir, the painters are doing that. Mind you, I didn't favor opening up the other house, but it wasn't for me to object. And when you failed to arrive, she said there was no point in delaying any longer."

She! The cold wind that had been gathering there blasted up his spine. "Lady Dragoner," he said.

"Then you *didn't* know." Edoard slumped against the doorjamb. "I should have listened to myself. I kenned something was wrong when she would never come out and say you had authorized the work, but she was always ready with answers that did well enough. Couldn't expect her to explain herself to a valet, could I? And besides, she don't look old enough to be sneaky."

"I know how she looks." Deceitful little baggage. "How long has she been here?"

"Came shortly after I arrived, with that battle-ax of a companion what calls herself Lady Hepzibah. They spend most days supervising the workmen and, I must say, doing quite a lot of work themselves. But they're staying at the Hôtel St. Pierre."

"You think she's there now?"

Edoard shrugged. "They left here not an hour past, but I got the impression they'd be back. Dunno for sure. Lady Dragoner said she was going shopping. For furniture."

"Sergeant Platt," Dragoner said, advancing on him and spitting out the words, "did it occur to you, for even one moment of rational thought, that if I were expecting my wife to join me in Paris, I might at some point have *mentioned* it to you?"

"Oh, aye." Edoard held his position, arms folded and one shoulder propped against the doorjamb. "But here she came, and me a valet. What would you have had me do? Toss 'er out on 'er bum?"

"If you can be this bloody impertinent with me, why not with my wife?" Wanting badly to hit something, Dragoner pounded a fist into the palm of his other hand. "Very well. I understand the position you were in. Now listen to what happens next. I want you to wait downstairs by the door. When they return, you will get rid of the old woman by whatever means required and send Lady Dragoner to me. And under no circumstances will you say anything to anyone of what has transpired here until I have devised a story for us to give out. We still have a job to do, or had you forgot?"

"As a matter of fact, your lordship, I've been kept busy doing our job while you were gone. The reports are in my bedchamber, which I've so far managed to prevent the ladies from entering. And I've spotted your hunting dogs most every day, watching the goings-on from the alley. By now they'll have put out the word to whoever pays them."

"I'm perfectly aware of that. Why else do you think my wife's indiscreet presence concerns me? It casts rather an odd shadow—wouldn't you say?—over my sterling reputation as a drunken gamester, seducer of women, and all-around wastrel."

"How about you wait until the spaniels are skulking in the alley and then *you* throw her out on 'er bum?"

"That's enough, dammit!" Dragoner began to pace. Until Delilah was gone and he'd made it obvious to everyone in Paris that she had no part of him, he would be able to accomplish nothing. Edoard was right. He had to toss her out.

This time it would have to be a clean break, and a harsh one. Oh, worse than harsh. When he was done with her, she wouldn't ever want him back. Not if he came to her and begged forgiveness for the way he had neglected her, which he had now and again imagined himself doing—madman!—during those halcyon days at Dragon's Hill.

He was surprised, furious as he still was, to realize how much he dreaded hurting her. But what choice had she given him?

"Be you finished with me?" Edoard asked, his voice marked with his own distress.

Edoard had done his best, Dragoner knew perfectly well. But Delilah had a way of rendering normally stalwart men to custard. "Go on downstairs," he said, "and keep watch. You may as well send the painters home."

"With the house painted only two-thirds down?" Edoard cast him a wry grin. "The neighbors are bound to complain."

Chapter 7

"For death-like dragons here affright thee hard."

Pericles
Act 1, Scene 1

"They were not following us after all," Delilah said, snatching a quick look over her shoulder before turning the corner. "I'm nearly certain they continued along the rue de la Paix."

"And what if they did?" Lady Hepzibah emitted a snort. "They trailed after us from Lord Dragoner's house in the first place and could be reasonably certain we were on our way back there. I am not mistaken, my dear. When we walk out in future, we shall take that Edoard fellow with us."

"If you think it best, of course. But I expect they simply live in this neighborhood and chanced to be going in our direction." Delilah halted, raising one hand to shield her eyes from the bright sunlight. "Good heavens. What has become of the painters?"

"Gone off for a long luncheon and a nap, I would imagine. Hired workers generally disappear when there is no one about to supervise them."

"But Georges and Bernard always bring lunch baskets from home. Oh, there's Edoard by the door. He'll know where they are."

Edoard, his thin lips white and his expression sour, came out to meet them in front of the scaffolding.

Delilah felt a jolt of apprehension. "Has there—"

"Lord Dragoner has returned, milady. He wishes to speak with you."

"Of course." Her stomach began turning cartwheels. "I shall go to him immediately."

"He specified a *private* meeting," Edoard said, his gaze moving to Lady Hepzibah. "It would be advisable, I believe, for your companion to return to the hôtel."

"I'll do no such thing!" Lady Hepzibah said, gathering her skirts with the clear intention of forging into the house. "Move aside, young man."

Delilah put a hand on her arm. "No, Heppy, please. Everything will be perfectly all right. But of course, you ought not to go back unescorted. Edoard will accompany you."

"And leave you alone with Dragoner? It does not bear thinking of! He is certain to be furious with you." Lady Hepzibah glared at Edoard. "He *is,* isn't he? Tell her!"

Edoard's face reddened. "I couldn't say, milady. He gave me instructions, and I am following them."

"And so shall we," Delilah said. "Think on it, Heppy. You must admit he has every right to be angry, and we shall only make matters worse by disregarding his wishes now. My husband means to ring a peal over me, that is all, and he quite understandably prefers to do so without an audience."

Her jaw set, Lady Hepzibah nodded curtly at Edoard. "Well, come along then. If the child is hell-bent to beard the dragon in his den, it's not for me to stop her."

Edoard, unmistakable sympathy in his eyes, bowed to Delilah before hurrying down the street after Lady Hepzibah.

Delilah looked up at the open windows, expecting to see her husband looking back from one of them. Heppy's voice, when she got her temper up, was the sound of a file on metal. But if he had been listening, or if he was watching her now, there was no sign of him.

She stood on the pavement a few moments longer, steadying her breath and locking her courage into place. Then, because there was nothing else to do but get it over with, she entered the house and began to climb the stairs. They stretched a considerable distance, it seemed, much farther than they had done before. As the heels of her half boots clicked on the newly-polished wood, the sound echoed from the ceiling and walls.

Rather like nails being pounded into a coffin, she thought, feeling suddenly as Marie Antoinette must have done as she mounted to the guillotine. Delilah grasped the railing to hold her balance.

She was being silly. Truly, what had she to fear? Nothing awaited her that she had not taken into account. After calculating the loss she might take against the prize to be won, she had willfully courted his anger, preferring rage to the indifferent charm he wielded at her like a rapier. Or perhaps he used it as a shield. Either way, it effectively held her at a distance. What choice had he left her but to force a confrontation?

Taking a deep breath, she unclamped her fingers from the banister and ordered her legs to carry her across the landing and up the next flight of stairs.

He was waiting for her at the open door of his bedchamber, standing with his arms at his sides, utterly motionless.

On seeing him, her first vagrant thought was that he needed a haircut. Strands of overlong black hair shadowed his forehead and draped over the collar of his shirt. He was wearing a dark blue riding coat, buckskin breeches, and scuffed boots. He must have arrived within the hour.

She kept moving, hoping he would greet her. But when she came near the door, he only stepped aside to let her enter and gestured to the sole chair, a plain wooden ladderback that had been placed in the center of the room.

There was to be a trial, then, or perhaps only the setting of a sentence. She passed by the chair and went to the open window, where she looked out and waited for him to speak.

A man pushing a wheelbarrow loaded with bricks paused to wipe his forehead with his sleeve. She saw a woman with a flamboyantly yellow gown and a preposterous bonnet walking with the help of a cane. Behind the woman, their tails raised like exclamation points, strolled five fat marmalade cats.

Finally she turned to face her husband.

He had moved to a spot inches from the door, which he'd left open, and stood with his shoulders propped against the wall and one knee drawn up. His arms were folded across his chest. It was a deliberately negligent stance, she realized, trying to read his face. But he'd chosen the one place in the room untouched by the light that streamed through the window. She could barely make out the bridge of his thin, aristocratic nose and the thrust of his jaw. Of his eyes, she could see only two flashes of white.

" 'Oh, full of scorpions is my mind, dear wife,' " he said, his voice deceptively mild.

She drew in a shaky breath. "Please, my lord. Don't do that today. Whatever you have to say to me, I would much prefer to hear it in your own words."

"You won't like them, I can promise you. But shall I come straight to the point? How ought a man to punish his wife for disobedience? No, let me try again. For out-and-out *defiance*?"

"That is the wrong word as well, sir. I have an excellent memory. You never said that I should *not* come to Paris."

"How neglectful of me. I had forgot your aptitude for slipping through loopholes. But make no mistake, madam. After today, no misunderstandings will remain between us. I mean you to understand precisely what I expect of you."

"You want me to return to England," she said.

"That, certainly, and a great many other things as well. But you'll not find it difficult to obey me. Indeed, before we are done here, I expect you will be more than eager to comply." One thumb lifted to rub against his chin. "But I am getting ahead of myself. To begin with, if you don't mind overmuch, perhaps you will satisfy my curiosity. What in the name of God *possessed* you to think I would welcome you here?"

This was not anger, nor anything so insipid as rage. She wrapped her arms around her waist against the force of it. "I never expected that you would," she said. "But once I was here, and when you'd got over being displeased, there was a chance you would let me stay. A slim chance, to be sure, but I thought it worth a try. The alternative was to wait for you in England, and I had already done that for six years. Did you ever mean to return?"

"Probably not. With the war ended, I am now free to be off on my travels again. You always forget, Delilah, that I was raised in boardinghouses, gaming houses, and inns. Every few months, a new city and new adventures. It is the life I prefer.

When my business in Paris is concluded, I mean to go exploring."

"I don't forget," she said quietly. "And I don't believe you. I think you hated that life."

He leaned his head back against the wall. "You *want* to think so. Did you also persuade yourself that I would accept what you offered in place of it? A house on the river, quite elegant enough to tempt an impoverished viscount. Money to unimpoverish— is that a word?—said viscount, money that you'd winkled from his father and invested in ships and estates and the devil knows what. Was I meant to be seduced by shillings and guineas?"

"Would you rather be poor?"

"If that is a condition of my independence, the answer is most assuredly yes. It was amusing, really, to watch you baiting the hook for a fish that had no intention of biting. A family dinner, replete with snot-nosed brats and flirtatious little sisters and lizards. 'Go to Dragon's Hill,' you said, trusting that the sight of it would inspire me to settle there and breed children of my own. You circled me like a nesting sparrow with twigs in your beak. Did you think I would fail to recognize that you were building a cage?"

His foot, the one that had been raised knee-level against the wall behind him, dropped to the floor. "Understand this, Delilah. I have been manipulated for the last time. I will not be put on a leash. You were mistaken to try."

There was an undercurrent of pain, she thought, in the cold river of his sarcasm. Or perhaps she heard what she wanted to hear. Probably so.

"For all that, sir," she said, "you are still married to me."

"And unable to do anything about it. Yes, I know. Your solicitor made that much excruciatingly clear. And I am sorry for it. Were there a way to set you free, short of taking a razor to my wrists, I would gladly oblige you. But as it is, we are yoked together in the chains of the law and must come to terms like other married couples who prefer to lead separate lives."

"That is *your* choice, not mine. If I may ask, what is it exactly that you dislike about me? My appearance? My temperament? My birth? The fact that I engage in trade and enjoy it?"

Even from across the room, she saw his muscles tense. But

he recovered quickly, waving a hand as if scattering a swarm of gnats. "I neither like you nor dislike you. In a number of ways, I have come to admire you. But that does not signify. The problem lies, and always has done, with me. Shall I tell you why?"

"I thought you had already done so," she said. "You wish to travel. You relish your independence. You resent being trapped in a marriage not of your choosing."

"All of that, yes. And now I shall show you the rest. It will not be pleasant, Delilah. I suggest you avail yourself of that chair."

"No, thank you," she said, taking a deep, shaky breath. "I feel small enough as it is."

With a shrug, he pulled himself away from the wall. "You won't mind if I move about? I feel restless of a sudden and, as you have surely noted, I am somewhat out of temper. I'll not come within a distance that threatens you."

She lifted her chin. "Am I meant to be afraid, sir?"

"Not particularly. But should you attempt to leave before I have done with my tale, I will most certainly stop you. Now where shall I begin? With the women, I think. As you might imagine, there have been a great many of them."

He made a turn at the bed and crossed directly in front of her. "I prefer married women, by the way, so long as they aren't married to me. During the past several years I've cuckolded most of Bonaparte's generals, who were kind enough to be off fighting the war, not to mention any number of husbands who were snoring obliviously in their own chambers while directly next door I was enjoying their wives. Parisian women, I must say, are remarkably good lovers. They have a talent for invention."

"It comes with experience," she said, determined to match him point by point. "You could teach me."

He looked surprised at the interruption. "Probably," he said, after a moment. "But I haven't the patience to instruct novices. And besides, you would be shocked."

She didn't think she would be, although she'd little idea what he was talking about. There had been little enough *invention* the one time he had taken her to bed. There had been little of anything at all, beyond a sharp pain that had surprised more than it hurt. She remembered the scratch of whiskers and the scent of brandy when he brought his lips to hers and took them away again, unwilling to kiss her.

"But my flagrant infidelity cannot be news to you," he said thoughtfully. "I understand that it has figured prominently in the London scandal sheets. Or perhaps you do not read them."

"Lady Hepzibah does. She has the papers delivered to the house and acquaints me with items of interest each morning over breakfast. I believe, however, that she skips over the lurid details."

"Then I shall do the same. You need only apprehend that the stories are true, or near enough to suit my purposes. But I do not wish you to leave here with any matter unresolved in your mind. You may ask questions if you like."

She examined a spot on the floor that the sanders had missed. In the center of it, a nail head required to be hammered down. She wondered if he had brought his fashionable Paris ladies to this ramshackle house and lain with them on the large, lumpy mattress she'd meant to replace, along with the tester drapes and the carpet. A rivulet of perspiration streamed between her breasts.

"No?" He passed close to her again, stirring the air. "Then I have a question for you. Before leaving for Paris, had you got word that I was to be stripped of my commission?"

At that, she looked over at him. He had come to a stop by the fireplace with his feet planted apart on the flagstone hearth and his hands clasped behind his back. A chilling smile curved his lips.

"I heard nothing of it." With care, she maintained a steady voice. "For what reason?"

"Oh, the usual ones, I suppose." He sounded amused. "Wellington failed to enumerate them in detail, but likely that was because he did not wish to offend his hostess and her guests. You'll hear all about it soon enough. We chanced to encounter each other at one of Madame de Staël's salons, where he lost his famous composure for the short time it took to drum me out of the army. There was mention of disgracing my regiment, cowardice was implied, and then he recollected where he was and turned his back to me. It would have been rather droll,

except that the girl I'd been cultivating all evening unaccountably lost interest in me. I had to go out and find another."

She, who rarely lost control, was losing it now. Her pulse
beat erratically, and her breath was coming in shallow gusts.

"You ought to be prepared," he said, his voice insufferably
kind. "I have been advised that some of my fellow soldiers are
telling tales out of school. By the time you return to London,
my assorted transgressions will be the talk of the town. Naturally your family will catch the worst of it. Perhaps you'll find
it easier to deal with the gossip if I tell you what really happened. Do you want to hear it?"

No! she wanted to shout. But he would tell her anyway. He
would not permit her to leave this room until he did. "Will it be
the truth?" she asked in a colorless voice.

"Oh, certainly. *Sans* excuses, *sans* theatrics, *sans* remorse."
He propped an elbow on the mantelpiece and rested his chin on
his hand. "The trouble with war, I quickly discovered, was that
strangers with whom I had no particular quarrel kept trying to
kill me. A tedious business, really, being shot at. I disliked it
nearly as much as I resented being ordered about by my superior officers, most of whom hadn't the sense God gave a cab-
bage."

She could well imagine how he had behaved. Dragoner was
not a man to suffer fools lightly.

"Wellington—Lord Wellesley back then—had me on the carpet for insubordination a dozen times. But in my misspent
youth I'd learned to speak a number of languages, so he often
employed me as a translator. And it occurred to him that I might
cause less trouble if sent out as an exploring officer. Do you
know what that is? But never mind. In brief, I was assigned to
ride into French-held territory and send back word of what I
saw."

She regarded him with astonishment. "You were a *spy*?"

His gaze shifted abruptly to the vacant chair, and then to the
floor. "Hardly that. Spies, if caught, are tortured for information
before being hung, or shot, or eviscerated. You can't think I
would put myself in the way of such unpleasantness. Exploring
officers wear full uniform precisely to avoid being mistaken for
spies. There is a protocol, you see, when gentleman officers are

captured. They have only to give their parole, which amounts to swearing they won't try to escape, after which they are invited to supper. They are even permitted to keep their weapons, and quite often directed to make their way to Verdun on their own. No guards. No escort. An officer's word, you see, is regarded as his bond. I am still amazed at it."

"But when you were captured," she said, confused, "they sent you to Paris."

"I made certain that they would. And so we are come at last to the kernel of my story. Have you realized yet that I *chose* to be made a prisoner? It required a good deal of planning, of course. If I failed to do the thing properly, I'd have been dispatched to Verdun, exchanged for a French officer, and all too soon there I'd be, back in the war again."

He resumed his pacing. "Unfortunately, my little drama required a pair of corpses to decorate the stage. Oh, you needn't worry. No lurid details. I shall take you directly to the last scene, in which I was pinned down behind some boulders with two luckless Spanish guerillas who had been serving as my guides. The French patrol that had driven us to ground shouted for us to come out. The Spaniards declined. Then came a shot, a scream or two, and silence. A few moments later I emerged from behind the rocks with my hands in the air."

"No," she said in a strangled voice. "You c-could not."

He appeared to brace himself. "Oh, but that's what happened. Mind you, I wouldn't be telling you of it now except that the story appears to have got out. I've no idea how. In any case, the Frogs took me in custody and had a look at the scene of my crime. They found my rifle, still hot from firing, and my bloody sword. Since one of the Spaniards had been shot and the other gutted—well, you may draw the natural conclusions. The captain of the French patrol did so and was exceedingly pleased with me. What's more, I chanced to be carrying rather a large number of gold coins, and made no objection when he appropriated them for himself. So now you know, Delilah, how I won the affection of my captors and got myself billeted in Paris while other poor sods were dying on the battlefield for God and country."

Coming to a halt in the center of the room, he lifted his hands like angel's wings and cast her a seraphic smile. "Still want to be married to me, sweetheart?"

At some point she must have moved, although she hadn't been aware of it. She was near to the door and he had seized her wrist and swung her around to face him. Her eyes burned, as if they'd been scoured with salt. Blood pounded in her ears.

"Wait here," he said. His voice came to her from a great distance.

She tried to pull away.

"Wait for Edoard," he said, holding her in place. "I'll lock you in if I must."

She looked down at the hand clutching her wrist. "Yes," she murmured. "They might have been following us. Heppy was sure of it. If I wait, will Edoard take me to the hôtel?"

He let her go. "Who was following you, Delilah?"

"Oh, I don't know. Two men." She felt unbearably tired. "It doesn't matter."

"Come," he said, one hand pressed against the small of her back.

Next she knew, she was seated on the chair, and he was at the door. She hadn't meant to speak to him, hadn't thought she could. But when he glanced over at her, the words crying in her heart found a soft voice. "How can it be true, sir? How can you have done such horrible things?"

His eyes, hard as polished stones, looked directly into hers. Then he was gone, the sound of his response burning in her ears.

" 'He hath confessed. Away with him! He's a villain and a traitor.' "

Chapter 8

"Why did you throw your wedded lady from you?"

Cymbeline
Act 5, Scene 5

Shortly before dawn, two of Le Chien Noir's brawniest waiters were directed to escort a gentleman through the rain-slick streets to his residence. Luckily the distance was not great. They had been required to support him like a poleaxed bull, as one of them remarked when the scaffolding came into sight.

Dragoner knew that he was drunk. For the second time in his life, he had deliberately meant to be drunk. It seemed only fitting, he thought dreamily, to end his marriage the way he had begun it.

At some point he found himself propped up against the scaffolding with one of his arms wrapped around a ham-sized neck. The other man went to the door and pounded on it.

The noise exploded in Dragoner's head. Letting go of scaffolding and neck, he sank to his knees on the pavement.

Sometime later, he awoke on his own bed. A shaft of light knifed through a narrow opening between the curtains, slicing across the room and scalding his eyes. He was still fully dressed, but someone had draped a blanket over him.

Lifting his head a fraction of an inch, he felt a pain so acute that he immediately settled back onto the pillow with a groan. Even that much sound thundered in his ears. He closed his eyes and watched the fireworks play, red and gold and green, against his sealed eyelids.

An excess of brandy had bought him a few hours of welcome oblivion, and this was the price of it. This and the substantial sum he had lost at dice, most of it to Jacques Batiste. Money well spent, he reckoned, and along with the brandy, a relatively cheap way of punishing himself.

Not everyone approved his tactics. Minette had loomed at his side throughout the long evening, disapproval flashing in her eyes whenever he directed her to refill his glass. Edoard would scold him as well. He could not silence his friends.

But his conscience, which had lately erupted like a phoenix from the ash heap, must quickly be put down again. What was the use of remorse? He had done what he had to do, and if some of what he had told Delilah could not stand up to close scrutiny, they had been necessary lies.

Or something of the sort. He could not think clearly.

The results were all that mattered now. She would return to England, perhaps grieve for a time, and then, resilient and tenacious little thing that she was, she'd cast him to the winds and find herself a lover.

He might have slept again. When he opened his eyes in response to the sound of a voice, he saw that the blade of light from the window was gone. Except for the flicker of a candle, the room was dark, and the pain in his head had settled to a low throb. He felt sweaty and miserable and in need of a chamberpot.

"They're out there again," said Edoard, helping him to sit up and swing his legs over the side of the bed. "I thought you'd want to know."

"Yes." Dragoner tried to focus his eyes. "What time is it?"

"Just gone eleven. If you wish to make their acquaintance, I've hot water ready for a shave, and a change of clothes laid out."

After four years running in tandem with the Yorkshire pig farmer turned soldier and spy, Dragoner was unsurprised that Eddie—Edoard—understood that he required something to do. The yokels who had been tracking him before he left for England were unlikely to prove much of a challenge, to be sure, but with any luck, they might provide a little amusement.

Skipping the shave, he used the hot water for a sponge bath, allowed Edoard to dress him, and tied his own neckcloth into a simple knot. Then, with a tall-crowned hat on his still-aching head and his sword-cane in hand, he exited the house like any other young man setting out for a night on the town. He sauntered as far as the corner, made the turn, and drew out his sword. The silver blade glittered in the light from the street-lamp.

Moments later, a head poked around the corner. The point of Dragoner's sword met it just below the chin.

"Good evening, gentlemen," he said in a friendly voice. "Won't you step into the light so that we can become better acquainted?"

The man held at sword-tip sidled into view, his forehead beaded with sweat.

"Venez ici, idiot!" he yelped when the sword pricked his neck. "He'll kill me."

Scowling, the other man emerged from the shadows. "How'd you know we was following you?" he demanded in an accent straight from the docks.

"I'm prescient," Dragoner replied. "Ask someone to tell you what that means. The gentleman who sent you, perhaps. Does he wish to make an appointment, or have you been harrying me to no purpose whatever?"

The men looked at one another. The fox had turned on them, and they clearly had no idea what to do about it.

"Nothing to say?" Dragoner inquired gently. "Then I may as well cut your throat and be done with it. Unless, of course, you would rather take me to someone who can answer my questions?"

"Now would be an excellent time," said Edoard, who had come around the corner with a pistol in his hand. "We can all go together."

The thugs, shuffling their feet, led their captors through a series of narrow streets and alleys that gave way to a few derelict buildings scattered alongside the river. In the windless August night, the air was heavy with the smell of fish, marshy ground, and sour wine.

Several dozen men, most with tankards in their hands, clustered around the trestle tables set up on a patch of weedy grass between two slate-roofed taverns. Dragoner heard the clatter of dice and the grate of angry voices. By one of the tables, a fight broke out. Men rushed over and encircled the combatants, shouting insults and placing bets on the outcome.

"They're bad-tempered because they're out of work," Edoard said. "Grevers, they be called. Most days you can see them demonstrating in front of the Hôtel de Ville. They come here at night."

"I'm overdressed," Dragoner said. "Will they object, do you think?"

"I'll tell them you're here so that I can show you off," Edoard said with a grin. "But you ought to have let me tie your neckcloth."

"Ivre l'Oie," grumbled one of the thugs, pointing to the tavern on the left. "But he might not be there tonight."

"Then let us find out. Edoard, wait here with our other friend. If he makes a fuss, you have my permission to shoot him."

The Drunken Goose smelled as if its namesake used it as a privy. The room they entered was low-ceilinged, dim with smoke from tallow candles, and exceedingly hot, which explained why most of the patrons had chosen to take their drinks outside. Dragoner counted about a dozen men slouched in groups of two or three over small square tables. A plump maid balancing a large tray gave him a saucy smile.

"There." The thug pointed to a table half concealed behind a worn tapestry screen. "Monsieur Beltrand. He's the one with yellow hair. Now let me go."

"Perhaps later." Dragoner took hold of his elbow. "I require an introduction."

Four men were seated at the table, three of them wearing threadbare army uniforms. They looked up, startled, and one of them reached inside his unbuttoned tunic.

"That won't be necessary," said the blond man, gripping his companion's forearm. "I have been expecting Lord Dragoner. Jervin, give him your chair."

Dragoner waved the boy back to his seat. "Don't trouble yourself. I'll not be staying." He focused his gaze on Beltrand, assessing the quality of his bottle green coat and yellowing linens. A man of means fallen on hard times, he decided, and one bent on avenging his misfortune. But his eyes were blurry with drink, and his fingers drummed nervously on the table until he saw Dragoner looking at them.

"If you were expecting me," Dragoner said, "where is your employer?"

"Who says I have one? And I didn't say we expected you *tonight*. Our invitation was meant to have been delivered at a more appropriate time."

"By the two oafs I keep tripping over? I take it you meant me to know I was being followed."

"Hardly." Beltrand glared at the inept spy who was making himself small in the corner. "I am not at liberty to explain, except to say that no harm was intended."

"Then let me guess what this is about. Half of Paris is embroiled in some plot or other. You've devised one of your own and thought I might be persuaded to join you. But first you had to make sure I was not already aligned with whichever side you have set yourself against." Dragoner glanced around the table. "Take no insult, gentlemen, but I fear we will not suit."

Beltrand lifted a hand. "You are willing to discuss the matter with my—*our*—employer?"

"Perhaps. But there are conditions. For one, your enterprise must come with money attached, or some other excellent reason why I would care to trouble myself with it. Furthermore, you will call off your dogs. I've no great objection to being followed, but it has become something of an annoyance."

His voice hardened. "What I will *not* tolerate is the expansion of your interest to a pair of harmless ladies who chanced to be doing some work on my house. They are none of your concern."

"We could not be sure," Beltrand said after a moment. "One of them is your wife."

"Thank you, but I was aware of that. If it matters, Lady Dragoner will shortly be on her way back to England. I want it made clear, however, that *no* woman of my acquaintance is to be distressed by your inept conspirators. You will deal with me directly or not at all."

"I shall convey your message," Bertrand conceded, his face filmed with perspiration. "We did not intend to disturb the ladies, I assure you, but the news that you were married came as a surprise. It had to be taken into account."

"I fail to see why." Dragoner lifted his cane to Beltrand's shoulder. "Do you know, I cannot quite decide if you are attempting to recruit me, or to lead me into a trap."

"Wh-what sort of trap? Why should we do any such thing?"

"You tell me." Dragoner wanted Beltrand, or one of the others, to give him an excuse for a fight. But the three soldiers had developed a sudden interest in examining their fingernails, the fat spy was cringing in the corner, and Beltrand only shrugged.

"Our plans are as yet unformed, but what we have in mind will put us all at risk. To that extent, we are each of us stepping into a trap. Are you willing to be contacted again, milord, or shall I inform the others that we must proceed without your assistance?"

"It makes no difference to me either way," Dragoner said, withdrawing his cane and moving away from the table.

A waste of time, he thought in disgust as he went to rejoin Edoard. "Let him go," he said, gesturing to the man who stood stiff as an icicle with Edoard's gun at his back. "But next time you see him, put a bullet in his head."

When the man had scampered off, Edoard slipped his pistol into his waistband. "Nothing?"

"It appears not. That lot couldn't find their way out of a snuffbox. Where shall we go now? I haven't asked what you discovered while I was in England."

"Only the usual," Edoard said, falling into step beside him. "Rumblings and grumblings. Anger and frustration, but most of it expended in fisticuffs or smothered in drink. There will likely be riots, but I don't see how we can anticipate them. Someone might turn his rifle on the king, or Wellington, or any one of a hundred targets. It's madness in the streets. If you want an organized plot, milord, you'll do better trolling for it among the nobs."

"I suppose so." Dragoner, his head throbbing, lapsed into silence.

Edoard led him back the way they had come, somewhat to Dragoner's relief. He didn't feel up to another confrontation, and thought he might be tired enough to sleep through the rest of the night. They were in sight of the scaffolding when he spoke again. "How did Lady Dragoner know I had leased the house next door?"

Edoard looked surprised. "I thought you must have told her about it. But come to think of it, she was poking around the statue. Said it was unsightly. Could be she tripped the latch and opened the panel. Anyway, she said that when the other house had been repaired and furnished, she would take up residence there. I did manage to talk her out of painting the exterior. Told her it was contrary to the lease." He gave Dragoner a sidelong glance. "I take it she's changed her mind about staying in Paris?"

"Yes." His stomach clenched. "You saw her safely to the hôtel?"

"Of course. On the way, she told me what she'd already purchased for the house to replace the things she'd had carted away. The bills will be sent to her. She made a point of that. I thought you had arranged it between yourselves."

"So we did," Dragoner said numbly. Trust his merchant wife to see that everything was tidied up. He was to have a carpet again, and perhaps a wardrobe for his clothes. And whenever he looked at his newly polished floors and painted walls, he would be reminded of her. Of how he had last seen her, white-faced and trembling, her eyes wide with pain. When he led her to the chair, her arm had been cold as marble. He could not bear to think of it. Of her. Not yet.

"Hire me a horse," he said abruptly. "Have it here tomorrow morning. I don't know how long I'll be gone."

"You're taking off *again*?" Edoard threw up his hands. "Any use me asking where?"

"I don't know yet. I need to clear my head, that's all." After a moment, he asked, "Did she go into my study?"

Edoard unlocked the door. "She went into all the rooms except mine," he said.

Dragoner had meant to put himself directly to bed, but that was impossible now. When Edoard was gone, he pulled on his dressing gown, took up a candle, and let himself into a small windowless room on the ground floor. At one time it had been used as a butler's pantry, or so he had been told, but now the shelves that lined the walls were filled with books. There was one comfortable chair set in front of a writing table, with a pair of standing candlebraces arrayed on either side to provide light for reading.

This had been his refuge since first he came to Paris, a place to hide when he needed to be alone. Even Edoard was not permitted to set foot here.

But Delilah had bustled in the way she always did, going where she wasn't wanted, intruding and manipulating and taking charge. He fully expected to find that she had rearranged his books, polished the shelves, and for good measure, upholstered the chair.

Nothing had been disturbed. The chair was as he had left it, with the cushion he employed to support his back in its usual place. A thin layer of dust coated the writing table, where a well-thumbed volume of Shakespeare's plays lay open.

What had he been reading before he left for England? He had not been in the room since then. Closing his eyes, he tried to remember. He had read all the plays so many times. When he could not think what else to say, he quoted lines from them.

He'd patched together an education from these books, and invented himself from bits and pieces of Shakespeare's characters. Whatever his circumstances, he could always become whichever character best fitted the role he was required to play. Soldier. Seducer. Lover. Spy. Villain. Fool.

Measure for Measure, he thought. The ignoble Angelo, smitten with a courageous virgin, has resolved to bed her. That she will be ruined matters to him not at all.

O you beast, O faithless coward, O dishonest wretch!

Opening his eyes, he saw that the play was indeed *Measure for Measure*. Then his gaze was drawn to a line that made him catch his breath.

He expelled it, extinguishing the candle, and lowered himself onto the chair. Darkness settled over him like a cloak.

Not far away, at the Hôtel St. Pierre, Delilah was sleeping.

Ever until now, when men were fond, I smiled and wondered how.

Chapter 9

"Love you the man that wrong'd you?"

Measure for Measure
Act 2, Scene 3

I don't want you.
For a long time, huddled on a chair by the window of her bedchamber, Delilah rehearsed the words in her mind. She wasn't certain Dragoner had ever said them, but everything he *had* said could have meant nothing else.

Heppy, after one look at her face when Delilah returned to the hôtel, gave her the solitude she had requested with her eyes. Speech was beyond her power now, as was the relief of tears. She could do no more than keep a silent vigil, mourning the death of her marriage, and her dreams, and the children who would never be born.

Time passed.

I don't want you.

The light faded and was gone. She sat, her arms wrapped around her waist, mindless and miserable as the night wore on.

Later, moonlight streamed through the window. Then the moon, too, vanished, but it had roused her a little. Other words, spoken words, came back to her.

Did you think I would fail to recognize that you were building a cage?

Understand this. I have been manipulated for the last time.

He must have thought it necessary to say those things. She had pursued him, and bound him in marriage, and refused to accept that he did not want her. She had come to Paris against his wishes. Pushed herself on him. She had forced him to be cruel. How else could he compel her to go away and leave him be?

This time, crushingly, he had succeeded. She believed him now. She would not trouble him again.

Dawn crept over the cloudless sky, apricot and pink and golden. The pigeons on the ledge began to stir, greeting one another with low, throaty noises. Light gilded their sleek feathers and bobbing round heads. She watched them rise on their twiggy legs, stretch their wings, and soar off into the morning.

With the sunrise, her last vigil had come to an end. It was the tenth of August, Dragoner's birthday. She wondered if he had remembered.

Rising less gracefully than the pigeons had done, she shuffled to the dressing table and gazed into the mirror. A sad little girl with shadowed eyes looked back at her. *Delilah. Oh, Delilah. You must rally yourself.*

She had before now made mistakes, suffered losses, and found new enterprises to engage her. She would do so again. But for the time being, she knew to concentrate on simple matters, taking one small decision after another. Wash her face. Brush her hair. Put on a fresh gown. Put on her lips a reassuring smile for Heppy.

First thing, she must speak with Heppy, who had doubtless been keeping a vigil of her own in the next room. They must make preparations for their return to England. There was packing to do, a carriage to be hired, a journey to be made. By the time she reached Calais, she would be herself again.

Slowly, she began to undress. But all the while, too late, came the words she ought to have said to him.

Yes, I did try to manipulate you. I thought it for your own good, but I now understand that I was using you to fulfill my own dreams. I had no right. I am sorry.

No, I don't want to be married to you. The marriage is over. On that, at least, we are agreed.

Somehow she had wound up seated on the floor, her arms wrapped around her knees, rocking back and forth. The watergates had opened, it seemed, and all the things he had said to her began scrolling through her mind. Line by line, as if exam-

ining a ledger, she dealt with each point he'd made and marked
it off.

Other women, yes. Of course. How could there not be?

She had been mistaken to suppose he still cared about
Dragon's Hill. Had he gone there, she wondered, as she had
asked him to do? If so, he never admitted to it. At one time, perhaps he had wanted a home, but now he preferred his travels.
New cities and new adventures. His parents had been
vagabonds, she should have remembered. That was the only
life he knew.

Taking him to meet the Benings had been another miscalcu-
lation. She had hoped that by introducing him to a settled, af-
fectionate family, she might lead him to imagine having one of
his own. Manipulation. Oh, yes. But he had endured patiently
what must have been for him a frightful afternoon and fled the
first moment he decently could. His anger, his repulsion, had
been left behind him in blood. Blood on a marble railing.

How had she forgotten that?

She moved on through all the forest of sarcasm and bitter
revelations, but when she came to the bottom of the ledger,
where he had spoken of slaughtering two men to win his way
into the graces of the French patrol, she ran into a wall. She re-
viewed the story again and again, shivering with the horror of
it, and still, and still, she refused to believe he had done any
such thing.

About this, if nothing else, he had lied to her. Or she was
fairly sure he'd done. She no longer placed any great reliance
on her instincts, which had been perfectly dependable until the
day she first cast eyes on Charles Dragoner and went spinning
off like a top.

How could he have done such a thing? The story had got out,
he said. The French soldiers who captured him must have spoken of it, and they had been there to witness what had occurred.

She debated the issue, reeling from one side to the other, but
at the end, she knew only that she could not let the matter rest.
Had her judgment been so flawed as he wanted her to believe?
Had she been wrong to keep faith in him for all these many
years?

With so little left to her now, must she also regret having loved him?

The clock on the mantelpiece showed half past ten when she went to the *secretaire* and wrote a brief, careful note. Then, wrapped in her dressing gown, she gave it to the servant who responded to the bellpull and asked him to have it delivered. She knew only the name of the recipient and not the direction, but he assured her that the hôtel manager would soon find it out.

Heppy came into the room as the servant left it, her face wreathed with concern. "Oh, my dear," she said. "What did that awful man do to you?"

"He told me to go home," Delilah said, mustering a smile. "I thought you'd approve. Have you had your breakfast?"

It wasn't to be imagined that Heppy would leave the subject of Lord Dragoner alone, not altogether. But she was uncharacteristically restrained with her questions while Delilah drank coffee and nibbled on toast and made vague responses. Heppy did not disturb her at all when she took a bath, except to inquire about the servant who had been dispatched with a letter.

Delilah deflected that question as well, since she had no real hope that anything would come of it. But not long after, a reply was delivered. If she wished to pay a call, said the neatly inscribed note, she would be most welcome at any time between two and four that afternoon.

Delilah set out for Clichy in a hired carriage at two o'clock, with the young servant to escort her and a disgruntled Lady Hepzibah left behind. She had put on the nicest of her gowns and wrenched her hair into a springy knot at the back of her head, but recalcitrant curls began breaking loose almost immediately. Most of the journey was spent pronging hairpins into her scalp, which kept her from worrying overmuch about what would occur when she reached her destination.

On arriving at a large house set in the midst of extensive gardens, she was ushered into a parlor and left to wait for a considerable time. Long enough, at least, to regret the impulse that had brought her here. By the time a maid arrived to lead her upstairs, she was quivering like a jelly.

The door opened to a pleasant, sunlit room. "Lady Dragoner," said the maid, stepping aside to let her enter.

She made an awkward curtsy in the direction of a plump, swarthy woman seated at a writing table. A pair of startling black eyes examined her with forthright curiosity, and the woman's lips curved over a pair of prominent front teeth.

"Lady Dragoner," she said. "You are most welcome." Madame de Staël set down her pen. "I am delighted that you have come."

"Thank you for receiving me, madame. I was, I know, most impertinent to ask."

"Not at all, my dear. Had I known you to be in Paris, you would long since have been invited here. Now make yourself comfortable and tell me how I may be of service."

"Is it so obvious that I mean to beg a favor?" Delilah asked ruefully as she perched on the edge of a delicate chair. "But it is, I believe, a very small one. I wish only to discover if there is any truth to a rumor I chanced to hear about an incident that supposedly took place at one of your salons."

Madame de Staël appeared unsurprised at the question. "It concerns your charming husband, of course. What exactly have you heard?"

"Very little, save that an unpleasant encounter took place between Lord Dragoner and His Grace the Duke of Wellington. Did you chance to witness it?"

"Indeed I did, along with many others. The incident was quite the talk of Paris for several weeks. What did you wish to know of it?"

Delilah unclenched her hands, which had fisted on her lap, and came to her feet. "In fact, I had hoped to learn that nothing of the sort had taken place. You must pardon me for intruding on your time, madame. It was a pleasure to make your acquaintance."

"Nonsense. You will sit yourself down, child, and tell me why you have not asked these questions of your husband. But perhaps I know already. *Le beau Dragon* is a difficult young man, *n'est ce-pas?*"

"He was the one who told me what happened," she said, returning to her chair. "The thing is, I didn't believe him. Not altogether. It seems impossible that he could be guilty of—"

The word *treason* lodged in her throat. Flushing hotly, she lowered her gaze.

A long silence followed, during which she felt Madame de Staël's intense gaze scouring her face. She should never have come here, she thought miserably. Dragoner would be furious if he learned of it. Not that she cared a fig about that. It made no difference now, what he thought of her.

She had been trying to sort out what she thought of him, was all. But willy-nilly she had fallen into a familiar trap, seeking excuses for his behavior and finding reasons to justify her regard for him. It had been a mistake. She must give up on him. She *must*.

"I have come to a decision," said Madame de Staël in a firm voice. "You require more information than I am at liberty to reveal, and only the duke can provide it you. But he is in Belgium, I fear, and likely to remain there for some time. Until his return, will you consent to be ruled by me?"

Delilah looked up at her in surprise. *Ruled?* Why should this formidable woman take the slightest interest in her? And she most certainly would not dare to question the Duke of Wellington about her husband. Good heavens!

"Madame," she said, "it is my intention to leave as soon as may be for England. My companion is even now making the arrangements."

"What? Leave Paris? *Quelle idée!* But you cannot remain at an hôtel, of course. I shall have rooms prepared for you here."

"But Lady Hepzibah—"

"Yes, a room for her as well. You will both be company for me in the afternoons. My mornings, you understand, are given over to writing. Have you read my books?"

"N-no, ma'am," Delilah replied, wretched with confusion and embarrassment. "Perhaps you did not know. My father is in trade."

"Well, what of it? Does it follow that you are illiterate? When you have read the books I shall lend you, I should like your opinion of them. But you needn't reply, of course, if it turns out to be unfavorable." Madame smiled. "In the evenings, you will attend my salons and add a welcome dash of English good sense to the conversation. Ah, but your wardrobe. What you are wearing will not do. Stand, if you please, and turn slowly around."

Sure she had been caught up in a whirlwind, Delilah found herself doing as she was told.

"It will take a bit of work," Madame de Staël pronounced. "But Madame Récamier will be delighted to assist, and when she is done with you, all of Paris will be charmed by the incomparable Lady Dragoner." She tapped her chin with her forefinger. "I see that you are nerve-jangled, my dear. Even, perhaps, a little afraid. But I see a great many other things as well, and they persuade me that you should do exactly as I say."

"But why? That is, I am honored. Except that it makes no sense you should pay me any mind whatever. And how could I stay? My husband expects me to return to England."

"I daresay. But we shall surprise him. And annoy him, I have no doubt. It will be good for him. And you are not a captive, child. Once you have spoken with the duke, you are free to stay or depart, however you are inclined." Her face grew solemn. "How will you learn the truth if you do not remain in France long enough to hear it?"

"*Is* there a truth I ought to hear?"

"*Mais certainement.* Have you the courage, Lady Dragoner, to put yourself into my hands for the next few weeks? It won't always be pleasant, but you will not regret doing so."

Delilah clung with both hands to the back of the chair. The coward in her was driving her to scamper home and lick her wounds in solitary misery.

But there would be her family to face. Explanations to make. Their well-meaning pity. Dear God, she did not want to be pitied.

Her breath caught painfully in her throat. Madame de Staël proposed to take her up like a lost puppy, which she supposed she was. But she had a new life to build for herself, one that did not include her husband. Why not begin that life here and now?

"I would be most grateful for your help," she said simply. "Will you tell me why you have offered it?"

In response, Madame de Staël beckoned her to the writing

desk and held up a small painting framed in ornately carved silver. The picture was of a dashing young man astride a large, haughty steed.

"My lover," she said. "John Rocca. He is twenty years my junior, handsome and gallant and not, I fear, overly intelligent. But he adores me, and one day, if he continues to importune me, perhaps I shall consent to marry him."

Delilah politely examined the picture. "I am sorry, madame. He is quite splendid, of course, but I do not understand what he has to do with my own circumstances."

"Why, nothing at all. I speak only of love, inscrutable love, which cannot be measured with logic or understood except in the silence of one's heart. It merely *is*, like the moon's call to the tides or the inescapable hold of gravity. We yield to it because we must."

"I see," Delilah said, although she did not. Love seemed to have very little to do with her.

Rising, Madame de Staël tugged on the bell rope. "You will come to me tomorrow morning," she said briskly. "I shall send my carriage for you. Are we agreed?"

"Y-yes, madame."

What else was she to reply? Gravity, however inescapable, could take lessons from Madame Germaine de Staël.

Chapter 10

". . . though I go alone, Like to a lonely dragon."

Coriolanus
Act 4, Scene 1

The countryside, baking under a ferocious August sun, stretched on both sides of the narrow road in shades of brown, green, and gold. Dragoner rode north, keeping well away from any route that might be selected by a traveler bound for Calais. More specifically, by a carriage containing his wife, who had set out for England that very morning.

He had made certain of it, stopping by the Hôtel St. Pierre on his way out of Paris. The manager assured him that Lady Dragoner and Lady Hepzibah had paid their shot and departed with their luggage in a fashionable coach. Unhappily, the gentleman had missed them by little more than an hour. And no, they had not left a direction where a message might be delivered.

At the news, Dragoner had nearly abandoned his own plans to travel. It no longer seemed urgent to escape the city, now that Delilah was no longer in it, and he didn't relish a long ride aboard the placid mare Edoard had procured for him.

"All there was," Edoard had said after not listening to his complaint.

Horses were hard to come by on either side of the Channel, it seemed. Émigrés and travel-starved aristocrats flooding into Paris hired every decent mount that hadn't been snatched up by officers of the occupying armies, which were strewn out across the Champs de Mars and the Tuileries.

The city where he had formerly moved with negligent ease no longer existed. Any number of places were closed to him now—the Champs Elysées, for one, where thirty thousand British troops had been quartered. If recognized by any one of them, he could find himself dangling from an improvised noose.

Fortunately he knew where to apply for a horse, although it had required him to impose yet again on the Comte de Marais, who kept an excellent stable at his estate near the village of Argenteuil. Augustin wasn't at home, but his shy young wife gave Dragoner leave to select a mount and sent him on his way with a wicker lunch basket.

He stopped to eat in the late afternoon near a listless stream that flowed alongside a hedgerow. There was one tree for shade, and a few cows nibbled dry grass in an adjacent pasture. Seated with his back against the trunk, he spread pâté on chunks of crusty bread and finished off a pair of roasted chicken legs, a pickled onion, a thick sandwich of ham and cheese, and an apple.

The flagon of wine he left alone, drinking instead from the stream. He was riding out, after all, to clear his head and, he hoped, to arrive at a decision about his future. Surely there was *something* he wanted to do. *Somewhere* he wanted to go.

Pâté and water, he decided after a time, insidiously transformed an otherwise cynical man into a maudlin brooder. Or perhaps it was the familiar experience of sitting alone on a country road, watching the sun arc toward the western horizon and waiting for a cloud of dust to signal the approach of a carriage.

On this quiet afternoon, he had no such expectation. Should a coach or a wagon come into view, it would have nothing to do with him. He needn't even look up, and there would be no heart-stopping disappointment when it passed him by.

He folded his arms behind his head, closed his eyes, and let the memories tumble free.

Papa had told him they were playing a game, rather like hide-and-seek, but only the family could know about it. He was to do as he was told, and if all went well, he would be rewarded with a treat. He'd liked the first part of the game. For two or three days in a row, Mama and Papa would go out of the inn wearing a great many clothes, one piece on top of another. They looked funny, but he wasn't to laugh.

Sometimes they took him for long walks, and he had to memorize the place where he was to hide and the way to get there from the inn.

He was the family decoy, they said, but at five, he'd thought they were calling him the family duck. That, too, made him want to laugh.

When it was time for the game to play out, the duck's task was to stay in the room after his parents had gone and wait until it was night and the inn was very quiet. Then, making sure that no one saw him, he would tiptoe down the stairs and let himself out. Sometimes it was hard to find his way in the dark, but he always managed to arrive at the place they had showed him. And eventually—often many hours later—the coach would come by and pick him up.

Only once, on his seventh birthday, did they fail to appear. He was sure he'd gone to the right spot. In the light of a big round moon, he recognized the stone barn and the little house across the field, and the tree beside the stream where he had been directed to wait. Papa had scratched a tiny C for Charles in the bark.

The sun rose, and still they hadn't come. Like a good duck, he stayed there all day, hiding behind the tree when strangers passed by. Above all things, he had been warned, he was never to seek help from strangers. He ate some of the berries that grew in the hedgerow, but they made him sick to his stomach. Later he found a bird's egg and sucked it dry.

When night fell, he dug out a hollow in the ground, lined it with field grasses, and curled himself into a shivering ball. He was afraid to go to sleep. What if they came, and didn't find him, and drove away? He listened hard for the sound of horses' hooves and carriage wheels.

Papa had always said that Dragoner men were brave and up to every trick, but it wasn't true. He was scared. And as the long night wore on, he thought that probably he would always be scared. Always alone.

By the time a battered coach pulled to a stop beside the tree, he was crying uncontrollably. Papa had hauled him inside and slapped him across the face. Tears were for babies, he said, and Charles was a stupid boy for mistaking the day. Mama said nothing at all.

He had not mistaken the day, of course. The game had been set for his birthday, with a special present to be given him after he escaped the inn. But there was no present, because Papa was in a bad mood. He had lost at the tables, Mama whispered later. Charles had no idea what the tables were, but he had learned what it meant to lose. He never cried again.

There were a number of surreptitious departures from hotels, inns, and posthouses before he'd grown too old to be an effective duck. Wary landlords took to securing him inside the room whenever his parents left him behind, so he taught himself to pick every sort of lock. If a door was firmly barred, he went out the window and slid down a rope made of sheets he'd knotted together.

It had all been excellent training, he supposed, for a spy. Over the years, Papa had taught him any number of useful things—how to gamble, how to make himself charming, how to lie. When Wellington had no further use for him, he could quite well take up where his father had left off, trading on his title and good looks. All the world, it seemed, opened its arms to a handsome aristocrat.

Another city, another adventure. That's what he had told Delilah, and perhaps it was the truth.

Amused, he watched a family of curious ducks waddle up the bank to where he was sitting. In the spirit of brotherhood, he fed them the remains of his lunch.

Now that he had come to a decision about his future, there was no point going on from here. But neither was there a good reason to go back. He would not be truly free, he thought somewhat irrationally, until Delilah had left Calais and crossed the Channel. Besides, he had never before been at liberty to explore the French countryside north of Paris, and the weather was exceptionally fine. He had a good horse to ride and an excess of energy to burn off. He was due a holiday.

After washing his face in the stream, he rolled his riding coat into a log of fabric, stowed it in his saddlepack, and continued north in his shirtsleeves and a buckskin waistcoat. Along the way, he decided to let his beard grow and masquerade as a half-pay French soldier named Charles Gerard.

The country folk welcomed him or spat at him, depending on how the French troops had behaved whenever they were bivouacked in the neighborhood. No one questioned his false identity. But all too soon, the peace of mind he imagined that he had found, or thought he'd pieced together, began to seep away. He had been fooling himself to think it would be so easy to escape responsibility. His journey had become a pilgrimage without a destination, and as the days went by, the shadows of his past lined up to accompany him.

He knew them by name, each and every one of the women he had seduced to elicit their secrets and caused to betray their husbands and their country.

He knew the names, too, of the men he had robbed at the gaming tables to cover his expenses. When necessary, he had cheated. While the war was on, his army salary seldom reached him, and even spies had to pay for housing and food. An upper-class spy required fashionable clothing, a valet, and money enough to give the impression he had a great deal more of it.

There were reasons for everything he'd done, but was there justification? Deception had become second nature to him. He could scarcely differentiate truth from falsehood, so easily did he lie. Even to himself, he lied.

Once or twice in his wanderings, he drank enough home-brewed ale at a farmhouse to sleep without nightmares. He spent hours sitting in the back pews of country churches, staring at the altar and the flame glowing inside the red lamp beside the tabernacle, unable to pray. He didn't know what to ask for, and had nothing to offer in return.

Sometimes, when there was rain, he spent the night in the churches. But when the skies were clear, he slept under the stars. They put him in mind of Delilah, the stars, bright and faithful and far beyond his reach.

One Saturday morning, invited to a wedding in a small village, he made the mistake of accepting. The bride was tall and angular, with dark hair and lapis-colored eyes. She looked not at all like Delilah until she smiled and showed two pert dimples. He fled.

When he crossed into Belgium, gossip had it that the Duke of Wellington could be found touring the countryside south of Brussels. Puzzled, he decided to see for himself and eventually picked up the duke's trail at Charleroi, where all became clear. He recognized one of the men traveling with Wellington as a colonel of the Corps of Engineers. Years ago, Dragoner had often ridden out with a party like this one, scouting for battle positions and seeking places where a river could be forded.

In a local tavern, for the price of a round of ale, he learned what the foreigners were up to. The Prince of Orange, not at all reassured by Bonaparte's abdication, was convinced that the French Army would quickly reorganize itself and mount an invasion of the Low Countries. At his request the English general had agreed to inspect aging fortifications and choose sites for new ones, which amused Dragoner's drinking companions no end. Prince Billy, they said, hadn't the money to build so much as a pigsty.

Wellington would know that, of course. So why the devil was he here?

Lacking anything better to do, Dragoner followed at a distance, keeping watch on the duke through his spyglass. The exploring party spent all the next day surveying the rolling countryside just south of the forest of Soignes, where there were no fortifications to inspect. Wellington rode off by himself for several hours, tracing every small ridge and slope as if visualizing how best to align his troops for a decisive battle.

Dragoner, concealed in a small orchard behind a farmhouse, reckoned the duke was enjoying one last chance to play at being a field marshal before taking up his duties as a mere ambassador.

Finally, as the late-afternoon sun gilded the rye fields and cast shadows over the orchard, Wellington gathered his companions and set out at a fast clip on the road that led directly to Brussels. Playtime, it seemed, was at an end.

Left to his own devices again, Dragoner wandered into a nearby village and took a room for the night, which he spent mentally composing a letter of resignation.

Flourish. Exeunt.

It was clear to him that he was no longer of use in Paris. Perhaps Wellington would consider releasing him, after which he would take himself off to Italy. Or to Greece. He might get a chance to fight in Greece, if the Turks went on making a nuisance of themselves.

Before dawn, he rode out of the village of Waterloo in a foul mood that lasted all the way to Paris.

Someone had finished painting his house, Dragoner noted without interest as he let himself inside and wearily mounted the stairs.

Edoard, one arm wrapped around Minette's waist and a gleam in his currant-black eyes, caught up with him on the landing. "Thought I heard you come in," he said, following him up the second flight of stairs. "There's news. Nothing urgent, though. Want to hear it now or later?"

"Tell him now," Minette advised, "while I put water to heat for a bath."

Dragoner, wishing both of them to the devil, dropped his saddlepack on the floor and collapsed face-front onto his bed.

It felt . . . different. For once, he failed to immediately sink between lumps of padding to the center of the mattress. No dust rose from the counterpane. For that matter, the counterpane was blue. The one he was used to had been a moldy green. He rolled over, sat up cross-legged, and looked around the room.

There was a new carpet on the floor. New curtains at the window. A new armoire against the wall.

"Nice, ain't it?" Edoard remarked cheerfully. "The workmen and suppliers had already been paid, so I let them in to finish the job. Didn't figure you'd object."

"No." What was the point? "You said there was news."

"Good and bad, as usual." Edoard's smile faded. "Beltrand—the fellow we met at Ivre l'Oie—is in contact again. His employer wants to meet with you. Word is that he'll be at the tavern every night this week. And I've been out and about, picking up on rumors. What I heard is written down the way you taught me. There might be something there worth following up."

"Such as—?"

Now Edoard looked distinctly unhappy. "Happen it's the usual," he said, lapsing into his Yorkshire drawl. "The newspapers have taken to calling the duke 'Lord Villainton.' He ain't even here yet, but already factions are scheming to kick him out. Nothing precise, though. No out-and-out plot I've managed to uncover. The sods are just now getting organized, but in a month or two, there will be trouble. Assassination, I expect, or a try at it."

So much for his letter of resignation. "And this is the *good* news, I take it?"

"You can read the other for yourself." Edoard went to the dressing room and returned with a small parcel, which he tossed onto the bed. "This was delivered the day after you left, and I'm guessing there's a letter inside." There was a long pause, followed by a gritty sigh. "In case not, I'd better tell you this much. Lady Dragoner is still in Paris."

The parcel had landed near his hand. Dragoner looked down at it, his heart suddenly pounding double-time. "Go away," he said. "Come back in ten minutes."

Half that time had passed before he could bring himself to untie the string and open the parcel. Inside the brown paper wrapping was a sealed note, which he put aside, and a small velvet-covered box. His hands were shaking as he opened it.

There, gleaming up from its blue velvet nest, was a pocket watch. And on its gold casing was engraved the Dragoner seal, identical to the one on his signet ring except that the image of the dragon was ringed with the motto of his family: *Dans L'Adversité, le Courage et la Foi.*

In Adversity, Courage and Faith.

Had any Dragoner ever lived up to that? he wondered.

Setting aside the box, he forced himself to open the note. It was brief, but hard to read because the words kept jumping around. He wiped his eyes with his sleeve and tried again.

"You should know," Delilah wrote, "that I have decided to remain in Paris for a time as the guest of Madame de Staël. I am sorry if it displeases you. Nonetheless, I require to speak with you before I return to England and hope you will do me the kindness to pay a call within the next few weeks. What I have to say will most certainly meet with your approval.

"As for the pocket watch, I had ordered it from Monsieur Breguet as a gift for your birthday and could scarcely return it after it had been engraved. Keep it if you like, or not."

There was no signature.

The air began spinning in dull gray circles. He folded his arms over his crossed knees and bent his head. She was here. She wanted to see him.

What could she possibly say that he would approve?

That they were done with each other? But that was clear as rainwater. He had no wish to hear her reaffirm it to his face.

That she meant to go away and leave him? But she hadn't gone away, had she?

Pretty, earnest, impossibly naïve Delilah. Delilah of the needle-sharp wit and the iron will.

No, he would not meet with her again. The last encounter had drained him of his last ounce of courage. There was none to spare for her now.

What's gone and what's past help should be past grief.

Should be. And wasn't. Shakespeare didn't always get it right. He was grieving anyway, and expected that he always would. If only—if only—he could be sure that she would not.

Of all the things he regretted, and there were too many of them to count, he was most deeply sorry that he had hurt Delilah. She ought to have met him before he became his father's duck, a player of devious games who grew up to play deadly games.

Before he lost his soul.

A rap on the door, swiftly followed by Edoard stepping into the room, compelled him to sit upright and produce a smile. "The bath is ready?"

"In the kitchen, m'lord. Are we going out tonight?"

Dragoner hated it when Eddie "m'lorded" him. "Why not? Perhaps our friends at The Drunken Goose have devised a scheme for us to foil."

Chapter 11

"Good Lord, what madness rules in brainsick men."

Henry VI, Part 1
Act 4, Scene 1

The rundown tavern on the riverbank had lost none of its dubious charm, Dragoner reflected as he made his way across the taproom with Edoard at his side. It was, however, considerably less crowded than before, the hour being early, and there was only one man seated at the table behind the tapestry screen.

Beltrand of the bright yellow hair, his hands wrapped around a battered tankard, was staring into his drink and looking decidedly morose.

"'Yea, watch his pettish lunes, his ebbs and flows,'" said Dragoner, tapping his cane on the screen.

Beltrand jerked to attention, sloshing ale onto the table. "*Qu'avez-vous dit?* My English is not good. And what is this? You have brought your *valet?*"

"Edoard gets out so seldom," Dragoner replied in French. "I am giving him a treat."

"He must remain here, then." Beltrand stood. "The gentleman you have come to meet is waiting upstairs."

"Unless it's the Pope waiting upstairs, I see no reason to leave my servant behind. You may have noticed that he carries a pistol. My regrettable aversion to meeting a stranger in a strange room, you understand."

Shrugging, Beltrand led them to a narrow staircase. "It's all the same to me. But you will find no strangers here. Only compatriots, bound to a common cause."

When they reached the end of a dim passageway, Dragoner and Edoard were ushered into a sparsely furnished bedchamber. Two men stood near the lone window, which was open to catch the breeze, and Dragoner recognized them from his first encounter with Beltrand. The young man—Jervin?—wasn't there.

He also recognized the lanky figure stretched out on the bed with his shoulders propped against the headboard.

Chuckling, Dragoner passed his cane and hat to Edoard and sank onto a rough-hewn chair. "Cards or dice?" he inquired silkily.

"But you have already plucked the last centime from my pocket," Jacques Batiste responded mournfully. "I meant to surprise you. Are you not astonished to see me here?"

"In fact, yes." It wouldn't hurt to give him the satisfaction. "I hadn't thought you cared a fig for politics."

"Nor *did* I, until France was invaded by foreign pigs. Take no insult. If the rumors are true, you have no love for your countrymen, nor any credit with them. Indeed, when you disappeared from Paris after your first visit to Ivre L'Oie, I could only presume you had fled their retribution."

"I shall probably have to, one of these days." Dragoner draped an arm over the back of his chair. "Am I wasting my time here, Batiste, or do you mean to provide a reason for me to stay?"

"Ah, the English. Always in a hurry. But we shall, as you say, come to the point." He frowned at Edoard, who was leaning against the closed door with a hand concealed under his coat. "You wish your servant to hear this?"

"That depends on what you have to say, of course, but a little talk of sedition would please him enormously. When not devotedly ironing my shirts, Edoard invents preposterous schemes to rescue Bonaparte from Elba."

"We are not so ambitious, I am afraid. Elba is far away. But Wellington is near, or soon will be. It is our intention to dispose of him." Batiste grinned. "I thought perhaps, given your recent contretemps with the ambassador, you might like to do the honors."

Dragoner confined his reaction to lifting a brow. "An assassination? To what purpose?"

"For my fellow Bonapartistes, it would be a gesture of defiance. A rallying cry as well, to those who believe our cause is lost. It is not. The people must be made to see that there is hope if only we unite against our foes."

After a moment's consideration, Dragoner called his bluff. "And someone will pay you to kill Wellington?"

"That, too," Batiste acknowledged, erupting in laughter. "So I'm not political, as you had already divined. But there's money to be had from those who are."

"No doubt. Should I assume you have a sponsor lined up, or are you still taking bids?"

Batiste sobered. "Naturally I am unable to divulge that information. Shall we speak frankly? We are not friends, you and I. Far from it. But we are both gamesters, and we need not be at odds with each other when there is a greater prize within reach. I called you in for two reasons. One, you've a better chance of coming near Wellington than I or any of the others. And two, for reasons of your own, you *want* to see him dead."

He leaned forward, fixing his eyes on Dragoner. "Am I mistaken, or would it not give you pleasure to put a bullet between his eyes?"

"Oh, momentarily. But then his bodyguards would tear me limb from limb. And you *are* mistaken to think I could get close enough to take a clear shot." Batiste was just another man in the middle, Dragoner was thinking, only a step above Beltrand. Who was orchestrating this half-baked conspiracy?

"Besides," he added, "killing the Duke of Wellington would make of him a martyr. Has your superior thought to the consequences? The Vienna Congress would impose war reparations severe enough to bankrupt France into the next century."

"Then what?" Batiste flung himself off the bed. "Unless we do *something*, our pockets—yours and mine—stay empty."

"How can I say, without knowing the intentions of the man who has the resources to fill them?"

They were going round in circles now. Nothing, Dragoner

thought angrily, would come of this unless he took the lead. But—the spy *creating* the plot in order to squelch it? He ought to walk out now, before the temptation grew too strong.

"There was another idea proposed," Batiste said with obvious reluctance. "But I can't see how it would work."

Dragoner, half risen, sank back on his chair. "Tell me."

Batiste had rambled on for several minutes before Dragoner put the pieces together. But they didn't quite fit. At the center was a gaping hole, which he reckoned could only be filled if he knew the identity of Batiste's superior and the reasons behind his determination to draw an Englishman—perhaps this particular Englishman—into his scheme.

A fairly reliable tingling at his spine had long since put Dragoner on his guard. Was *he*, and not the duke, the focus of all this attention? It seemed unlikely, on the face of it. If someone wanted him dead, why not set a band of thugs on him in the street? Fire at him from an alleyway? He made a fairly easy target, most of the time. Until now, he'd had no cause to expect an ambush.

Well, it didn't really matter. Whatever this was about, he had already resolved to see it through. Help it along, if need be.

"Let's see if I have this straight," he said, interrupting Batiste midsentence. "You propose to steal works of art looted by Napoleon and brought to France, and make it appear that Wellington has reapporpriated them for himself."

"Something of the kind. It was a suggestion offered by someone else. I don't like the idea."

"No? Perhaps you have not given it the proper consideration. Should the plan succeed, Wellington's appointment would be withdrawn and he left with no choice but to slink home to England in disgrace. A nice touch, that. I find a good deal of merit in the idea. But how do you intend to put the blame onto him?"

Batiste held out his hands. "Who knows? It's bound to be easier than walking out of the Louvre with an armload of paintings."

"Oh, I shouldn't think you'd get away with that." Honestly, this was all too simple. The planning, at any rate. Dragoner was less certain this lot of imbeciles would manage to follow through with the plan, even if he drew them a map, but he would have to leave the execution to them. His leash, the one held by the duke, stopped short of wanton criminal activity. "Not everything Bonaparte brought to France is contained in the Louvre, you know."

Beltrand spoke up. "We can't break into government buildings. Or Malmaison, or the houses of the emperor's friends."

"Certainly not. But were you aware—no, I don't suppose you were—that provincial museums were established by your emperor so that common citizens could delight in the booty of war?" By coincidence, Dragoner had explored two or three of them on his travels in the north of France. He smiled. "It was little enough to give the people, don't you think, in exchange for their sons."

"Where are they, these museums?" Batiste looked positively exuberant. "How well are they guarded?"

"Really, you'll have to do *some* of the work," Dragoner said. "But if you've no idea how to go about it, I might lend you Edoard for a time. Inventive fellow, my valet. He will expect to be treated as befits my own rank, you understand. And in return, perhaps he'll teach Mr. Beltrand how to tie a neckcloth."

Mr. Beltrand glowered.

"Excellent!" Batiste, evidently imagining himself in the throes of invention, began to pace. "When we have the locations, I'll dispatch my people to steal whatever they can carry away. Anything we don't need for our plan can be sold. I know a place to store the goods. It will be well, I think, if the thieves are wearing uniforms of the English army. They can be seen in the vicinity before the museums are robbed." He turned to Dragoner. "Yes?"

"If you have a way to come by the uniforms, I expect they would direct suspicion where we want it placed."

"Oh, with a dozen duels being fought each day in the Bois de Boulogne, we've only to strip a few corpses. What else? What else?"

Batiste's eyes held the demonic fire Dragoner had often seen from across the gaming tables at Le Chien Noir. When caught up in such a passion, he inevitably went too far. And lost. But he was, unfortunately, quite right about the bodies strewn hither and yon after irresponsible duels. Sometimes it appeared that disgruntled French officers had set out to win the war after it was over by picking off their English counterparts one by one. There were, of course, plenty of French uniforms to be found in the Bois de Boulogne as well.

Perhaps Edoard would be able to talk Batiste out of his most radical notion. But for the present, Dragoner merely settled back, awaiting the inevitable questions.

The first came straightaway. "Wellington would only want the most valuable items," Batiste observed, eyes wide at his own brilliance for thinking of it. "But I'm no connoisseur. How do we choose?"

"Perhaps your sponsor?" Dragoner suggested delicately.

"I don't know. He wishes to remain above reproach, should anything go wrong. Not that it will. I mean to see that it doesn't."

Batiste appeared to be taking this business more personally than the circumstances would warrant. Or maybe not. He had always aspired to a position in society that he could not afford to maintain, given his addiction to gaming. And in that, he was not unlike hundreds of other younger sons lacking an inheritance or the prospect of gainful employment. Dragoner had always wondered, though, how Jacques Batiste, a perfectly healthy specimen of young manhood, had managed to avoid conscription into the army. Had his brother exerted a bit of aristocratic influence?

"Much of my life," said Dragoner reflectively, "has been spent in travel. An extended Grand Tour, if you will, one that has included most of the great houses and museums in Europe. I expect that I can distinguish quality from dross. When you have assembled a stash of paintings, statues, and whatnots, I shall examine them and select the items to be foisted on Wellington. Will that do?"

"You have a way in mind to accomplish that? The foisting, I mean."

The inevitable second question. "I believe so. But until you have done your part, mine is irrelevant. I suggest that you lose no time getting about it, Jacques." He used the Christian name deliberately, to imply a bond where none existed. "Once Wellington has established himself in Paris, he will be all that much more difficult to dislodge. And too, I imagine your sponsor will grow impatient if you have nothing specific to tell him when he quizzes you."

Batiste's lips tightened. "He'll not be disappointed. One week, or at the most two, so long as you—or your valet—tells us where the museums are located. Directions to those nearest to Paris will suffice."

Rising, Dragoner stretched broadly and pretended to stifle a yawn. "Well, it's not quite so simple as that," he said. "We have not yet established how I am to be paid for my services, nor how the spoils are to be divided when we sell the leftover *objets d'art*. Not to mention that while Edoard is working for you, he cannot perforce be working for me. I shall expect compensation."

"We can do without your servant," Batiste said huffily.

"Oh, but you can't. He is the most valuable thing I have to offer. The linchpin, if you will, of our plan. Like your sponsor, I find it in my own interest to distance myself, given that I walk on eggs as it is. If I am driven from Paris, you understand, I cannot help you in any way."

"Yes, yes. But let us settle the details now, between us. We are the principals."

"To the contrary. You answer to someone else, and I do not. Tomorrow night Edoard will return here and deliver my terms, along with an accounting of how he proposes to be of assistance to you. If you find what you hear unsatisfactory, send him back to me and that will be that. I'll not expose you, should you choose to proceed without my cooperation."

Dragoner moved to where Batiste was standing and clapped him on the shoulder. "I have no love for Wellington, as you know. Even without financial reward, I would be delighted if you brought him to his knees." He grinned. "Of course, should you manage to fill your pockets with ill-gotten gains, I shall be waiting at Le Chien Noir to empty them again."

After a moment, Batiste produced a barking laugh. "I have no doubt of that. But my luck is due to turn. Keep it in mind."

"Oh, I do, Jacques. I always do. Your skill has never been in question. Only bad luck has brought you down. As it will me, I am certain, one of these days. But we both play—do we not?—because gaming is in our blood. There are worse ways to live."

He had hoped the gesture would seal something between them, but when he had reached the door, which was opened by Edoard, Batiste spoke again.

"And what of your wife?" he asked, a false note of indifference in his voice. "Is she a factor?"

"Why, how could she be?" Dragoner turned, heat burning under the mask of surprise on his face. "What has she to do with this?"

"Nothing. Or something. A week ago you told Beltrand that she was returning to England. But you left Paris the next day, and she remained."

"So I am told. She was taken up, it seems, by Madame de Staël, who does not approve of me. I imagine they dissect my character over breakfast and enumerate my faults during lunch. What of it?"

"Do you mean to see her while she is here?"

More and more puzzling. And ominous. What could it matter to Batiste? Dragoner chose his words with care. "I haven't decided. One brief call, perhaps, to express my displeasure. I told her to go home, and she has failed to obey me. But then, she ignores me as studiously as I do her. So long as she stays out of my way, she may do as she likes."

"There is no love between you? And no heir, I understand." Batiste shook his head. "I wonder that you have not divorced her."

Dragoner was surprised into a laugh. "Trust me, I would if I could. But I married her in England, where the law requires an Act of Parliament to detach a man from a wife he doesn't want. I expect that when she's done shopping and cavorting in Madame de Staël's salon, Lady Dragoner will trundle home to her family where she belongs. I wed her for the dowry, you know, and I've long since spent it all. She is of no use to me now."

"But her family has money?"

Why did he persist? "None I can put my hands on," Dragoner said unhappily. "Her father is ambitious, but when I failed to elevate him into society, he cut me off. Perhaps he will succeed in marrying one of his other daughters to a more cooperative aristocrat. Meantime, is there a reason why we are discussing my personal affairs?"

Batiste shook his head. "None. None. I was curious, that's all. My apologies."

Unclenching his hands, hoping Batiste had failed to notice them, Dragoner tossed him an amiable smile. "Be kind to Edoard. Don't forget. From here on out, he speaks for me."

Chapter 12

"The blackest news that ever thou heard'st."

The Two Gentlemen of Verona
Act 3, Scene 1

In the parlor where, two months earlier, he had waited to be humiliated by the Duke of Wellington, Dragoner sought among Madame de Staël's guests for his wife.

The doors had not been closed to him—Delilah would have seen to that—but navigating the crowded grande salon was not an experience he looked forward to repeating. When their gazes fell on him, people moved away as if he were carrying an infectious disease.

Madame herself, ensconced on her Grecian sofa, had spared him a keen glance before turning her attention elsewhere, but she must have suspected why he'd come. Not long after, a servant approached him with word that Lady Dragoner could be found in an adjacent parlor.

He paused at the door, scanning the guests for a glimpse of disorderly hair and outlandish dimples. Eventually he spotted the Comte de Chabot, or rather, his back, and beside him the Prince de Talleyrand, Minister for Foreign Affairs, leaning negligently on his cane. They were standing at the far end of the room, speaking to someone who made Talleyrand laugh. After a moment, he bowed and moved away, revealing a slender figure wearing a gown of muted gold.

Dragoner almost failed to recognize his wife. This was not the wan creature he'd last seen seated on a straight-backed chair, her arms wrapped around her waist, tears streaming down her cheeks. The transformation stunned him. She was beautiful. Radiant. As sophisticated as any patrician French courtesan assured of her own desirability.

Someone must have introduced her to a fashionable modiste. Some *man*, he corrected sourly. Only a male would have selected that shamelessly low-cut, indecently clinging dress. She looked as if she had been dipped in a pot of honey.

And Chabot was standing too close to her. Infuriatingly close. Dragoner fought a primitive compulsion to launch himself at the Frenchman and plant him a facer.

A few heads had turned in his direction, and voices began to still. Delilah glanced over then, her expression friendly and markedly impersonal. The nightmarish scene in his bedchamber might never have happened. He was looking at a stranger.

Appearances must be preserved, he supposed. At least twenty people were observing this encounter with avid curiosity. Slipping a polite expression onto his face, he strolled over to where she was standing, poised as an Egyptian temple cat, regarding him with a notable lack of interest.

He bowed, and because it would annoy her, said, " 'What, my dear Lady Disdain! are you yet living?' "

" 'Is it possible Disdain should die,' " she replied smoothly, " 'while she hath such meet food to feed it as Signior' . . . well, I suppose I must say 'Signior Dragoner.' "

He blinked.

And then he saw that Chabot had moved even closer to her, his lapels all but resting on her bare shoulder. Like a ram in rut, he was staking out his territory.

Ferocious willpower held Dragoner's feet in place while all the rest of him thrummed with primal male instincts of the brutish kind.

"Ah, it is Dragoner," said the comte, unaware that he was moments away from an ugly death. "I was under the impression Madame de Staël had barred her doors to you."

"Plainly you were mistaken," he said, years of experience supplying an automatic response to his lips. "She is inexplicably fond of me. But as it happens, I am here on this occasion to speak with my wife. You won't mind, I am sure, if I claim a few minutes of her time."

"Certainly not, so long as you return her to me." Chabot's long-fingered hand settled on her shoulder in an unmistakably possessive gesture. "I shall be waiting for you, *chère* Delia."

Delilah smiled up at him. "I am counting on it, Gustave. You promised to teach me how to play billiards."

She called him by his Christian name? Black spots danced before Dragoner's eyes. Never once had she addressed her own husband as "Charles." Not that he wanted her to, of course, having no desire to be on intimate terms with his wife. But neither did he relish the idea of Delilah on intimate terms with another man. With *any* other man.

Stepping forward, she slipped her arm around his elbow. The touch shot through him like an electric current. His brain sizzled and went blank.

She had led him through a door and down a long passageway before he came to his senses and detached his arm. "Where are we going?" he asked, putting a space between them.

"To the gardens," she replied, maddeningly at ease. "I know of a spot at the far end of the formal garden. Unless someone else has claimed it, we can be private there."

A number of people, in clusters of two or three, were sitting on marble benches or walking along the paths of the parterred garden, enjoying the balmy August night. Overhead, a crescent moon, thin as a fingernail paring, hung amid a blaze of winking stars. Behind a potted orange tree, a man and a woman drew together in an embrace. Dragoner looked away.

Gravel crunched under his feet as Delilah guided him beyond the formal gardens and into a shadowy copse. From one of the tree branches, a nightbird sang. He heard the sound of splashing water and the chirp of crickets. Then they emerged into a clearing lit by a circle of torches, and he saw a round marble fountain with the statue of a dancing nymphet at its center. A nude nymphet, poised on the ball of one foot, her other leg extended behind her. Water streamed from her outstretched fingers, and from her mouth, and yes, from her nipples.

From fairies and the tempters of the night, Guard me.

The very air was charged with erotic tension. Beside him,

within reach of his hands, Delilah's breasts gleamed in the torch-light. He ought not to have come here.

She turned to face him, her dimples flashing as she smiled. "You read my letter! I confess myself amazed."

Along with a number of other things he disapproved, she had learned sarcasm. All in two short weeks. "I was probably drunk at the time," he said, defensively matching her tone. "And I expected the letter to be from someone else. I had thought we were finished with each other."

"As did I. My first inclination was to flee back to England, lick my wounds, and go on as I had done before. But on reflection, I realized that new opportunities were scattered all around me, waiting to be gathered up. Are you outraged to find me still in Paris?"

He was outraged, that was certain, although he could scarcely put the reasons into words. "You are free to do as you like, of course. And should I command you to leave, I doubt you'd pay me any mind."

She made a noncommittal gesture. "In the usual course of things, sir, there is little likelihood that we shall encounter each other. You needn't fear I mean to plague you."

"I am delighted to hear it," he said, resisting a childish impulse to check the time so that she would see he was emphatically *not* carrying the pocket watch she had given him.

No longer smiling, she drew closer to the fountain. "What you told me about yourself, my lord, was excessively difficult to hear. Unbearable, really, and even now, I don't believe the half of it. But you may be sure that I have taken your point. You do not want me. I understand fully, and I accept it."

A dull ache settled in the back of his throat. "You continue to misunderstand, then. I was merely giving you the reasons—some of them, at any rate—why you ought not to want *me*. You became infatuated with the wrong man, is all. What I want or do not want is immaterial."

Mist, caught up by the breeze, settled over her hair like diamond dust. "I should greatly like to know what that is," she said. "I wonder if *you* know. But it is no longer my business, if indeed it ever was. I interfered in your life and persisted in doing so long after you made it perfectly clear the marriage was abhorrent to you. I imagined that if only I worked hard enough and invested all of myself in creating a home for you, I could make myself indispensable. I thought that I could somehow *earn* your love. But of course, I was mistaken. Love cannot be bought and sold in the marketplace. It can only be freely given, from the heart."

Cords tightened around his chest. Had she *loved* him? It didn't bear thinking of. She had desired him, no more than that. Over the years a great many women had desired him. He had grown accustomed to it. But love had never entered into his brief affairs, not even those he had enjoyed without ulterior motives. There must have been a few, although he could not recall them at the moment. It felt as if he'd been selling himself, one way or another, for all of his life.

She moved away, to the other side of the fountain. "I beg your pardon," she said. "I did not mean to dredge up the past. I only wished to assure you that I have put it behind me, and to thank you for compelling me to face the truth."

"Is that all, then?" He desperately hoped it was. She had *thanked* him, bugger all, for being a monster. For being cruel to be kind, which was, of course, the justification he had used to still his conscience. Who would have thought he still had one?

When she failed to respond, he forced himself to look over at her.

"I'm afraid there is more," she said at last. "You need to know why I have remained in Paris and what I mean to do here. If I am successful, you see, I shall eventually require your help."

He closed his eyes. It wasn't over, then. " 'How now, fair maid,' " he said lightly. " 'There is some ill a-brewing.' What will you have me do?"

Her sigh was audible. "In fact, Lord Dragoner, I have set myself to procure the only thing you have ever asked of me. You should know straightaway that I am not doing it for your sake, but for my own. I am speaking, you must already have realized, of a divorce."

The word hit him like a fist. It was the last thing he had expected her to say. "Given our circumstances," he said slowly, "I thought a divorce impossible to acquire."

"And so it was, practically speaking. But only because I had

failed to commit adultery. Without evidence that I had done so,
you had no grounds for a suit. But you soon will, for I intend to
provide both a co-respondent and witnesses who will testify in
court that they observed me *in flagrante delicto*. Or I mean to
try. There is no certainty I'll attract a lover, even in Paris, but at
least here I am able to cast my net. You understand that I am un-
welcome in London society on account of my birth and your
lamentable reputation."

Stunned, Dragoner blurted the first thing that came to mind.
"Not *Chabot?*"

"No? Well, at this point, he's only one of several candidates.
Frenchmen seem to delight in flirting, and I've too little experience to know if one of them is actually trying to seduce me. But
it's true that Gustave has been most attentive, and I suspect him
to be somewhat careless where morals are concerned."

"Of that you may be sure. Already he has buried two wives,
who coincidentally died not long after he had run through their
fortunes. I doubt you are sufficiently wealthy, my dear, to buy
him for yourself."

She flinched, or he thought she did. It was hard to tell through
the water streaming down between them. "But I only mean to
rent him," she said. "Assuming that he is amenable to a short-
term business transaction, of course. And if he is not, I'll find
someone else. You needn't concern yourself with the prelimi-
nary arrangements, my lord. When everything is in place, I shall
contact you again and ask for your cooperation. I am sure you'll
not withhold it."

She sounded a bit less certain at the end of that pronounce-
ment, as well she might. Never mind the ultimate goal. She was
asking his leave to have an affair with Chabot. No. She had
flatly declared her intention of doing so.

Chabot in bed with Delilah. Chabot touching her body.
Mounting her. He was an experienced man. He would give her
pleasure, as her husband had never done.

"You dislike him," she said. "I could tell when the two of you
met. But I trust that will not prove an obstacle. Indeed, when
comes the time to denounce us in court, you will be all that
much more convincing."

"Of course I dislike him. He is a womanizer, an opportunist, and a scoundrel. He survives by trading on his title and a certain degree of charm."

"You failed to mention that he is astonishingly handsome," she said. "In fact," she added with a decidedly feline smile, "you might as well have been describing yourself."

That rocked him on his heels. "Has it occurred to you," he fired back, "that you habitually set your sights on the wrong men?"

"Oh, yes. I can scarcely deny it. We have already agreed that I made a terrible mistake by marrying you. But I am wiser now. This time I know very well what I am about. And if Monsieur le Comte is in fact a rogue, he will nicely serve my purposes. I can hardly ask a decent man to mire himself in a divorce proceeding."

"You keep assuming I will agree to sue for divorce," he said. "What if I refuse?"

"But why should you? I'd offer to pay you for your trouble, except that you would take insult. Naturally I shall cover every expense—court fees, solicitors, travel for the witnesses and the like. And I will ask nothing from you. Nothing at all. Dragon's Hill is already yours, as is the river house and the investments I have made on your behalf. I want only my freedom, sir. You cannot begrudge me that. You would not be so mean-spirited."

He was such a tangle of unfamiliar emotions that he was sure mean-spirited must be among them. Along with fury and jealousy and resentment, and a vague sense of longing as well, although he couldn't put his finger on what it was that he longed for.

What is't I dream on?

Light from the torches had transformed the water spray into a curtain of gold. Beyond it stood Delilah, her hands loosely clasped, her head lifted to the sky.

He circled the fountain to where she was, and when she turned to face him, his pulse raced. For the space of a few heartbeats, he came perilously close to kissing her.

The sensation passed, leaving him chilled.

He said, "It always comes down to the price of things, does it not? A divorce will cost you your reputation, Delilah. Your family will pay dearly as well."

"Do you imagine I have not considered that? My father has a letter from me explaining what I mean to do and the reasons for it. Should he advise me not to proceed, then I shall likely fold up my tent and go home. But I expect him to give his approval, however reluctantly. He will understand, you see."

"Then help *me* to understand, Delilah. Why in the name of heaven are you doing this?"

Torchlight spilled over her face.

"For a child," she said softly. "For a family of my own. For a chance to be loved." Giving him a slow, sad smile, she lifted her gaze to a spot beyond his shoulder. "The odds are greatly against me, of course. Even if I managed to secure a divorce, which will be more difficult than I have made it appear, what sort of man would fall in love with a certified adulteress? Perhaps I will never meet such a man. But how will I know unless I try?

"The thing is," she continued after a pause, "I think a man—the right man this time—would not be disappointed in me. I have a great deal of love to give, you know. I simply need to redirect it to where it is wanted. In any case, my lord, I intend to make a new life for myself. For the opportunity to have children of my own, fathered by a man who loves me, there is nothing I would not dare."

He raised a hand, thinking to touch her cheek, and let it drop again. He had no right to touch her. And what was there for him to say to this remarkable woman, whose life he had effectively ruined? However often he'd told himself that she had entrapped him, the blame was entirely his. He had trusted a father who had betrayed him a hundred times. Been greedy to have his estate restored. Given no thought whatever to the young girl who stood beside him at the altar and vowed to love and honor and obey a man who had already laid plans to desert her.

He wished it undone, and her free, and himself sealed in a cold dark cave where he belonged.

Nothing goes right; we would, and we would not.

Her voice, when she spoke, trembled with fear. "Do you mean to deny me, sir?"

"No, Delilah," he said. "Not this time. When you need my help, send for me."

Chapter 13

" 'Tis a most gallant fellow. I would he loved his wife."

All's Well That Ends Well
Act 3, Scene 5

All in all, Delilah reflected a few days later, things were not going too badly.

Once she had recovered from Dragoner's glee at the prospect of being rid of her, she flung herself into the social circus with what her father would have described as zealous pigheadedness. But then, she required to be adamant, and purposeful as well. There was a crucial investment to be made in a man who would do her will and not make overmuch trouble about it, and that combination of virtues had thus far eluded her.

There had been plenty of gentlemen, though. Yes indeed. She scarcely knew what to make of the attention accorded her at salons and dinner parties and balls. As Madame de Staël's protegée, she was welcomed everywhere, and on one memorable afternoon, she had been presented to His Majesty the King. A very plump gentleman, to be sure, but he had kind eyes and a wry wit and spent several minutes speaking with her about England.

Even Heppy was pleased with her, most particularly because she had severed contact with her husband. Unaware of her true intentions, Heppy encouraged her to be extravagant at the shops and, for once in her life, to simply enjoy herself. Meantime the acerbic Lady Hepzibah had gathered a considerable court of her own. Most were ladies of her own age, but there

were several gentlemen as well, and one of them had quite a
gleam in his eyes. In consequence, Delilah was often free of her
companion for entire evenings at a stretch and left to get about
the business of finding a properly improper man.

Sometimes, if briefly, she wished that Dragoner were present
to see Delilah triumphant. But when such petty thoughts bub-
bled to the surface, she quickly squashed them down again. It
would be better to give him no thought at all, but under the circumstances, he could not help but be present in her mind. And
of course, the Comte de Chabot made frequent reference to
him.

With the comte, it was difficult to know how to go on. In
some ways he was easily handled, and like so many gentlemen,
he was especially susceptible to flattery. It gave him pleasure to
teach her to play billiards, and she had endured a number of
lessons at his Paris hôtel, crooning over his brilliant shots while
deliberately missing when it was her turn at the table. As her
brothers could have informed him, Delilah had long been the
reigning billiard champion of the Bening clan.

At other times, though, she surprised a look in his eyes that
spoke of lust mingled with something very like derision. But
then he would smile, and put his hand on the small of her back
to lead her into a dance or escort her into dinner, and be perfectly charming for hours on end.

After a particularly late night in company with him, she spent
a long time wondering if it would be better to devote less attention to the comte and more to the several other gentlemen
who had shown interest in her. The sun had risen before she put
the matter aside and buried her head into a pillow, no closer to
a decision than before.

It was past ten of the morning when the maid awoke her with
a knock on the door and carried in a tray of coffee, which she
set across Delilah's lap. On the tray was a brief note from
Madame de Staël.

"The Duke of Wellington has sent word that he will be
pleased to meet with Lady Dragoner this afternoon at two
o'clock."

Oh, heavens. Oh, no!

Madame de Staël had once promised to seek an appointment

for her with the duke, but in the weeks that followed, Delilah had put it from her mind. And what did it matter now, what she had intended to ask him?

After dressing quickly, she hurried to the room where Madame de Staël was taking her breakfast, only to be met by a frowning face and a wagging finger.

"Do not think to cancel the appointment," Madame said before Delilah could speak. "Yes, I know precisely what you are thinking. But His Grace has made time in his schedule for you, and it would be immeasurably rude to decline his invitation. I shall accompany you, of course, and Lady Hepzibah may come along if she wishes."

"But I—"

"We shall depart at one o'clock, and if we arrive early, so much the better. You will require a few minutes to compose yourself, and I have been curious to explore the new embassy." Madame de Staël gestured Delilah to sit across from her. "It won't be so bad, you know. The duke has a fondness for the company of pretty young women, especially if they are intelligent. You need only speak plainly to win his respect."

"Have you forgot the subject I had intended to address?" Delilah shivered. "He cannot wish to have a conversation, plain or otherwise, about Lord Dragoner. Not that it signifies. I'm sure I'll not be able to utter a single word."

"Nonsense. I had the message from him yesterday, as a matter of fact, but feared that if I told you then, you would not sleep a wink last night for fretting about it. Now you have time only to bathe, arrange your hair, and select a suitable gown. The apricot muslin, I think, and I shall lend you my filigree necklace." Madame de Staël spread butter on a segment of baguette and handed it to her. "But first, you must have a light meal to settle your stomach. And while you are eating, my dear, I shall tell you how best to conduct yourself with the duke."

By the time Madame de Staël's carriage turned onto the rue du Faubourg Saint-Honoré, Delilah's stomach had been invaded by a squadron of butterflies.

"The Hôtel de Charost," Madame de Staël was saying to Heppy, "was formerly the home of the Princess Pauline Borghese. Something of a tramp, she was, but I give her credit for joining her brother in exile when she might have stayed in Paris and done well for herself. Beautiful women generally do."

A footman let down the steps and Madame descended, still talking, as she had done all the way from Clichy. To soothe Delilah's nerves, it was to be supposed, although so far the effect could not be perceived.

"Wellington did well to snap up the property when it went on the block," she said as the three ladies were ushered into the foyer. "I hope he didn't pay too much for it. Your government will stand the cost, to be sure, but I dislike seeing the Bonapartes stuff their imperialistic pockets with other people's money."

Delilah closed her ears to the monologue and hung back as Madame de Staël and Heppy were greeted by a young army officer with dark hair so much like Dragoner's that she went cold to see it. When his white-gloved hand lifted to smooth back a lock that had strayed over his forehead, she nearly wept.

Today, perhaps, she would discover that she had been altogether mistaken in his character. Perhaps he was, indeed, a blackguard and a traitor. It seemed more than likely to her now, after what she had learned of him since becoming a popular guest at society entertainments. Even so, to have his villainy confirmed by the Duke of Wellington was certain to be a crushing blow.

She hoped she wouldn't cry in front of him.

Madame de Staël touched her arm. "Brace up, young lady. The duke is free now and will speak with you immediately. This nice young man will lead you to his office, while Hepzibah and I enjoy a turn in the garden. Remember now—speak plainly."

The officer with hair like Dragoner's led her upstairs, opened a door, and stepped aside to let her enter. Across the room, seated behind a large desk, was the impressive man she had come to see.

He looked not at all like the duke of her imagination. She had expected an elaborate uniform with gold lace and fringed epaulets and a great many medals, not the plain blue frock coat and simple white stock he was wearing.

He rose, smiling. "Lady Dragoner. Come in. Come in. There's a chair for you. I beg your pardon for the clutter. We have only just taken quarters here, and disorder is the rule."

Delilah remembered to curtsy before sinking into the chair. He sounded so . . . so *cheerful*. And openly delighted to see her, if the gleam in his alert blue eyes could be trusted. The sins of the husband, it seemed, were not to be visited on the wife.

"How are you finding Paris?" he asked in a hearty voice. "Too crowded, I daresay. Can't move in the streets without tripping over an Englishman."

"I like it very well, Your Grace." She looked down at her fingers, which were twitching like spider legs on her lap. "But I mustn't impose on your time. You were most kind to permit me to come here."

"Not at all. I was frankly curious to meet you. Now, tell me what I can do for you."

Speak plainly, Madame de Staël said in her ear. She lifted her chin. "I wish to ask . . . that is, there have been rumors about . . . oh, dear."

His eyes gentled. "Rumors about your husband? Yes, I know. They cannot help but distress you. It is entirely my responsibility, of course, but when we began this endeavor, I was unaware that Dragoner had a wife. Perhaps I ought to have known it, or inquired, but I did not. Surely he has explained what we are about? And you disapprove, I take it. Can't blame you. It's all a muddle now, isn't it?"

Indeed it was. She had lost the duke's meaning early on, when he spoke of his responsibility. "Lord Dragoner sailed for the Peninsula shortly after our marriage," she said. "I next saw him only a few weeks ago. There has been little opportunity for explanations."

"Oh, yes. Oh, yes." Wellington leaned back in his chair. "It is often that way for soldiers. Until my return to England for the Victory Celebrations, I had not been home for near a half-dozen years. War makes strangers of families, I'm afraid. Last I saw my sons, they were squalling infants, but they're strapping young fellows now. And Kitty—that's m'wife—means to join me here when I'm settled, but I don't expect she'll stay long. She don't like crowds."

Delilah nibbled at her lower lip. What was there to say in response to so *personal* a confidence? The spiders galloped
across her lap and clutched at her knees.

"Well, that's nothing to the point," said the duke. "The thing
is, my dear, I can do little at the moment to quash the gossip.
For your sake, I am sorry for it. But I hope you understand that
it is now my duty to ingratiate myself with the French, who
have no reason to love me. They would love me even less to
know I had planted a spy in their midst."

She was nearly rocked off her chair. Dragoner a *spy*?

But that would explain everything, of course. Or, no. Not
everything. Not why he had gone to such trouble to make sure
she believed the worst of him.

Really, she ought to take her leave now. The duke had told
her what she had come here to learn. Her husband had not betrayed his country. He was, as she had always believed, an hon-
orable man.

She ought to feel better, having that affirmed, and she supposed that she did. Her judgment was proven sound after all.
Only her heart had gone wrong.

"Shall I release him?" Wellington asked, a look of concern
on his face. "I can do that much, if you wish it. He has told me
often enough that he would be ineffectual in Paris after the war
ended, and I expect that he is right. I have been selfish to hold
him here."

"He would not leave," she said, "until he was sure that he
could no longer be of service to you." It was an automatic thing
to say. They had been speaking at cross-purposes since first she
arrived. And it was her fault, for not speaking plainly.

"Your Grace," she began, uncertain where the sentence
would end, "if you can spare me a few minutes more, I should
very much like to know precisely what happened when Lord
Dragoner was captured."

"He hasn't told you?" Wellington frowned. "But then, it is
the nature of spies to be cautious. And Dragoner, of course, has
special reason to know how a woman's tongue can wag. Take
no insult. He must have feared that, hearing the gossip and
knowing the truth, you would try to defend him."

"I will say nothing to anyone, Your Grace."

"Of course. I only meant that you should not judge him too harshly. And I see no reason to withhold the story from you now." Wellington clasped his hands on the desk. "An interesting young man, Dragoner. He caught my attention early on. Reckless, I must say, and always at the front of the line. Charged at anything that moved. His men were besotted with him. Followed him wherever he led. I had to pull him out of his regiment and send him off as an exploring officer before he got them all killed.

"But that's not what you asked me." The duke smiled at her. "For a considerable time, I had wished to insert a spy into Paris. Now and again a captured officer ended up there, but he was never let to stay for long. It was Dragoner who figured a way to compromise himself with the Frogs, and by the time I learned about it, the thing was done."

"Lord Dragoner acted without your approval?" she said, picking her way through the thorns.

"Let us say rather that he discerned an opportunity in the field and seized upon it. At great risk to himself, of course, heedless young rascal that he is. But it was a devilish clever plan, and it worked, and he has since proved enormously valuable to me. Does that ease your mind, my dear?"

"Yes, Your Grace. For the most part. But you see, I heard that he had k-killed two men—allies, not the enemy—which seems to me a great deal more vicious than clever."

"Ah." The duke templed his hands. "Well, that's the story that got out, to be sure. The truth is known only to me, two or three of my officers, and the corporal who rode with your husband that day. As for the Spanish guerrillas, they were originally found dead not far from a well. I expect the French had poisoned it. A not uncommon tactic, I'm afraid."

Light-headed with relief, Delilah closed her eyes. He hadn't murdered them. He hadn't. And she had known it! Except that, for a time, she had not been sure. She had lost faith in him after all. Guilt twined around her chest, holding her breathless.

"I beg your pardon," said the duke. "This is not a fit tale for a lady to hear."

Her head shot up. "Oh, no, Your Grace. Please continue. Really, I'm not in the least given to swooning."

Clearly reluctant, he made a gesture of accord. "If you wish it, then. But briefly. After so many years, I can scarcely recall the details. Dragoner and Corporal Lakeford had located the dead men's strayed horses and were returning to camp with the bodies draped over them when they spotted a French patrol some distance away. They propped the corpses upright on their saddles, and Lakeford separated himself, keeping watch as Dragoner drew the attention of the patrol and made as if to run from it. Then he took refuge behind an outcropping of rocks, set up the scene he wanted the Frogs to discover, and waited for them to find him."

"I know this part," she said. "He made it look as if he had killed the Spanish gentlemen. He shot one of them and ran the other through with his sabre."

"Well!" The duke gave her a look of surprise. "You have heard more than is generally known, I must say. It cannot have been pleasant for him, of course. But in the end, all unaware, the two guerrillas gave laudable service to their country. I expect they would have preferred such an outcome to death by poison and no more than so. In any case, Dragoner was taken up by the French and Lakeford slipped away to deliver the news. We retrieved the Spaniards, by the way. They were provided Christian burial and their families eventually located and told what had occurred. Dragoner instructed Lakeford to insist on it."

He leaned back in his chair. "And so, my dear, that is the whole of it. The French were humbugged and Dragoner given leave to remain precisely where I wanted him, in Paris."

Delilah regarded his face through a sheen of tears, willing them not to fall. Tears of joy, yes, to have all her doubts about her husband swept away. But they were tears of grief as well. How *desperately* he must have wanted to be rid of her, to fill her head with such reprehensible lies.

"Thank you, Your Grace," she said, bemused at the calm tone in her voice. Delilah the Woman of Business, bless her steely heart, had taken control of Delilah the Rejected Wife. "You have been most inordinately patient and kind. Might I ask one more favor? Will you not tell Lord Dragoner that we have spoken on this subject?"

"Very well," he replied after some thought. "Indeed, I have no contact with him, save for the reports he smuggles onto my desk. And of late, quite frankly, they have provided little information of consequence. Would you rather I sent him home? I can easily do so."

"Oh, you must not! Certainly not on my account. It is true that by coming here, I have been that most dreadful of creatures—an interfering wife. But he need not know of it. Yes?"

The duke whooped a disconcertingly raucous laugh. "Yes," he said when he had composed himself. "Was there anything else, Lady Dragoner?"

She rose and curtsied. "Only my thanks, again, and my apologies for claiming so much of your time. Good day, Your Grace."

He caught up with her at the door, taking her arm in his. "I shall see you out, my dear, and on the way, you can give me the benefit of your advice. It concerns a matter of diplomacy, in which I suspect your skills overmaster my own."

Her murmur of protest was ignored as the duke led her briskly down the passageway, talking all the while. "Bonaparte, as you may know, brought to France the treasures of the countries he invaded and conquered. Now it is our business to see them returned where they belong. But just lately, the pope has insisted that I keep a certain statue of considerable value as a gift. What do you think? Shall I retain it in the spirit of friendship with which it was offered, or risk offending His Holiness by sending it back?"

Stolen art! Why would he address this particular subject with her? Did he know that she had associated herself with—? But no. How could he? She tempered her voice. "Who else would you offend, Your Grace, by accepting the statue?"

"Well, there's the nub of it." He cast her a look of approval. "The Duchesse de Duras said t'other night that if I sent the gift to London, England would have one statue the more, but one man the less. Do you concur?"

"In fact, sir, I do. However innocent the circumstances, I believe that in your position as ambassador you must be, like Caesar's wife, above reproach. And the pope will no doubt be glad to have his statue back. There is little so satisfying as the making of a grand gesture without being compelled to follow it through."

Another whooping laugh from the duke, which caused her nearly to trip over her skirts. "Then back the statue goes," he declared. "A veritable Portia, you are. Dragoner chose well. And now I am reminded of something."

He drew her to a halt and gazed solemnly into her eyes. "When I can, as soon as I possibly can, I mean to see his reputation restored to him and all credit given for his service to England. He will hear none of it—the young man has a melancholic view of the future, I'm afraid—so I am telling you instead. I will make certain he is exonerated. And honored. You have my word on it."

Chapter 14

"O world, thy slippery turns!"

Coriolanus
Act 4, Scene 4

For Dragoner, the next fortnight passed in a red-tinted haze.
Somewhere in the city, with Chabot or with some other
man, Delilah was laying the groundwork for a divorce. And no
doubt laying herself out on a bed to commit adultery, which she
did every night in his tormented imagination.

To think of it was unbearable. Not to think of it was impossible.

Edoard spent his time in company with Jacques Batiste and
his cohorts, returning home only to deliver an occasional written report. Dragoner was rarely there to receive it in person. He
did not care to be at home. His house carried Delilah's scent
and the visible traces of what she had left behind her—the carpets, the curtains, and most particularly the new mattress on his
bed. When he slept, he did so in the chair in his study.

He kept himself busy in the drawing rooms of Parisian society, sniffing out conspiracies, finding nothing more blameworthy than general discontent. Watered wine, the sort he had
drunk at Le Chien Noir, was a thing of the past. He drank, like
so many other fools, to forget, and discovered, as every fool before him had done, that memories could not be drowned in
wine.

Once, at a ball given by the Duchesse de Duras, he caught a
glimpse of his wife. Incandescent in a gown of buttery silk, she

moved gracefully through the figures of a contradanse, smiling at each of her partners as if he were the only man on the planet.

There would be, Dragoner was sure, no lack of co-respondents for Delilah's divorce.

He took himself to the room set aside for gaming, lost heavily at cards, and kept an eye out for Chabot, in a mood to eliminate at least one contender for his wife's favors. But the comte failed to appear, and when he returned to the ballroom, Delilah was nowhere to be seen. He decided they had gone off together.

The next morning, when his head was splitting from the aftermath of a rendezvous with a bottle of cognac, Minette accosted him in his dressing room. Of late she had taken residence in Edoard's bedchamber, he knew, but she had come and gone from her work at Le Chien Noir without disturbing him. Preoccupied with his own misery, he had scarcely noticed her.

There was no failing to notice her now. She snatched the razor from his hand and slammed it on the dressing table. Soapy water sloshed over the rim of his shaving basin. Astonished, he turned on the stool to look at her.

She glared at him, fire in her eyes. "And what, I ask myself each day that goes by, is it these imbeciles think they are doing? But Edoard will not say, the little time he spends with me, so I know it cannot be good. I think you must explain, Dragoner. I shall give you no peace until you do."

He released a sour-tasting breath of air. "Damned if I know any more, Minette. In the beginning, there might have been some point to it. I'm not sure. Then I tossed the whole business in Eddie's hands and left him to follow through. It's nothing of importance, really, a matter of stolen art and an absurd plot to make it appear the Duke of Wellington was behind the theft. I expect that little will come of it."

"You have lost your wits! The both of you!" She threw up her hands. "When Edoard is gone, he is busy stealing these arts, yes?"

"I'm afraid so, but only so he can record precisely what was taken and from where. He is providing me with lists. We'll return everything where it belongs."

"I care nothing for that. What if he is caught, eh? What will become of him then?"

Heat scorched the back of his neck. She was right. She was right. "That won't happen," he said after a moment. "You know Edoard. The ground could open under him and he'd find something to hang on to."

"But it is *you* pulled away the ground from him. And you do nothing but drink, and snarl like a dog with a broken leg each time I have tried to speak with you."

He had no recollection of her approaching him, but she might have done. If she said so, it must be true. "I am sorry, Minette. It's all gone wrong, my fault, and I'll put an end to it. Have you any idea where I can find Edoard now?"

"He was already gone when I came home last night. Before you came home as well. But he left a note on your bed, which I have opened and read." She pulled a wrinkled sheet of paper from her pocket and threw it at him.

Dragoner picked it up from the floor where it landed and scanned the message. There was to be one last raid on a provincial museum, Edoard had scrawled, after which Batiste had been instructed to stop pressing his luck. It wasn't clear if the robbery was scheduled for the night just past or the one ahead. In any case, Lord Dragoner was requested to come on Sunday to where the goods had been stored and select the items to be sent to London under the auspices of the Duke of Wellington. He should bring with him the name of the recipient and his direction. At that time, decisions would be made about the best way to sell off the remainder of the goods and how the profits were to be distributed. At the bottom of the page was a sketchy map with an X marking the place he was to go.

On Sunday. Tomorrow.

He refolded the paper and placed it next to his wallet and house key on the dressing table. "Minette, thank you. I'll see to it this benighted scheme is overturned before any more harm can come of it. And it's time for Edoard to leave my service altogether, don't you think? He will do far better without me."

"*Oui. Far* better. But don't you understand? He will never leave you so long as he thinks you need him. And he will continue to think that until you prove to him that you do not. You

must come to your senses, Dragoner. The war is over. The time
for spying is over. You cannot replace the good service you
have done with children's games!"

With that declaration, which struck him like a bayonet in the
chest, she flounced from the dressing room. The door crashed
shut behind her.

For a time he sat where she had left him, staring blankly at
the wall.

Children's games.

At all costs he must separate Edoard from this misadventure.
And from the Dragon.

A few hours later Dragoner paid the jarvey who had driven
him to Montmartre and set off on foot for the building—he
didn't know what sort to expect—indicated on his map. He
passed flint mills and grain mills, now closed, and squat stone
buildings where supplies and tools had been stored, and the occasional workman's residence.

Soon the landscape changed dramatically, grass and trees
giving way to yawning pits studded with outcroppings of stone.
These were the gypsum quarries, abandoned several years earlier because the excavations had begun to undermine the hills
of Montmartre. His destination lay not far beyond the blackened pit, a surprisingly impressive two-story house with a
good-sized stable and a few shade trees. It looked to be deserted.

Except for the faint moaning of wind through the quarry and
the occasional call of a rook, all was still. He had decided to approach the house openly, as one of the merry band of thieves
come a day early to play his part, and expected to find at least
one man standing guard over the loot.

But no one came out to meet him when he approached the
front door. The small hairs at his nape prickled a warning. He
circled to the back of the house and tried the kitchen door,
which was unlocked.

Inside, the kitchen resembled a carpenter's shop. The butcher
block was littered with saws, hammers, and nails, and on the
floor were wooden boxes in various stages of completion. He

saw the remains of a meal on the trestle table and smelled bacon and sawdust.

Warily, he let himself from the kitchen into a narrow passageway. To his right was a staircase, and directly across from him, slightly ajar, was a door. He approached it and looked into a large room that had become, evidently, the repository for the stolen goods. In one corner, stacked like cordwood, were rolled carpets and tapestries. Paintings were arrayed two and three deep along the walls. The center of the room was crowded with tables, all of them covered with porcelain plates and figurines, clocks and lacquerwood boxes, and even a small mummy case. Light poured from the windows onto Murano glassware, silver trays and epergnes, candlesticks and samovars, and gilt torchères.

Dear God, what had he done? If Batiste was permitted to spirit these things away in the boxes being manufactured to transport them, they would be lost forever.

He moved into the room, examining more closely the items he had caused to be stolen. There was little here of significant value, but the whole lot, even sold on the black market, would net a considerable amount of money. The ploy to discredit Wellington had almost certainly been a sham. He wondered if it had ever been a factor in Batiste's plan, or, rather, the plan of whoever it was originally proposed the idea.

At the beginning, Dragoner had suspected Batiste's older brother, the Comte de Chabot, only to dismiss the idea. The brothers openly despised each other. Had done so for years. Later he had wanted to believe, for personal reasons, that Chabot was behind the scheme after all. But he soon dismissed those suspicions as well. He was too experienced a conspirator to let adolescent jealousy rule his wits. Or so he had told himself.

Now he was coming to think his first instincts had been on target, and that he had been wrong to ignore them.

A moment later, he was sure of it.

Across the room, a door swung open and Chabot stepped through it, an amused smile on his face. "Ah, it is not a bumbling policeman after all! When I heard someone enter from the back door, I naturally threw myself into hiding. But then I realized that, by now, a policeman would have knocked something onto the floor and broken it." He made an expansive gesture. "So, what do you think of our treasures? Have we done well?"

Chabot was far too confident, in the way of a man who has been dealt all kings and aces. Dragoner propped both hands on his sword-cane. "Moderately well. The others are gone to acquire more knickknacks for the collection, I presume?"

"That, and to arrange for their transport from Paris. But we were not expecting you today, Vicomte. Our appointment was for tomorrow afternoon, was it not?"

We? Who else was in the house?

Dragoner gave an indifferent shrug. "As it happens, I have other plans for tomorrow. Does it matter? I can as easily select items for Wellington from the current display and give you the direction where they are to be sent."

"Dear me. I had forgot about Wellington. He will simply have to do without, I'm afraid. Why toss away a portion of our profits for the sake of a meaningless political gesture? No, no, we shall sell everything. And I fear, too, that your services are no longer required. I have found someone else to put a value on our treasures and suggest suitable markets where we might dispose of them." He turned slightly and held out his hand. "Do come in, my sweet, and join us."

Smiling, her blue silk skirts twirling around her, Delilah swept into the room.

Dragoner's heart stopped beating. He should have known. He should have known. In league with her lover, she had been part of this all along.

She brushed Chabot's fingers with hers, a gesture of intimacy, before she passed him by to stop directly in front of her husband. *"Bonjour, mon cher mari."* She dipped a mocking curtsy. *"Comment allez-vous?"*

He gripped the silver dragon at the hilt of his walking stick, ordering his heart back to work and his lungs to start breathing again. "Your French is improving," he said.

"For that I must credit Gustave. He is teaching me." Her brows lifted. "But you look displeased to see me here. Are you offended that he has selected me, and not you, to evaluate our merchandise?"

"Why would I be?" Dragoner glanced at Chabot, who was watching this encounter with narrowed eyes. "It will spare me a tedious afternoon poking around in search of something worth more than the price of a smoked ham. By all means, the honor is yours. But I wasn't aware that you knew the least thing about art. Even inferior art."

"Oh, I don't," she agreed cheerfully. "But I know what a credulous English merchant might be convinced to pay for something—*anything*—that Napoleon thought worth plucking from its owners and bringing home to France. Intrinsic value does not signify, sir. It is the market value that counts. Within six months I can sell every item in this room at enormous profit, including the tables and chairs and wall sconces and possibly the balls of dust on the floor. Do you doubt it?"

He did not, mercenary little witch that she was.

She began to roam among the tables, picking up a figurine here, a salt cellar there, as if wholly preoccupied with her calculations. She paused by a display of dueling pistols and jeweled daggers, her brow wrinkled with thought.

Unable to look at her any longer, he forced his attention to the problem at hand. Chabot.

The comte was moving in his direction, a benevolent smile on his face. "I believe you have underestimated your wife," he said. "It is no wonder she wishes to divorce you and come to me instead. *Has* come to me, as you can plainly tell. But she has assured me that you will have no hard feelings, since it was you first proposed a separation. Or have I mistaken the matter?"

"I don't want her, if that is what you mean." Careful not to be obvious about it, Dragoner sought a way to leave his vulnerable position, his back exposed to anyone who might appear at the passageway door. But with Chabot coming at him, his only path was to the spot where Delilah was standing, contemplating a silver-chased bowl.

Indolently, following her example and the route she had taken, he developed a fascination for the objects spread out over the tables. There was no immediate threat from Chabot. His hands were empty, and his tight-fitting coat gave no evidence of a concealed weapon.

"Did you wish to *marry* her?" Dragoner asked, putting astonishment in his voice. "I am more than willing to let her go, but she will bring nothing to you but herself. What money we have between us, I mean to keep."

"We shall see," said Chabot, making the turn into the scatter of tables. "More immediately, I am concerned with the outcome of this so charming foray into crime and the disposition of what we have stolen. And I ask myself, what is to prevent you, in a fit of pique, from informing on us to the police? Considering that you are to have no share of the proceeds, I mean to say. Except for mentioning the existence of the provincial museums, you have done nothing to justify being cut in. Wouldn't you agree?"

"Do you expect that I will? An idea is worth far more than the efforts of your lackeys to follow it through. And I could scarcely inform on you—could I?—without incriminating myself. Surely, gentleman to gentleman, we can arrive at a suitable arrangement. I've already given you my wife, after all."

"An ante into the gaming pot?" Laughing, Chabot came to a halt several feet away, his arms folded behind his back. "I think, rather, that she came to me of her own volition. And she is most certainly providing me everything a man could possibly desire."

Control was slipping away. Breathing heavily, Dragoner met Chabot's mocking eyes. "Then I shall leave her to you," he said with the last bit of nonchalance he could muster. "And all of this as well." His gesture overturned a candlebrace. "As you say, my contribution to the scheme was insignificant, and with the plan to disgrace Wellington fallen by the boards, I have no reason to concern myself any further. I daresay that at some future time, I shall win my share of the profits from your brother at Le Chien Noir. Shall we call it even, then? My wife for your brother's purse?"

His move to extricate himself from the tables was blocked by the still-smiling Chabot. "A fair exchange," the comte said affably. "But don't go yet. I have not described to you what I have done to the lovely Delilah, and what I mean to do. She is quite out of the ordinary. Starved for a man capable of satisfying her, in fact, and—"

"Enough!"

Dragoner raked the sword from his walking stick and leaped at Chabot.

He was felled midair. From behind, something crashed against his head. As he dropped, he caught a last glimpse of Delilah's arm following through after striking the blow. Then all went black.

Chapter 15

"See the coast clear'd, and then we will depart."

Henry VI, Part One
Act 1, Scene 3

Dragoner came awake slowly, fighting his way through a
wall of pain and nausea until he thought he might be conscious. It was difficult to tell. When he succeeded in opening
his eyes, nothing changed except that the darkness seemed to
grow more intense.

Panic brought his head up like a shot. But there was nothing
to be seen, assuming, of course, that he was capable of seeing.
Breathing heavily, he willed himself to remain calm and gently
lowered his head again.

His cheek met splintery wood. He lay still for several minutes, taking careful inventory of his body. Most of it ached, as
if he'd gone several rounds against Gentleman Jackson with his
hands tied behind his back. They were, in fact, stretched out in
front of him, and manacled. He moved his wrists, feeling the
scratch of rusty metal against his skin. There was a chain as
well, attaching him to something beyond his reach. He wasn't
yet ready to find out what it was.

The floor seemed to be moving. He gave that some thought.
The entire room, if it was a room, swayed right and left. It
rocked up and down. Only slightly, to be sure, but he could distinguish the motion as separate from his own dizziness.

He was on a ship, then, chained and shackled. Brought down

by a blow from his wife and brought here, no doubt, by her lover.

Listening closely, he heard the faint creaking of wood and, from somewhere overhead, the sound of voices and an occasional burst of laughter. After a time he distinguished three separate timbres, all male, but there might be others. For all he knew, Delilah was up there with them.

Treacherous little Delilah, who was certainly living up to her name. She hadn't shorn his hair, it was true, and he hadn't been chained between two pillars, but in every other way she had rendered him powerless. And heartsick, although he couldn't afford to dwell on that.

There had to be some way out of this. His feet weren't bound, for what that was worth, but the manacles were tight around his wrists. There would be no wriggling free of them.

He forced himself to relax and gather his strength. Once or twice he nearly slipped back into the release of unconsciousness, and came to understand that his greatest battle would be fought against his own weakness.

The trouble was, he didn't really mind dying. What was death, after all, but oblivion without a hangover in the morning? Even so, he did object, keenly, to being trussed up and butchered like a capon.

Concentrate.

With his ear pressed against the deck, he evaluated the swaying motion and realized that the ship must be at anchor. It was marginally good news. Then, raising himself to hands and knees, he traced the chain to a heavy metal ring protruding from the wall about six inches above the floor. Seizing hold of the ring with both hands, he gave it a hard yank. Not unexpectedly, it failed to budge.

Next he ran his fingers over the rough-hewn walls—the parts he could reach—and concluded he was imprisoned somewhere midship, in a small storage compartment that doubled as a brig. He located a door, firmly locked, and came to the end of the chain. Heading the other direction, still feeling along the wall, he met only a corner and more wall.

Sinking back on his heels, he pulled at the ring again and swore under his breath when it slipped from his sweating hands. Someone had removed his gloves, probably because the manacles would not fit over them.

He was considering what to do next when he heard, from behind him, a distinctive scraping sound. Turning, he saw the barest glimmer of light where the floorboards met a door on the opposite wall. He was certain the light had not been there earlier.

The scratching came again, and he crawled toward the door as far as the chain would permit him. "Who—?"

Shhh.

"What is—?"

Shhh!

He got the point. Somewhat bemused, he watched a shadow break the sliver of light. A thin object slid under the door, followed by another. Then, after several attempts, a larger object came through.

He dropped to his belly and stretched out his hands, but the gifts lay well beyond his reach. In the dark, he couldn't even make out what they were. Moments later, a small comb slipped under the door and pushed the other objects in his direction. Still not close enough. He pulled against the manacles, raising blood to his wrists, but it was no good.

It eventually occurred to him to try with his feet. *Idiot!* Quickly he reversed himself and slithered backward, probing for the objects with the toe of his boot. The process was slow and frustrating. Now and again he raised up and looked to see if he'd succeeded in drawing them closer, but the light didn't reach far enough for him to tell.

Be methodical, dammit! He put his toe against the far side of the door and drew it forward, repeating the motion inch by inch until he had reached the other side. Then he turned to see what he had gleaned.

For the first time, dull-witted as he had been these last few minutes, it dawned on him that he *could* see. Relief flooded through him. And on the other side of that door was an ally, although he was doubtless a prisoner as well. Could his captors have brought Edoard here?

The objects were now close enough to take hold of, although he had to trace them with his fingertips to decipher what they were. Two hairpins, unless he was very much mistaken. Not Edoard, then. And glory be, a knife, small and slim and pointed like a stiletto, but with a razor-sharp blade.

They were precisely what he required. Turning again, he made himself comfortable and set to work picking the lock that held the manacles in place. Like the irons that banded his wrists, the interior of the lock was encased in rust. He punched at the encrustations with the tip of the knife, breaking loose the worst of them, but was soon compelled to stop. He'd had to hold the knife by its blade, and wound up doing more damage to his fingers than to the rust.

Next he braided the hairpins together. Individually they hadn't the strength to turn the mechanism, but when knitted together, as he soon discovered, they were deucedly hard to manipulate.

It had to be Delilah, he thought as he worked. What the devil was going on? She was the one who clipped him on the head, and the sight of her hand swinging down was the last thing he remembered before waking up in this cabin.

It was a long while before he was able to free his hands. When the lock kicked open, he quietly lowered the manacles to the floor and approached the door on his knees. He assumed it to be locked and the key missing, or Delilah would simply have opened it.

Sitting cross-legged, he swiped the perspiration from his forehead with his sleeve and set to work again with the hairpins. There was no sound from the other side of the door. This time the lock, like most of those he had picked when escaping to meet with his delinquent parents, gave way with relative ease. The door swung open, and he saw Delilah on her knees directly in front of him, one finger lifted to her lips.

Keep silent, she was telling him. He nodded.

She lifted three fingers and pointed overhead. Three men, then, as he had suspected.

"Chabot?" he whispered. "Batiste?"

"No." She exaggerated the movement of her lips, showing him how to go on. "I'm locked in as well. They said it was for my safety, while they make arrangements."

"Where are we?"

"Anchored a few miles from Paris. We were ferried aboard on a skiff, but it took Batiste back to shore. He's gone to bring the merchandise to the ship."

Dragoner rubbed one of his shredded wrists, deciding which of his questions could not wait. "Are they armed?" He pointed overhead. When she looked puzzled, he formed his hand into the shape of a pistol.

She nodded vigorously.

So much for trying to overpower them with his fists and a knife. It would have to be a surreptitious departure, then, and a speedy one. "How long since Batiste left?" He moved his arms as if pulling oars.

"About two hours," she mouthed. "You must be gone before he returns."

"Yes." He could scarcely bring himself to ask. "And you?"

After a moment, she shook her head. "I'll wait here. Is there something you require? A diversion?"

She had to repeat the last word several times before he understood it. Ought he to leave her here? She didn't seem to be afraid, but he had less faith in Chabot's intentions for Delilah. Not that she would necessarily come with him, even if he insisted, and when it came right down to it, his chances of escape weren't good. With a female in tow, they became practically nil.

She leaned forward and put a hand on his arm. "Can I help?"

"Thank you. No. Keep safe." He remembered that she must appear guiltless. "Fix your hair," he advised. Red-gold curls had pulled loose from her crown of braids when she removed the two hairpins.

For a time he simply looked at her, at the wide hazel eyes dilated with concern and the smooth skin dusted with freckles and the lips that curled upward at the corners even when she wasn't smiling. It might be the last time he ever looked on her face, Delilah's sweet, impertinent face. He missed the dimples. He would miss her as well, if he survived.

"I'll lock you in," he said, moving back so that he could close the door. Alarm flashed across her face, checking his motion. Then he heard the thud of feet against wood.

Delilah reached for the door as he turned and dove for the

manacles. The cabin went dark. He clasped the irons loosely around his wrists and stretched facedown on the floor.

All three men had come for a visit, and they were in high spirits. Two of them spoke dockside French, but the third voice, with its schooled diction, was one he knew. Dragoner suspected he was about to pay the price for all the times he'd insulted Jean-Marie Beltrand.

A key rattled in the lock. Oaths. The lock was resisting. Then the door swung open.

"Look there," one of the men said with a chortle. "I told you so. He's dead to the world."

Dragoner smelled garlic, onions, and cheap wine as someone bent over him.

"Maybe he's *really* dead. It would save us the trouble."

"We'll see," Beltrand said.

A booted foot plowed into Dragoner's side. He rolled with the blow, keeping his body limp. The next kick was harder. When the third came, he managed to strangle a cry of pain but could not help drawing up his knees.

Fingers seized hold of his hair and pulled him head and shoulders off the floor. A hand slapped him across the face and back again. He knew he was about to break. And when he did, they would make damn sure he was unconscious. No escape for him then, he reminded himself, tasting blood in his mouth. Hold out. Hold out.

His head was slammed back against the floor.

"Batiste promised I'd be the one to kill him," Beltrand grumbled. "But I want him looking me in the eyes when I do. He's breathing, anyway. And we'd better keep to our orders or we won't get paid."

"I'd settle for the girl," said Garlic-Breath. "We're to have her later. Why not now?"

"You're too drunk," the third man said with a laugh. "So am I."

"And *I* think Batiste will keep her for himself. It's our ship, and we haven't seen a sou for the hire of it. I say they'll cut us off when they're done with us. We ought to take what we can get now."

There was a scuffle, and Dragoner thought a fight was about

to ensue over his prone body. He was too muddle-brained to figure a way to exploit it.

"Merde!" Beltrand shouted.

More noises Dragoner could not decipher. Someone stumbled over his outstretched leg and swore loudly. He felt himself drifting into a place where none of it mattered.

The door slammed. The key turned in the lock. They were gone, he decided when the footsteps and voices faded. It hurt to draw breath, and he feared some of his ribs had been broken. If so, he was as good as dead.

I'll settle for the girl. We're to have her later.

He had to get Delilah away from here.

Moments later she was leaning over him, brushing the hair from his eyes.

He rolled onto his back, staring up at her. Blood trickled from his mouth and down his chin. When Beltrand kicked him, he had chewed at his tongue to keep from screaming, which now struck him as an exceptionally stupid thing to have done.

"Can you swim?" he asked.

"Yes." Rising, she began to peel off her dress.

She had understood instantly what would be required of her. He struggled to a sitting position and began to loosen the buttons on his waistcoat.

Delilah, out of her dress, poked him on the shoulder. "Knife," she said.

He pointed to his left boot, where he'd stuffed it when he heard the men coming. She removed the knife and pulled off both his boots, which he doubted he could have managed by himself.

"They kicked you," she said, still careful to make no other sound. "Where are you hurt?"

He made a vague gesture at his chest. "Ribs. Cracked, I think. Or bruised. It's not so bad."

She ripped into her dress with the knife, cutting long strips of fabric from the skirt. "I'll wrap you up," she said. "When I've got the bandages ready, we'll get you out of your coat."

He removed it himself, slowly, evaluating the level of pain. The best he could say of his ribs was that, by contrast, his head barely troubled him now. And there were none of the sharp, stabbing pains that would mark a splintered bone or two, which had been his greatest fear.

His shirt would have to come off as well, because it would catch the light. He tugged it from the band of his trousers, unbuttoned the cuffs, and was about to wrestle it over his head when Delilah came to help him.

"You had better stand now," she said when he was free of the shirt.

His legs, at least, were functional. On his feet, he lifted his arms at her direction and stood quietly while she encased his chest, mummy-fashion, in strips of blue silk. She had to lean into him each time she reached around his back, her bare arms brushing against his skin as she worked. Under any other circumstances, he thought somewhat dreamily, the experience would have been erotic. The light fragrance of perfumed soap floated from her hair. Her lips were inches from his own. His thoughts began to drift in impossible directions.

He jerked them quickly back into place. The next few minutes would tell if they were to live or die.

She tied the last knot with such force that he nearly yelped. "You'll do," she said.

"Thank you," he replied, choosing short words so that she could read his lips. Probably they couldn't be heard if they spoke aloud, and whispering would surely be undetectable, but Delilah had set the rules for their conversations. He saw no reason to override them.

"Pay attention," he said. "If the men are aft, we can steal to the bow and lower ourselves down the anchor chain. That would be best. But if they are forward or midship, we'll have to run for it and dive overboard. Go deep, because they'll use their guns. Then swim for your life. It will take about a minute for them to reload. They're drunk. But they might have extra weapons."

"I understand." She sat beside him and drew off her shoes.

When she lifted her chemise to unclasp her garters and roll down her stockings, he turned his head away.

The chemise was too long. It would impede her when she was swimming, and the corset would have to come off as well. He couldn't imagine why she wore it, slender as she was. He moved behind her, untied the laces, and unwrapped them from the metal hooks.

She must have been reading his mind. When he took up the knife, she stood patiently while he dropped to one knee and began sawing away at her chemise. Words had become unnecessary, it seemed. He held out his coat and she slipped her arms into the sleeves, apprehending that the dark fabric would make her less visible in the moonlight. She would know when it was time to shed the coat.

Lady Dragoner was a resourceful young woman, and for as long as she continued on his side, he had absolute confidence in her. But she had turned on him once, and might well do so again. The next time, he did not mean to be caught unaware.

Taking up the braided hairpins, he hunkered by the door and immediately encountered an obstacle. The key had been left in the lock. He could push it out, of course, but it would make a clatter when it landed.

Delilah was leaning over his shoulder, watching him. With gestures and a few words, he explained the situation.

She appeared to be thinking it over. "Wait," she said. "Get back."

Moments later she was stuffing the remnants of her dress and chemise under the door. There was barely a quarter-inch of space between it and the floorboards, so she had to use the stiletto to prod the material through. "It might help," she said, moving aside. "Go ahead."

Good girl, he thought, jabbing at the key with the hairpins. It resisted, snagged on a protrusion of rust, and finally gave way. He heard a muffled thump, and silence. Carefully, he began to draw the fabric in. He rather expected the key to remain behind, but it rode along and slipped under the door with ease.

After unlocking the door, he turned to Delilah. "I'll go first, to see where they are. If I am caught, go back to your cabin and pretend to be hurt. Tell them I attacked you. Understood? I'll wave my hand if it is safe for you to follow me."

Unable to resist, he put his fingertips against her cheek. "We can do this. Don't be afraid. And don't try to help me if things go bad. Just get away as best you can. Promise me you will."

Her eyes blazed into his. "I'll do what I must," she said.

Dragoner crept from the cabin, holding to the shadows as he took his bearings. He was in a short, narrow passageway, dimly lit by a filthy lantern attached to a hook on the wall. Directly ahead he saw an angled ladder bolted to the floor, and above it, a glimpse of sky.

The ship was fairly large, badly maintained, and at least a half-century old. A derelict vessel for hire, he suspected, for the price of a barrel of wine. He smelled rotted fish, stale smoke, and decaying wood.

Splinters dug through his stockings as he padded to the steep ladder and mounted it soundlessly. He could hear the voices of his captors, who sounded even more sotted than before.

When the top of his head reached the level of the hatch, he paused to listen. They were playing some sort of game, he decided after a time. There were curses, laughter, and an occasional shout of triumph. Cautiously, he took another step and lifted his head.

The men had settled themselves on the poop and were bent over, their backs to him, apparently tossing dice. Save for two lanterns suspended from the boom, the deck was lit only by a three-quarter moon and the stars.

He looked up. Clouds scudded across the sky, not very many of them, but now and again, the moon was concealed. Dropping back a step, he beckoned to Delilah. She joined him quickly, her expression composed.

"I'll go first," he said, pointing the direction he meant to take. "Count to twenty and follow me."

From the tug of the current on the ship, he knew the anchor was to starboard. After making sure the men were still absorbed in their game, he waited until a cloud passed across the moon. Then he mounted to the deck, sped to the bow, and crouched between the windlass and the bulwark. The anchor line was a rope, he saw, and not the chain he had expected. What if—?

A wraithlike figure, doubled over to half its height, flitted to where he was waiting. He lost no time helping her out of the jacket, which he stuffed under a tarp while she climbed atop the cat head. Then, taking hold of her under her arms, he lowered her onto the taut anchor rope. When her nod told him she had a firm grip, he ducked behind the windlass and watched through the hawsehole, his heart in his throat, as she slithered down the rope and into the water.

She immediately turned onto her side and propelled herself toward the shore. She was fighting the current, he could tell, drifting downriver with every stroke. Soon he lost sight of her.

The men continued to laugh and swear, oblivious to what was taking place not very many yards away. Dragoner threaded the stiletto through his bandages and waited for another helpful cloud. When it came, he vaulted the railing and lowered himself hand over hand down the rope.

The chance was too good to pass up, he had already decided, and perfectly safe for so long as the men went on gaming. He drew out the knife and, clinging to the rope with one hand, began to saw through it just below the waterline.

It soon became evident that he had underestimated the difficulty. The rope, as thick as his forearm, was stiff with salt and parceled with tar cloth. When one hand grew tired he shifted to the other, worrying with every slice that Delilah would run out of strength before she made it to shore. He should have told her to wait for him to descend. They ought to have made the swim together, in case she required his help.

He hadn't thought it out, hadn't thought clearly enough, and now it was too late to catch up with her. It had been too late from the moment she struck out on her own.

One by one, strands of the cabled rope began to unravel. His chest throbbed and his wrists hurt like the devil, but he kept at it until a bare half-inch width of hemp attached the ship to its anchor. The current would soon take care of the rest.

After securing the knife, he kicked against the hull to propel himself forward and began to swim. It was more like paddling, because the sound of splashing water would draw the men to the railing. Moonlight flooded over the river, exposing his bare shoulders and back to anyone looking in his direction.

It was hard going. Like Delilah he had to struggle against the current, which swept him forcefully along the path the ship would take when it broke loose. Whenever he checked, the trees lining the shore did not appear to be any closer.

Redoubling his efforts, he plied through the water, using his legs because his arms had begun to fail him. The pain of moving them was all but unbearable now.

A shout brought his head up. Turning, he saw the ship, now a considerable distance away, begin to swing around. The anchor rope had snapped, and the Seine had taken control of the vessel. Settling into the current, it began moving downriver at the speed of a trotting horse.

By now clear of its path, he flopped onto his back to watch the spectacle.

Voices rang out across the water.

"Take the tiller!" "The sails. Lower the sails!"

When the ship drew nearer, he saw two figures scurrying about on deck. Beltrand swarmed up the mast to cast off the gaskets.

Close to enjoying himself, Dragoner treaded water as the sloop floated past him and detected panic on the faces of the louts who had intended to rape Delilah.

It was possible they'd get control of the ship before it ran aground, but with a fair idea where he was, he knew that the Seine made another of its tight loops not far away. With only three drunken men to crew and virtually no wind to help them out, even dropping the sails would be of little use. He expected the ship to careen onto the riverbank and break up, which would please him enormously.

Setting his sights to shore, he focused all his energy on what remained to be done.

Fairly soon he reached shallower water, and when his feet touched bottom, he slogged his way through the mud until he met solid ground. Then he dropped to hands and knees, drawing in great gulps of air.

Between the weeds and grass alongside the bank and the woodlands lining the river was a familiar riding path. He had traveled this way a number of times, to borrow a horse from the Comte de Marais or to return it. There were no buildings or landmarks on either side of the river, but he knew the area reasonably well. If Delilah had come to shore nearby, she was unlikely to encounter anyone at this time of night.

He thought of how she had looked, descending the rope in a thin chemise that concealed nothing, especially when it pulled up over her thighs and all the way to her waist. He knew precisely how any man who came across her was likely to react.

Standing, his arms wrapped around his waist against the pain, he called her name without much hope. Were she close to hand, watching for him, she would have come forward by now.

An owl hooted. Water lapped against the muddy shore. A light breeze stirred the dry grasses.

He made his way to the path and followed it downriver, the direction the current would have carried her.

Chapter 16

"Alas, the way is wearisome and long!"

The Two Gentlemen of Verona
Act 2, Scene 7

Delilah came near to shore without the strength to move another inch. Bobbing in the shallows, she wiped her eyes and pushed clumps of tangled hair behind her ears.

For as far as she could see, woodlands covered the landscape on both sides of the river. There were no lights or buildings in view, nor could she make out the outline of the ship.

She had told Dragoner that she could swim, but she had only done so a handful of times, and in a waist-high pond at that. The current must have borne her at least a mile downriver before she managed to break free of it. Dragoner, much stronger than she, would have reached land a considerable distance from here.

If he had not been recaptured. If his injuries had permitted him to descend the rope and swim away.

She refused to consider any more *ifs*.

Shivering, she dragged herself out of the water and across a rock-strewn path. Taking refuge behind a tree, she dropped to her knees and sat back on her heels, wondering what next to do. Beneath the trees, the undergrowth was dense and thorny. If she went in search of Dragoner, wearing only a sodden chemise that adhered to her body from shoulders to midthigh, she would be forced to use the path and expose herself to the sight of anyone who chanced by.

But she could hardly remain where she was, could she? Standing, she wrung out the frayed ends of her chemise and was about to step from behind the tree when she heard noises coming from the river.

Someone was shouting. Another voice shrieked an oath. And then, to her amazement, the ship floated by.

Lanterns swung from their hooks, casting golden beams across the water. A man was clinging to a mast and wrestling with the sails. Another man was pulling at a rope, to no apparent purpose. She had the barest glimpse of three frantic faces before the ship swept from view.

Good heavens!

She could not even begin to conceive what had happened, although she suspected that Dragoner was behind it. He would certainly have taken the opportunity, if one presented itself, to wreak vengeance on Monsieur Beltrand and his pair of monkeys.

When the lights from the ship had faded, she emerged from her shelter and set out purposefully along the path. It was hard going. Small bits of gravel, sharp as broken glass, dug into her bare soles. She moved onto the softer ground near the river, but there were rocks there as well, along with weeds that tripped her up whenever she failed to watch where she placed her feet. Now and again, as clouds swept over the moon, she was forced to halt until the sky cleared again.

During one particularly long pause, she thought that she smelled smoke. Then the frail breeze shifted direction and she lost the scent. Cautiously, she returned to the path and proceeded slowly, watching for a break in the trees.

Sure enough, about twenty yards down, she saw a narrow opening and followed it to a wide clearing. Directly ahead was a small cottage, with smoke filtering from the chimney above a room dimly lit by what she suspected was a banked fire. No lights shone from the other two windows, which were set into solid stone walls.

It must be well past midnight by now, and the residents were surely asleep. From its paddock a cow lowed a greeting, and pigeons rustled in a nearby dovecot. But all of her attention was drawn to the line stretched between two trees at one side of the cottage and the clothing that had been hung on it to dry.

A minute or two later, her feet raw after a mad dash away from the cottage, she paused to draw on the homespun trousers and shirt she had purloined. The pants were tight on her hips, loose at her waist, and reached far past her ankles. She rolled them up, and did the same with the overlong shirtsleeves. She had snatched a pair of thin dishtowels as well, and used them to rub her hair dry before wrapping them around her feet and knotting the corners at her ankles.

As shoes went, the dishtowels were nothing to boast about, but they would provide a small cushion against the rocky path. She set out at a fast clip, feeling very much better with clothes on her body.

The sky had cleared, and stars blazed overhead, marking the path as she trudged along on her makeshift footwear. Now and again she was forced to stop and retie the knots. It seemed to her that she must have gone well past where the ship had been anchored, but it was impossible to be sure. Path. Trees. River. No distinguishing landmarks.

Where was Dragoner? If he had escaped the ship, would he not have come looking for her? She took to watching the river-bank, fearing to see his body washed to shore. But she would know if he were dead. Wouldn't she?

Please, God. Please, *dearest* God.

"Who's there?"

At first, she thought it was her imagination. But the voice came again, louder this time and unmistakably his.

"Put your hands in the air. I have a gun."

She remembered that she was wearing trousers. "It's me!" she called. "Delilah."

Some distance away, a dark figure emerged from behind a tree. After a moment's pause he broke into a run, moonlight flashing off his face and bare shoulders as he sped along the path.

Limp with relief, quivering with joy, she waited for him.

When he was only a few yards away, his arms opened, and for a breathless moment, she thought that he meant to embrace her. But then, just short of reaching her, he halted as if he'd slammed into a wall. His arms dropped to his sides. He was breathing heavily, the air rasping in his throat.

Of course he wouldn't touch her. The intimacy they had shared in the ship's cabin had not survived their escape.

It was what he wanted, so she planted her hands on her hips and threw him a jovial challenge. "What kept you?"

His laugh was forced and probably hurt his injured ribs. "I'm a poor swimmer," he said. "While you were shopping, you should have bought a shirt for me."

"I didn't think of it," she said honestly. "If you like, we can go back and take one from the clothesline. The farmhouse is no more than a mile from here."

"But in the wrong direction. We have a long walk ahead of us, Delilah. Are you up to it? Tell me the truth. If not, we'll go to your farmhouse and ask the family to take you in for the night. What money I was carrying was taken from me, but I can give them my ring as security."

"They already have my sapphire earbobs," she said, moving to his side. "I left them by the door in exchange for what I am wearing. How far are we from Paris?"

"We're going to Argenteuil," he said as they began to walk. "The village is three or four miles from where we are, and I have a friend who lives close by. His estate borders the river, so there's a good chance we won't encounter anyone before reaching it. You can remain there while I return to Paris."

She opened her mouth to object and closed it again. This was hardly the time for a debate.

Her resolve lasted for about a mile, at which point the silence had become unbearable. "I saw the ship go by," she said brightly. "What happened?"

"Beltrand was in a hurry to get somewhere, I suppose. We needn't worry about him, or the two jackals keeping him company." He looked over at her. "Why are you limping?"

"I'm *not* limping." Both her feet hurt too much for her to favor either one. "I'm dodging. You are taking up more than your share of the path and cannot seem to walk in a straight line. But if we can spare a few moments, I wouldn't mind retying my slippers."

Instantly he was crouched at her feet and fumbling with the knots. "What the devil are these? Dish towels?"

"I think so." She examined his feet. "They are holding up

better than your stockings. Perhaps I ought not to have removed your boots."

"They were too heavy for swimming," he said, lifting one of the towels. Dark stains were clearly visible in the moonlight. He brought the towel to his nose and sniffed it. "This is blood, Delilah. Your feet are bleeding."

That was hardly news to her. And he had been treading on the same sharp rocks. His feet had to be bleeding as well. "Not so very much," she said, grabbing the towel and bending to wrap it around her foot again. "If walking becomes a problem, I can always take to the water and swim to Argenteuil."

He stood, gazing down at her while she secured the knot and rewrapped her other foot. She was on her way up, a little unbalanced, when he scooped her in his arms and set off down the path.

"You can't do this!" she protested. "Put me down! I'm perfectly able to keep pace with you, sir. If you try to carry me, we'll never get where we're going."

"Yes, we will." His eyes were focused dead ahead. "But if you want to help, Delilah, please shut the hell up. And for God's sake, stop squirming."

She stilled instantly. One of his arms was supporting her back, and the other held her around the knees. She could not begin to imagine how he was bearing her weight or what it must be costing him to do so. Realizing that she was rigid as a fencepost, which was only making it more difficult for him, she concentrated on relaxing her muscles one by one.

She wasn't supposed to move. But after a time, thinking it might help, she draped one arm around his neck. When he didn't object, she lowered her head to his shoulder.

He proceeded steadily along the path, the sound of his breathing harsh in her ears. The whiskers at the side of his jaw rubbed against her cheek. She felt the pulse at his throat and smelled river water in the dark hair tickling her forehead. She wanted to cry because she was so happy to be this close to him, and because he was suffering for it.

She never failed to hurt him, one way or another.

Chapter 17

"... but let it rest. Other affairs must now be managed."

Henry VI, Part 1
Act 4, Scene 1

In the light of the carriage lantern, Delilah studied her husband's closed face. She could not determine if he was sleeping, but his eyes were shut, and lines of weariness had gathered on his forehead and at the corners of his mouth.

To her surprise, he had said not a word when he opened the door of the coach and found her already there. He hadn't needed to, she supposed. His scowl had made perfectly clear what he thought of her most recent act of disobedience. Then, after speaking to the driver, he had climbed inside, settled into the far corner, folded his arms across his chest, and proceeded to ignore her.

Well, what had he expected her to do? Remain in the care of the Comtesse de Marais while he gallivanted off to heaven knew where? When he deposited her with the comtesse and vanished to speak privately with the comte, it was as if he had put her altogether from his mind.

That was not, of course, a situation that could be permitted to endure.

The comtesse, a shy, sweet-natured young woman, had been no match for Samson Bening's daughter. By the time Delilah emerged from a quick bath and allowed her feet to be smeared with salve and bandaged, Madame had been persuaded to give her the loan of a gown, a pair of demiboots, and a servant to smuggle her into the carriage.

Dragoner had borrowed clothing as well, she noted, from the tall, plump Comte de Marais. The black coat, its sleeves rolled up, hung loosely on his frame, and the trousers were secured around his slim waist with what looked to be a neckcloth. There was a pistol stuffed into the makeshift belt, and she detected next to it the stiletto she had given him. Plainly, he was anticipating trouble.

For a mile or two she let him be, expecting that he would eventually break the silence if only to comb her down. But he seemed content to complete the journey as he had begun it, his isolation so acute that he might as well have been in another country.

It was up to her, she supposed. As ever, she must be the one to pursue, and demand, and interfere. She was the one who always got him into difficulty—the marriage, for example, and the trouble with Chabot. Yes, she was in part responsible for that. She had a great deal to answer for, and explanations to provide, and did not fancy there would be another opportunity any time soon to converse with him.

"Well, sir," she said, her throat raw from swallowing a large portion of the Seine, "what is to happen now?"

After several moments, his eyelids lifted. "Before or after I strangle you?"

"Oh, before, I should think. Where are we going?"

"First to Clichy, where I shall instruct Madame de Staël to clamp you in irons. After that, my intentions are none of your concern."

"Rubbish. I have, don't you think, earned the right to see this through? Had I not slipped you my hairpins and my knife, would you not still be imprisoned on the ship?"

"Did I forget to thank you?" He raised a quizzical brow. "Consider it done, then. But do not expect me to confide in you, Delilah. You have been playing both sides of the board."

Her heart cramped. "Yes, I know that it appears so. But there were reasons. Will you permit me to explain them?"

"Could I prevent you?" An unpleasant smile quirked his mouth. "You see, I do learn from experience. But yes, you may as well go ahead. The story will help pass the time until we arrive at Clichy, which I expect we'll do within half an hour."

"Then I'll talk fast," she said with a flutter of relief.

"I prefer that you start with Chabot," he suggested while she was deciding where to begin. "It appears that your ill-fated marriage has taught you nothing, my dear. Against all reason, you have taken up with yet another dissolute rounder."

"No. That is, I was altogether content with the one I had, but you had cut me off. It's quite true, though, that for a time I lost my balance. Madame de Staël swept me into a world I had never thought to enter, you see, and recruited her fashionable friends to prepare me for it. Madame Récamier selected my new gowns and provided a magical cream that turned my hair from straw to, well, to hair. My schoolroom French was polished up. I was given lists of names to memorize, along with descriptions of the people I was likely to meet and the subjects they preferred to discuss. And when Madame de Staël was persuaded I would not disgrace her, she admitted me to her salon."

Dragoner was regarding her with mild disapproval. But then, he had always presumed her to be socially ambitious, and here she was, busily proving his assumptions correct.

"And the very first night," she went on hurriedly, "I met Monsieur le Comte de Chabot. Along with a number of other gentlemen, to be sure, and they were all exceedingly kind. If you must know, I quite enjoyed their attentions. Never before had I received a compliment from a gentleman, or been the object of an admiring glance. I fear that it all rather went to my head."

"How convenient," he said without inflection. "All those men buzzing around you, and you in search of a co-respondent for a divorce proceeding."

"Yes, wasn't it?" She had learned, painfully, to counter his sarcasm by playing along with his more outrageous remarks. "The comte was most particular in singling me out, so naturally he became my prime candidate. And after making the necessary inquiries, I learned that he was in debt up to his ears, out of favor with the new regime because he had toadied up to Bonaparte, and in search of a wealthy female to exploit. He suited my purposes exactly. Oh, and I gave him to believe that I suited his."

"Because you thought you could outmaneuver him." Drag-oner shook his head. "I could almost pity the poor fellow."

"The thing was," she said, soldiering on, "he began hinting at a somewhat radical solution to both our problems. His need for money was immediate, and I could provide him none be-cause you, of course, control our extensive fortune. Which, as you know, does not exist, but I may have implied otherwise. In any case, a divorce would not come soon enough, if it came at all, to pull him out of River Tick. He was subtle, or imagined that he was, but I could hardly mistake his intentions."

"Shall I guess? In order to wed the fair maid, he must first slay the Dragon. A time-honored stratagem, if not terribly in-novative. Would you have married him, Delilah, had he suc-ceeded, or simply thanked him for his trouble and gone on your way?"

"I hadn't decided," she said. "And my own wishes became immaterial when he discovered that I am sprung from common stock. After that, there could be no question of making me the next Comtesse de Chabot."

"Not even for the vast fortune you would supposedly bring him? I thought he was in no position to be overnice about his next wife's birth and breeding."

"One would imagine so. But being penniless has had no ef-fect whatever on his superb conceit, and he continues to fancy himself the Grande Seigneur. Marriage was out of the question early on, as I explained, but he had some use for me nonethe-less."

"I daresay." He turned his gaze to the window. "You may spare me the details."

The raw note in his voice took her by surprise. Then she re-membered deliberately giving him the impression, the night they spoke in the garden at Clichy, that her relationship with Chabot had progressed beyond mere acquaintance. It was to punish him, she supposed, that she had misled him. She had been angry then, and hurt. She had wanted him to know that other men found her desirable, even if he did not. And at Mont-

martre, of course, Chabot had taunted him with false accounts
of their intimacy.

"There are none," she said, her cheeks burning. "No details.
We were never lovers."

His head swung around. For the barest moment she imagined
that he was relieved to hear it. A kernel of hope began to sprout
deep inside her.

"His loss," Dragoner said, watering the new plant with words
that she chose to accept—regardless of how they were intended—as reassuring.

But there was no time to waste now. The coach had picked
up speed as the roads improved, and she was finding it increas-
ingly difficult to make clear what had been a complicated series
of developments. What she had done was straightforward
enough, but telling him *why* would require her to change the
subject altogether. She decided to go on from where they were
and leave the rest for later.

"We became business associates," she said. "Having learned
that I engaged in trade, Chabot naturally sought a way to take
advantage of my experience, and I had reasons of my own to
encourage him."

"Business?" Dragoner, sounding amused, linked his arms
behind his head. "Fencing stolen works of art, you mean.
Naughty Delilah. I very much doubt your father would approve."

"You must never tell him!" she said with considerable alarm.
"Not that you would, I am sure, considering that you were the
one who stole them in the first place."

"Oh, that was Batiste," he said. "I merely told him where
they were to be found. And really, in all that stockpile he accumulated at Montmartre, one would be hard put to locate a single item worth more than, say, a few hundred francs. When
Bonaparte set up the provincial museums, he made sure that
nothing of significant value was sent them."

"Well, I had no idea where the loot was coming from, you
know. And I didn't mean to sell anything unless I had to."

"No?" He frowned. "Then what the devil did you imagine
you were doing?"

"Isn't it obvious? I was trying to find out what *Chabot* was doing. Even after he lost interest in making me a widow for his own purposes, he remained quite willing to help me dispose of you in exchange for my services as a broker. Or so he said, if not in so many words. He was to keep all the money, at any rate, and I was left to deduce how I might profit from the endeavor."

"I see. And having drawn the obvious conclusion, you chose to proceed." He brought his right hand to the pistol at his waist. "I'm rather glad I thought to bring this along."

"*Do* stay on course!" she snapped. "It was evident that once he'd decided to eliminate you, he meant to go through with it—with or without my assistance. So I gave it him, or pretended to, in the hope of finding some way to stop him."

"Indeed." In the flickering light of the carriage lanterns, his face seemed to have gone on fire at the edges. "You were attempting to save my life. And that would explain why you hit me on the head with—what was it? A vase?"

"A brass figurine. And yes, as a matter of fact, it *did* save your life. You must not have seen him, but there was a man at the window with a gun. I didn't know he was there either, until you launched yourself at Chabot. Then I saw an arm go up, and saw the gun at the end of it, and knew he was about to fire. So I grabbed the figurine and whacked you."

She had begun to shake again. Since it happened, she had relived that moment a thousand times, and each time it set off an earthquake inside her. "The blow might have killed you, I know," she said, locking her hands together. "But the alternative was a bullet in your back. What else could I do?"

When at length he spoke, his voice was soft as ashes. "I'm sorry. I have misjudged you. I didn't understand."

"No. How could you? But do you understand now? If I was to deceive Chabot, I had to deceive you as well."

"I would say," he murmured with the faintest of smiles, "that you might have confided in me from the start. But as we both know, I have never given you reason to trust me."

"I have always trusted you," she said. "Or *nearly* always, even when a sensible woman would have consigned you to perdition. But shall I tell you what happened next?"

"Some of it. We have little time. Why didn't Chabot kill me then and there?"

"He almost did." She shuddered. "You had spoiled their original plan, you see, by coming to the house a day early. They had intended to dispose of you at the quarries, making it appear you had been drinking and steered your vehicle over the side. Your body was to be found with some of the loot, to put suspicion for the thefts onto you and leave them free to sell the rest. But the goods had not yet been boxed and taken away, so they elected instead to stow you on the ship and deal with you later. It would be best, of course, if the merchandise was to vanish into England, which is where I came in. Or so I thought. Mr. Batiste had objected to my involvement from the first, and must have persuaded his brother that I would eventually prove a liability. He saw me at your house in Paris, I think, and concluded we were not truly estranged."

The carriage hit a bump, rocking her sideways. Dragoner put out a hand, but she recovered before he could touch her. She did not want him to touch her now, not while her thoughts were in such a jumble. "I took the stiletto from one of the tables," she continued in a rush. "And I accepted their reasons for stashing me on the ship because I needed to be there to help you escape. That's all. You know the rest."

"But at first, Delilah, you refused to leave the ship with me. Why was that?"

She sighed. "I thought, at the time, that Chabot had no reason to distrust me. I expected to have another chance to escape him. And I feared that you would not make it to safety with me along to slow you down."

After a silence, he said quietly, "I couldn't have made it without you. I would have had no reason."

Her heart jumped.

But his thoughts had already turned elsewhere. "And Edoard? What had they in mind for him? What *became* of him?"

"When the others returned with a wagonload of loot, Batiste said he had gone home directly after the robbery. He was meant, I believe, to make certain you came to the hideaway at the proper time."

Dragoner appeared to relax slightly. "Good. One thing more, if you don't mind. It is inconsequential now, to be sure, but I find Chabot's resolution to dispatch me rather astonishing. We were the barest of acquaintances and had no quarrel I am aware of. Take no offense, but it seems unlikely that he would commit murder for your sake, whatever he may have implied to the contrary."

"I cannot account for his motives," she said. "But he once mentioned that you had seduced his wife."

"Ah. In fact, that is not the case. But she might have told him that I did. Even so, the comtesse died two years ago, and from all accounts, he cared nothing for her when she was alive. Batiste, on the other hand, has never fared well in my company. On that score, I suppose Chabot could regard me as an enemy, but the brothers are known to loathe each other. It wouldn't surprise me if, at the end of the day, Chabot meant the both of us to perish."

She gave that some consideration. "It's possible, you know, that he simply required a target for his rage. There are people— I have met a number of them while conducting business transactions—who cast the blame for their own misfortunes on another person for the most nonsensical reasons. An imagined slight, perhaps, or a perceived insult. I believe a number of duels are fought over such trifles."

"Just so." Smothering a yawn, he rested his head against the squabs and closed his eyes. "The next time I meet Chabot, I shall simply have to ask him for an explanation."

"Good heavens, sir! You cannot mean to confront him?"

"Indeed I do. Briefly. Then I mean to shoot him."

"That will be most helpful, to be sure." The violence in him must be contagious, because she felt a sudden urge to kick him on the shin. "Are all gentlemen so prodigiously irrational? I did not go to considerable trouble on your behalf, I'll have you know, only to watch the guillotine lop off your head."

"You needn't fear that, Delilah. Every day in the Bois de Boulogne or a convenient courtyard, you can hear the clash of swords and the explosion of gunpowder. One more duel, I assure you, will scarcely be remarked upon."

"Well, I shall remark upon it! You cannot go around shooting people, Dragoner, even if they deserve it. It would be the sensible thing, surely, to report him to the authorities."

"Oh, certainly. The word of a disgraced Englishman—and even the undisgraced are not so popular in France these days—against the shocked protests of an aristocratic family that probably dates back to Charlemagne. Most efficacious. No, we shall not leave this matter to the uncertain hand of justice, my dear. Had you forgot what those louts had planned for you? I have not."

"Nor I," she said. "But you are speaking of revenge, sir. An act of vengeance will punish Chabot and the others far less than it will harm you."

When he smiled, his teeth gleamed in the lamplight. "I rather doubt it."

"Please yourself, then," she said, infuriated with him. "But your ramshackle conduct will not meet with Wellington's approval."

His eyes shot open. "I beg your pardon?"

"There's no use either of us pretending, sir. I know why you were sent to Paris, and have learned the truth about the circumstances that brought you here. I have, in short, spoken with the duke."

"The devil you say." His tone was quietly menacing. Leaning forward, he propped an elbow on his knee and rested his chin on the back of his folded hand. "Is there no end, madam, to your impertinence? Your effrontery? Your damnable meddling?"

"Not so far," she admitted. "And I cannot say that I am sorry for it. I have fought for my marriage, for your heritage, for the children I long to have and, just lately, for our very lives. Would you expect me to have done otherwise?"

After a space, he gave a resigned shake of the head. "I wish that you had chosen better, is all."

Then, surprising her, he rapped on the panel. The driver reined in to receive his new instructions, and the coach set off again.

"You are not taking me to Madame de Staël's house?" she asked with undisguised relief.

"No indeed. I dare not leave you to run wild. You may remain, under Edoard's strict protection, at the house you so kindly decorated for me, while I go on about my business."

Chapter 18

"Who cannot be crushed with a plot?"

All's Well That Ends Well
Act 4, Scene 3

Because the carriage, emblazoned with the crest of the Comte de Marais, would draw more attention than he wished to attract, Dragoner instructed the coachman to wait for him at a location several streets from his house. The borrowed boots rubbed blisters on his already torn feet as he walked, Delilah on his arm, the rest of the way.

Although the sun had risen some time ago, the narrow street lay in shadows between the rows of tall houses. It was Sunday morning, he remembered after wondering why there were so few people out and about. They passed a man with several long baguettes in the crook of his arm and a milkmaid with her pole over her shoulders, but otherwise the neighborhood lay hushed in Sabbath repose.

"I haven't a key," he told Delilah when they approached the door. "Our friends not unexpectedly emptied my pockets. Indeed, I'm rather surprised they left me with my ring."

"To enable the authorities to identify your body, don't you imagine?"

He suppressed a laugh. She was out of humor with him, he couldn't help but be aware, because of the impending duel. Assuming that he managed to locate Chabot, of course, who by now must have learned that his ship had unaccountably sailed. Whether he knew his prisoners were no longer aboard was less certain, but Dragoner had been keeping a wary eye on the streets and his hand on the pistol. If Batiste and his associates were looking for him, they would certainly come first to the house. Delilah, he had already determined, would be safe enough for a few hours in one of the rooms next door. Then, his business with Chabot concluded, he meant to personally escort her to Calais and chuck her on a boat for England.

When there was no response to his knock, he tried again more forcefully. Edoard was a light sleeper and ought to have responded well before now.

"I have more hairpins," said Delilah, visibly brightened by this turn of events. She knew he would not leave her here without a watchdog.

"Don't get your hopes up," he advised, knitting two pins together and hunkering down in front of the door. "I'll take you back to Clichy if I must. Or I could tie you up and lock you in the cellar."

"It's so nice to be wanted," she replied amiably. "Won't you require a second for your duel? I would be pleased to negotiate a settlement."

He took a moment to glare at her before returning his attention to the lock. "If you want to make yourself useful, my dear, keep your eye on the street. Especially the alley across the way."

"I have been," she said.

It was a good lock, unfortunately. He had seen to the installation of it himself. But that was several years ago, and it was somewhat worn with use. After several minutes, it finally yielded to his probing and he was able to raise the latch.

Light streamed into the dim foyer when he pushed the door open, revealing stacks of boxes and other indeterminate shapes blocking the passageway that led to the back of the house. He drew out his pistol. "Wait here," he said, pushing Delilah to one side.

He rose from his crouch and cautiously stepped inside. Wooden boxes, yes, and picture frames stacked one against the other. Papier maché carnival masks, brightly painted, leered at him from atop the boxes. One was hung from the newel post, and another had been suspended from a candle sconce.

My very own provincial museum, he thought with a mental tip of his hat to Chabot.

His instincts thrummed a warning. There was someone in the house. His gaze went to the staircase and followed it up to the landing.

Poised there, a gun held between her hands and pointed shakily at the open door, was Minette.

"It's all right, Minette," he said gently. "All is well."

"No." Her voiced quaked. "Move out of the way. There is another—"

"Delilah. My wife. Only the two of us. Show yourself, Delilah, and latch the door behind you."

After a moment, Minette hurtled down the stairs and flung herself into his open arms, sobbing uncontrollably. He was stunned. Minette, who feared nothing and no one, had never in his presence lost her composure. At his back, he felt Delilah remove the pistol from her hand.

For a time he simply held the weeping girl, smoothing her hair, very much afraid of what she might have to tell him.

"Brave girl," he whispered as her shaking began to subside. "Will you sit here on the stairs with me now?"

"I am sorry. I am sorry." She sank beside him and clutched at her knees. "Where is Edoard? What has become of him?"

She didn't know, then. He was not, after all, lying dead in the house. Dragoner steadied himself.

"I haven't seen him since Friday morning," he said. "When you are able, tell me what has happened since then."

Delilah passed Minette a handkerchief.

"*Merci,*" she said, wiping her eyes. "I was worried for you as well, but you are here. Perhaps he will return soon." In her distress, she mingled French and English as she spoke. "He was to meet me at Le Chien Noir last night, but he never arrived. He is sometimes very late, if you have put him to work, and so I waited until nearly dawn before coming to look for him."

She gestured to the clutter in the passageway. "These *things* were here. I thought perhaps he had brought them, or you, but the door had been left unlocked. He would not have been so careless. Later, I found a key on the floor."

"That was mine, I expect. It was taken from me yesterday. Did you find anything else?"

A shudder ran through her body. He wrapped his arm around her shoulders and drew her closer. "What else, Minette?"

"Blood," she said. "Over there, spattered on the wall. Perhaps some, a few drops, on the stairs and the landing. I could not be sure."

They were both thinking the same thing, he knew. Edoard's blood.

"I expect someone cut himself while unloading all this trash," he said, fairly certain Minette would not believe him. Second only to Delilah, she was the most intelligent female he had ever met, and the most courageous. He looked over at his wife, who was examining the bloodstains on the wall.

"We should hurry," she said. "Chabot meant these things to be found here. I think he will make sure that they are."

"Yes." He stood and helped Minette to her feet. "There is a coach standing by not far from here. Gather what you need while I change clothes. Then I shall see you and Delilah to a safe place." He brushed a kiss against her cold cheek. "I'll find Edoard, my dear. I promise you."

The women followed him up the stairs, Delilah walking beside Minette with an arm around her waist. They veered off at the first landing while he proceeded to his bedchamber and began to unwrap Marais' neckcloth from his waist.

Not long after, he heard a loud banging from downstairs. Shouts. He could not make out the words. Delilah and Minette erupted into the room.

"Police," said Minette breathlessly. "You must go. Quickly!"

He took her arm. "We'll go together."

"Don't be stupid. I am known to be your mistress. I will be angry and confused. I can deal with these imbeciles. Go. Find Edoard. *Go!*"

Dragoner, well acquainted with Minette's intransigence, knew better than to cross her now. Giving her a wink for luck, he grabbed Delilah's hand and towed her down the passageway. Behind him, he could hear Minette flinging apart the window shutters.

"Qui est-il? Que voulez-vous?" she called, her voice sleepy and impatient.

"Nous sommes la police. Ouvrez la porte!"

His hand found the lever that tripped the panel concealed behind the statue of Zeus, and Delilah, who had been through it at least once before, crawled in ahead of him. He followed and secured the panel before taking the lead again. It occurred to him that, in her frenzy to redo both his houses, she might have removed the ladder.

But there it stood, precisely where he had left it. Climbing swiftly, he reached the ceiling, raised the trapdoor, and pushed himself onto the roof. From there, on his knees, he turned back to help Delilah ascend.

She was still standing where he had left her, gripping her skirts.

"Come on!" he demanded in a harsh whisper. "Move!"

Tentatively she approached the ladder and mounted it in careful increments, as if imagining it would collapse under her at any moment. When she was close enough, he seized her under the arms and pulled her onto the roof.

After securing the trapdoor, he pointed the direction they were to go. "Follow me," he said. "Keep low. You can be seen by anyone looking up. Pretend you're a snake."

Her eyes, swimming with tears, looked back at him. "I c-can't. You go ahead. I'll stay here."

"The devil you will!" He examined her more closely. She was trembling like a jelly. "What's wrong?" he asked, gentling his voice. "I know the roof is steep, but we haven't far to go."

"I'm afraid of h-heights," she said. "They won't find me up here. I'll stay until you come back to get me."

"Slither, Delilah. I won't let you fall." He struck out across the roof, not looking back. There wasn't time to soothe or encourage her. If they were to escape undetected, it would have to be while Minette kept the police occupied at the house.

After a few moments he heard the small sounds of her progress—the scrape of leather, the rustle of her dress, the swift puffs of nervous breath as she wriggled over the slate shingles. He smiled. Delilah, tenacious Delilah, would not be left behind.

But the worst, he knew, was yet to come. She would require every jot of her remarkable courage for the descent.

When he approached the balcony of the deaf woman's house, he saw that there were no pedestrians on the street below. Good luck, for a change, but it wouldn't hold for very long. He swung over the side of the roof, dropped onto the balcony, and hunkered down. From above him came a gasp.

Delilah's face, white as a peeled radish, appeared above the gutter. "Oh, I can't," she mouthed, the way they had done on the ship.

"Turn and sit. Hurry."

"N-no." But she had already begun to reverse her position. Gingerly she edged forward, her skirt scrunching up beneath her, until her legs were dangling in the air.

"Don't look down," he said. "When I give the word, slide another few inches and let go. I'm right here. I'll catch you."

"Ohhh," she moaned, closing her eyes.

He stood upright, positioned himself directly under her, and opened his arms. "Now!"

There was a moment's delay. Then, her face wrinkled with concentration, she slipped the last few inches and pushed off.

Instead of dropping, she had propelled herself outward. He jumped back to catch her, his waist hitting the balcony rail as she slammed against his chest. The wind went out of him. He heard a crashing sound in the street.

Gripping her tightly, he brought them both to the floor and rolled over until she was pressed against the glass door with his body wrapped around her, shielding her from view. He looked over his shoulder. From this position he couldn't see the street, but anyone standing on the pavement across the way would be able to spot the two figures huddled on the balcony.

He must have knocked something off the rail. Damn. There had never been anything on it before, and he had been so focused on Delilah that he'd failed to look in that direction. The noise was bound to draw someone out to see what had caused it.

He turned back to Delilah, shivering in his arms, and brushed his knuckles against her cheek. "I'm sorry," he said. "We nearly made it."

"I c-can't breathe," she whooshed, shoving at his arm.

Immediately he lifted himself while she slid away from the door and under him, still panting for air. Then he settled again, keeping most of his weight on his elbows and knees, hovering over her as if they were about to make love. The thought struck him with mordant irony.

"What do we do now?" she whispered.

"I don't know. Wait here, I suppose."

"Good." A smile curved her lips. "Under no circumstances could you have persuaded me to jump off this balcony."

There were voices in the street now, male voices, coming closer. He put a finger on her lips and bowed his head.

Another sound then, to his left. He looked over and saw the French window moving away from him. An orange cat appeared in the opening, paused for a moment to examine him, and padded across his back. It was followed by another cat, and another. Next came two feet wearing slippers. They, too, stepped across him, not using his back as a roadway as the cats had done. He felt the brush of fabric over his hair.

"Mauvais chat!" said an irritated female voice. *"Qu'avez-vous fait?"*

Rather sure exhaustion had launched him into a dream, he held still while another feline settled atop his buttocks and began, he thought, to groom itself.

Cautiously he turned his head and saw a violently purple dressing gown that spread itself wide as the figure wearing it raised an ear trumpet and propped a wrinkled hand on the railing. Next to it, delicately poised on the narrow rail, was a large marmalade cat.

"Y a-t-il un problème, madame?" a man called from the street.

His sluggish mind, suddenly unable to cope with the French, began translating bits and pieces of the conversation. There was something about a pot of geraniums, and a *vilain chat* that that knocked it into the street. Apologies for creating a disturbance from the woman, and questions about any unusual activities in the neighborhood from the men. Men with authoritative voices, Dragoner noted, compelled to shout because the woman kept complaining that she could not hear them.

"Go into the house, my bad children," she instructed at one point, lifting the cat off the rail. "Shoo. Inside. All of you!"

Delilah plucked at his sleeve. "That's a cue, sir."

"Right."

In a tangle of arms and legs, they rolled themselves through the French windows onto a thick carpet and scrambled behind an overstuffed sofa.

Outside, the bizarre interrogation continued. Had she seen any strangers? *Non.* Heard any odd noises. *Non.* And how could she have heard them, deaf as she was? The cats got out where they weren't supposed to be, that was all. And ruined her geraniums, the wicked creatures. Her precious babies. She must feed them their breakfasts, *n'est-ce pas?*, and have her coffee, and take them for their walk.

Delilah, sitting back on her heels, had begun to laugh somewhat wildly. "Is this truly happening?" she asked, gasping for breath and laughing again. "Have I gone mad?"

"We both have," he said. And then, because she needed to be calmed or because he could not help himself, he took hold of her shoulders and drew her to his aching chest and kissed her.

It was, at first, a rough embrace and a wooden kiss, but then she went soft and pliant in his arms, and her lips were warm, so warm, open to him, fervent and yielding, and he lost himself in her.

Until he remembered. Not gently, he put her away and turned to one side, burying his face in his hands. The sounds from the balcony were drowned by the blood pumping in his ears.

Fool!

"It is permitted," she said after a time, "for a man to kiss his wife."

Nothing goes right; we would, and we would not.

"Is it permitted," he murmured, "to keep her?"

A short silence. "That, too," she said.

He came abruptly, unwillingly, to his senses. Lifting his head, he looked at her over his shoulder. "But no. I'm sorry. We were, for a moment, gone mad. That is all. You want a divorce, and so do I. We mustn't forget, either of us, who and what I am."

Her eyes, which had been wide with hope, perhaps it was

hope, or some other impossible emotion he was certain to dash, lost all their brilliant light. Her lashes fanned down, but not before a tear escaped to carve a silver path down her cheek.

He wanted, then, to die. But, of course, nothing came easily just from wanting it.

"Ah, ah, where have you gone?"

Startled, he looked up to see the woman from the balcony swooping around the sofa in a flurry of purple taffeta and yellowed lace.

"*Voilà!* As I thought. It is the nice young man who passes so often over my roof and thinks of my balcony as a staircase. But come out, come out, and be comfortable. The *gendarmes* have gone off, shaking their heads. For all their trouble, they found only a broken pot of geraniums and a lunatic woman. Come. You needn't stay on the floor."

He stood, his limbs protesting by now every exertion imposed on them, and held out his hand to Delilah. But she rose gracefully, without his help, and curtsied to the woman.

"We owe you our thanks," she said with a warm, untroubled smile.

He watched it with considerable awe before remembering to bow. "Indeed, yes, madame."

"Oh, you needn't shout," the woman replied, tossing her ear trumpet onto a table. "My hearing is perfectly fine, unlike my arthritic knees and weak eyes and poor digestion. It is a great trial, I assure you, when the body grows old before the mind. But I burn with curiosity. Let us all sit and tell one another what we have been doing."

With that she dropped onto a chair, her robe puffing out over the carpet, and welcomed two cats onto her lap.

A third joined Delilah when she settled on the sofa, and the other two curled around Dragoner's ankles as he continued to stand where he was, his mind spinning off in a thousand directions. "I thought you were deaf," he said stupidly.

"Pah! I only pretend to be, so that I can ignore people when they grow tedious. And one hears all the best gossip that way, you know. Also," she added with a sly grin, "one hears young gentlemen pouncing about in the middle of the night."

"I have disturbed you," he said. "Please accept my apology. I didn't know."

"Disturbed? Dear me, no. I do not sleep well, another curse of advancing years, and you have provided a good deal of excitement where there was none before. We have endlessly conversed, my friends and I, about you, trying to guess why you sometimes do not use your own door to leave your house. Monsieur Colbert believes you to be a burglar. Madame Ricot is sure you are plotting to overthrow the government. Bonaparte, Bourbon, either one. She cannot keep in her head who is in charge these days. The others have even more outrageous theories, but it is all nonsense, what they say of you. They do not know that you are an Englishman. Which means, of course, that you are a spy."

He glanced at Delilah and caught her smothering a laugh.

Dear God. What next? But this wily old lady had saved them, at least for the moment, from the police, and it seemed there was no use keeping up a pretense. "I'm not saying you are right, madame, but would you mind if I were a . . . something of the kind?"

"Oh, it's nothing to do with me," she returned with a shrug. "I watch, I listen, I enjoy. I prefer the mystery, *vouz comprenez*. It is enough that today I have had a small adventure."

"It may bring trouble," he warned. "The police have been told that I stole some things they have already found in my house. I doubt they will give up until they have found me as well."

"And the young lady," she said, turning her gaze to Delilah.

"My wife." The words hurt his tongue to say. "She has no part of this. It is by accident that she became involved, and my first concern is to see her to safety."

"Well, then," said the woman, "we shall put our heads together and find a way to extricate the both of you. What fun! I am, by the way, Madame Forbanne, a widow of no consequence with only cats for my babies. You are Lord Dragoner, I know. And I am delighted to make the acquaintance of your wife. She is very lovely, and most brave to have jumped off the roof as she did."

"Yes, I was," Delilah said. "And I mean to walk out of here

on solid ground, thank you, even if it puts me in the hands of the police."

"To be sure." Madame Forbanne returned her attention to Dragoner. "I was most surprised that you came by here again this morning. So soon and in daylight, too, which you have never done before. Well, those very irritating policemen would account for that, I suppose."

"Again?"

She frowned. "Was it not you dropped off my roof last night? I rushed to the window, but you were gone before I lifted the curtain."

Suddenly weak at the knees, he lowered himself on the sofa next to Delilah. "Edoard," he said in a rush of breath. "Thank God."

A warm hand settled over his. "He got away then," Delilah said. "We must tell Minette."

"Yes. When we can." Relief made him dizzy, made him want to shout. He had thought, he had been sure, that because of the mistakes he'd made, his nearest friend was dead. If he could now make sure that Delilah escaped unharmed, he would ask nothing more of a suddenly merciful heaven.

He looked up to see two dark eyes, bright as a bird's, fixed on him. Madame Forbanne, a most unlikely angel. Had he the strength to move, he would have knelt at her feet.

"I have an idea that may get you out of here undetected by those most tiresome policemen," she said. "But I do not expect that you will like it."

Chapter 19

"Shame and confusion! All is on the rout."

Henry VI, Part 2
Act 5, Scene 2

Madame Forbanne, it soon became apparent, was in no great hurry for her adventure to come to an end. "First we shall have coffee," she declared, bustling off to the kitchen before Dragoner could rally himself to protest.

"We need to get out of here," he grumbled. "Any time now, the police will start knocking on doors and interrogating the residents."

"But why would they?" Delilah asked reasonably. "It's not as if we are known to be in the vicinity. They'll be watching for us, or for you, at any rate, to come strolling home unmindful that your crime has been discovered."

She was probably right . . . except for that bloody geranium pot. And if they searched his house carefully, it wasn't impossible they'd locate the panel behind the statue. Delilah had found it easily enough.

He leaned back against the sofa, letting his eyes close. She was still holding his hand, he was aware, and he ought to remove it. But the exertion was too great, or perhaps he didn't want to offend her again.

"How shall we get word to Minette?" she asked after a time. "I think we must try. She was terribly worried about Edoard."

Who may have run into more trouble after escaping the house, Dragoner thought, especially if he'd gone looking for

Batiste. "I don't see how we can," he said. "The police would examine any message we sent, and I won't put Madame Forbanne at risk by asking for her assistance."

"I suppose not." Delilah's hand had tightened on his fingers. "There is a resemblance between them, I noticed. Well, I had never seen Minette before today, but they both have dark hair and brown eyes. Is Edoard her brother?"

His eyes flicked open. "Hardly that. These days he out-Frenches the French, or likes to think he does, but when he's not putting on airs, Sergeant Eddie Platt is purebred Yorkshireman."

"Good heavens. He's not your valet, then?"

"He is that, and a good many other things as well. Friend. Constant irritant. Fellow spy. Minette also works for me, after a fashion, although I cannot pay her."

"I see." Delilah let go his hand. "Well, I don't expect she would require to be paid."

"No, although I hope to make it up to her one day. She has had a difficult time of it. Her parents are long since dead, and both her brothers were conscripted when they were practically children. No surprise that they failed to survive their first battle. It's a common enough story in France—a million or so men fallen in Bonaparte's war and their women left to scrabble for a living. Minette is a most uncommon female, though. I expect you would like her."

"I rather doubt it," she said under her breath.

He wasn't supposed to hear that, he was fairly sure, but he'd got used to reading her lips. "Why not? She can't have offended you in so short a time. And in case you've forgot, she stayed behind to deal with the police while we did a runner."

"Yes. For your sake." Delilah's back was stiff as a plank. "I am sorry, sir, but I cannot help disliking her. You have had mistresses, I know. Lots of them. You've made that point to me often enough. But it's one thing to hear about them in the abstract, so to speak, and quite another to come face-to-face with one of them in your very own house. Good grief. I even bought you a new *bed!*"

She erupted off the sofa, scattering cats across the carpet.

"And I did like her at first, which makes it even more awful. Until she said what she said."

"When? What the devil gave you the idea she and I—?"

"You were there. 'I am known to be your mistress,' she said. I could hardly mistake that, could I?"

"Apparently so," he muttered, earning a blistering glare from his offended wife. His *jealous* wife. And why did that please him? It shouldn't. He had done much worse things than bedding Minette, and he had wanted Delilah to know it. How else to disillusion her? But in this case, a friend was involved. Or rather, not involved.

"*Known* to be," he said. "Minette required a plausible reason to make free of my house, and to be seen in my company at some of the fairly disreputable places I've had reason to go to these last few years. That's all. It's Edoard who is her lover. They plan to marry one day."

"Oh." Delilah's face had gone scarlet. "Oh," she said again. "I have made a fool of myself, haven't I? And for no reason. Probably I met some of your mistresses at Madame de Staël's salon and didn't even know it."

No doubt. But he refrained, this time, from saying so. "A misunderstanding, Delilah. Put it from your mind."

"Yes. I will. Of course. I'll go help Madame Forbanne with the coffee."

She looked to him like a wilted flower as she made her slow way from the room. His heart caught. It had been regrettable to hurt her when he didn't know her. But now that he did . . .

"I've an errand to run downstairs," said Madame Forbanne, a purple butterfly flitting by him and gone before he had started to breathe again.

Delilah arrived shortly after with a tray, which she set on the low table in front of the sofa. "We are to have help from her friends," she said. "I'm sorry. I couldn't stop her."

Any more than he had ever been able to stop Delilah. Females ought to rule the world, he thought, accepting a cup of coffee from her hands. Or perhaps they did, in their way.

The coffee was strong and bitter, even with the sugar she had piled into it. He took a fluffy croissant from the tray and bit into it. His stomach roiling, he set the croissant back on the plate.

"You have to eat," Delilah said. "Don't make me stuff it down your throat."

He knew when he was overmatched. He ate. And began to feel better almost immediately, of course.

Madame Forbanne returned with her arms full of clothing, and atop the mound, he saw a shaving razor. She dropped the lot onto a chair and began to sift through it. "You won't be easy to fit," she said. "Stand up, will you?"

"Certainly, if you wish it. But perhaps you would kindly tell me what you have in mind?"

"Soon enough. If none of these will do, I must apply to Madame Miret, who is a wicked old woman. And she sleeps until noon. Up. Up!"

He set aside his cup and stood, aware of Delilah watching him with an amused expression on her face. Next thing, Madame Forbanne was holding a shapeless swath of fabric to his shoulders and looking down to see how far it reached.

"Too short," she said, tossing it aside and returning to her pile for another specimen, also gray. This time, when she measured it to him, he took the trouble to lower his gaze and see what it was.

He saw skirts.

"Dammit, this is a dress!"

"Why, of course it is." Her bird-bright eyes fixed on him. "What did you think? That you could walk out of here clothed as a man? The police are *looking* for a man. They will stop any man they see and interrogate him, yes? But they have no reason to trouble two women on their way to church this Sunday morning. And that is what the pair of you will be, when I am done with you. Now keep still while I work."

Still? He was frozen with humiliation. And all the more so because she was perfectly right. Accustomed to disguises, he could have borne this one well enough, he supposed, had Delilah not been here to witness it.

She was wise enough to keep silent, although she might as well have spoken because he knew precisely what she was thinking. After the third gown had been tried and found wanting, unable to resist, he stole a glance in her direction. She had picked up a cat and was holding it to her breast, all her attention focused on it, demure as a nun.

The fourth gown pleased Madame Forbanne, lengthwise, although, as she said, he must try it on for fit. "Happily, you are slender," she chirped, "and not overly tall. Your wife should change into one of these dull gowns as well, I believe. In the one she is wearing, she is far too attractive. An amorous policeman is likely to notice her, which is the last thing we wish, *n'est-ce pas?*"

Having lost the capacity to speak, he nodded.

"Well, then," said Madame Forbanne. "She may select a dress while you shave yourself. Those manly whiskers would give you away in an instant. There is hot water in the kitchen, and soap, and I have borrowed Monsieur Colbert's razor. I shall bring you a mirror."

Not long after, perched on a stool, she watched him shave. "My Henri had a beard like yours," she said. "He was, for the most part, a nasty man while he was alive. But now that he is gone, I remember only the pleasant moments. He had to shave twice a day, Henri, but he was no good at it, so after a time he let me take the razor to his chin. Sometimes it was all I could do to keep from slicing his throat." She laughed. "But he was an excellent lover. A woman forgives many faults when an excellent lover takes her into his arms. Such fools we are."

He cut himself twice, once when she said that and later, when she spoke of Delilah.

"Your wife has love in her eyes," she said. "It sparkles like sunlight on water."

She said more, a great deal more, but he closed his ears to her words. Like Madame Forbanne, he, too, could pretend to be deaf. And what did she know of anything, after all? She saw only a young man and a young woman in the throes of an adventure. Of course they would appear to be bonded, he to Delilah, and so they had been for, what? Ten hours, more or less. Ten hours united in a race to survive.

If he retained any doubts that their high drama had eroded into farce, they were quickly dispersed. The shaving completed, Madame Forbanne instructed him to put on the dress while she located the accessories he would require.

"No female fripperies," he called as she vanished into her bedchamber.

Delilah must have gone there as well to change her gown, which left him alone in the parlor with a handful of gray cloth and the problem of stuffing himself into it.

It ought to be a simple matter. In his time he had removed any number of gowns from cooperative ladies. But now that he thought on it, he had never remained long enough to help them dress again, which was an altogether different procedure. Swearing profusely, he examined the shapeless mass with all its tapes and flaps and buttons, unable to decide how they were meant to come together. Well, someone else would have to do the honors. At length, having determined front from back and stuck his forearms into the sleeves, he attempted to pull the gown over his head.

When he heard Delilah and Madame Forbanne come into the room—more exactly, when he heard them laughing—he was hopelessly entangled. Half in and half out of the dress with his face smothered in cloth, he stood still on command while one of them tugged here and there until his head popped out. He took a welcome gulp of air.

For all Madame Forbanne's efforts, the greater part of the fabric remained snarled above his waist. "Naughty boy," she said. "You are still wearing your shirt! It is no wonder your arms will not fit into the sleeves."

The dress was pulled off, followed by the shirt, and Madame clucked to see the dark bruises on his shoulders and the bandages wrapped around his chest. They were not the remnants of Delilah's gown—he should not have liked to explain blue silk—but the plain linen bands that Marais' valet had provided him.

"All those lovely muscles," she said admiringly, touching his arm. "The sleeves may not accommodate them even yet. But we shall try."

This time the dress settled over him with relative ease, although his arms felt like sausages encased in the tight sleeves.

After securing ties and buttoning buttons, Madame stood back to consider the results. "You must take care not to move your arms overmuch, or you will rip the seams. But the hem is a suitable length, or near to. You cannot, of course, wear those boots."

"I'll remove them," Delilah said. "I've had practice."

He sat on a chair while she pulled them off, her expression schooled to the polite impassiveness he remembered from the solicitor's office. In her dove-gray dress and with her hair twisted in a knot at her nape, she looked rather like the head-mistress of a school for proper young ladies.

"This will soon be over," she said, rising. "And aren't we fortunate to have the assistance of Madame Forbanne and her friends?"

"Oh, indeed." He scowled at his bare feet and the folds of skirt across his lap. "You can imagine my delight."

But he took to heart her message, resolving to make no protest whatever was done to him from here on out. Delilah's fate, as well as his own, depended on the success of this masquerade.

Not unexpectedly, his good intentions were immediately put to the test. Madame Forbanne returned with two amorphous objects, lavender in color, and wrenched them with considerable difficulty over his cut and blistered feet.

"I knit the slippers myself," she said, "to wear when my ankles swell up, although they were never designed for feet so large as yours. But the skirts will cover them well enough, I suppose, unless someone looks too closely. Rise, if you please, and let us see what remains to be done."

With growing dread, he obeyed, feeling rather like a mannequin in a dressmaker's shop. His sole consolation was that Edoard had made his escape and was not here to see this.

"You have no bosom, of course," Madame pointed out unnecessarily, "but a shawl will conceal the deficiency. And a bonnet, of course, will camouflage your lack of womanly hair." She circled him, making obscure noises in her throat.

Delilah, a cat in her arms, regarded him with a degree of sympathy. "We could," she said, "surrender to the police and take our chances in the courts. I don't expect they would guillotine us straightaway."

She meant it, he could tell. If he decided to put an end to this charade, she was ready to deal with the consequences. From the depths of his gloom, he mustered a smile. "We have discussed this already," he said. "All in all, we've a better chance of eluding the police in the streets than extracting ourselves from a cell at Saint Lazare after they've nabbed us. But, thank you."

Their eyes met, and held. To keep her at his side awhile longer, he realized with a start, there was nothing he would not do.

With too much blood and too little brain these two may run mad.

Madame Forbanne shook her head. "It's no good. Your shoulders are too wide for the rest of you. We must create something to balance them." Off she went in a rush.

He had an awful feeling she meant to contrive for him a pair of breasts. But when she returned, there was nothing more threatening in her hands than a rounded wicker basket and a length of twine.

His relief lasted as long as it took her to thread the twine around the rim of the basket and clip it off with two pieces dangling from each side, at which point she looked up at him with a demonic glint in her eyes. "I am very much afraid, Lord Dragoner, that you are about to find yourself with child."

"Oh, what a good idea!" Delilah exclaimed before he could start swearing aloud. "That is just the thing. Isn't it, sir?"

Certainly. The heir to the Dragoner title would be a basket. Why not? And what else could he do but concede with entirely spurious grace? But, for causing him this supreme humiliation, he was all the more determined that Chabot must die. Slowly. With a bullet in his unpregnant stomach.

His skirts went up, held by his pernicious wife, while Madame Forbanne attached the basket to his belly. Next came a frilly bonnet on his head, all lace and ribbons and a clutch of faux cherries dangling over the brim. Then a fringed paisley shawl was draped around his shoulders, and he was shown how to conceal his hands in the folds of it. There was no hope, Madame informed him, of finding gloves to fit.

At least she had not demanded that he remove Marais's saggy trousers, although she rolled up the cuffs as far as his knees. With pants on his legs, he thought he might just make it through this ordeal. He was less pleased when she pulled strands of his hair from under his bonnet and made little curls of them, plastering them to his forehead with some sort of glue. When that indignity was followed by rouge on his cheeks and lips, he'd had enough.

"No more," he said tightly. "Send me out as I am."

"I'm done," she said, clapping her hands with delight. "Come into my bedchamber and see in the mirror how well you look."

"Oh, I think not." He glanced over at Delilah, who had put on the simple bonnet given her and tied the ribbons under her chin. Why was he the one afflicted with lace and cherries?

But he knew why, and credited the bizarre old woman for knowing it as well. The colorful hat would call attention from his face, which could not bear too close a scrutiny, and his swollen belly would serve much the same purpose. As disguises went, this one was a corker.

"Now if a policeman approaches you," Madame Forbanne was saying, "you must simper and be shy. Keep your head down and allow your wife to do the talking. Make up a story between you while I dress myself, because I shall go out before you with my cats. We are to provide a distraction, *n'est-ce pas?*"

A few minutes later, clad in stunning pink, the old lady led them down the stairs.

Dragoner was conscious of the doors on the second and first levels of the house cracking open as the residents in the lower apartments stole a glimpse of what they had helped to create. He couldn't bring himself to acknowledge them, garbed as he was, but Delilah smiled and murmured words of gratitude. She always knew exactly how to comport herself under any circumstance, which never failed to impress him.

When they reached the front door, cats swirling at his feet, Madame Forbanne turned to him. "*Bonne chance,* my dear friend. As I walk out, I shall pray that you come to safe harbor."

He took her hands and brushed a kiss on her papery cheek. "*Vous êtes un ange, ma petite.* I shall never forget you. And one day, I promise, I shall see you rewarded for all you have done for us."

"It will be enough," she said, "if I live long enough to see your sweet wife with a child in her arms and you with joy in

your eyes. For now, wait here until Madame Ricot gives you
the signal to depart. She is watching at her window for curious
policemen. *Au revoir, mes amies.*"

"I remember her now," said Delilah as Madame Forbanne
swept out the door with five cats, their tails aloft like masts on
a ship, trotting happily behind. "I saw her once from the window of your house. It was the day you returned from England."

Her voice, limned with sorrow, faded off at the end.

He would have taken her hand, except that he had been told
to keep his own buried under the shawl. "I'm sorry, Delilah,"
he said. "I was a monster that day. I thought it necessary to be."

"Yes. Of course. We needn't call it to mind again."

Her smile did little to ease the stab of pain in his heart.
*Leaked is our bark; And we, poor mates, stand on the dying
deck . . .*

"You may go now," said a whispery voice from behind one
of the partly open doors. "Godspeed."

Blinking against the bright sunlight, Delilah's arm tightly
wrapped around his, he made his way to the pavement and
minced—it felt to him like mincing—to the corner. Head down.
Small steps. Take care the knitted slippers stay under the skirts.

As they crossed the first street, Delilah took on the role of
lookout. "There's a policeman at the corner opposite us. Now
he has stopped a man who is carrying a satchel. We're past him.
I see no one in uniform at the next corner."

The police, he supposed, would be concentrated near his residence, which faced onto the street at the other side of the block
of houses. There were a number of pedestrians, some strolling
idly and others arcing off the pavement to pass the slow-moving
ladies. He heard the occasional murmured greeting and once,
Delilah drew him to a halt while she exchanged observations
about the pleasant weather with an old gentleman. Dragoner
buried his face in his shawl until she led him on again.

"It would have been rude not to stop," she said. "And we
don't wish to appear in a hurry."

They crossed another street without incident, and a third.
Then Delilah gripped his arm. "A policeman is walking to-
wards us. Here. Use this." She pressed a large, lace-edged
handkerchief onto the shawl just over his hand. He snagged it

best he could and raised it to his chin. It smelled of powder and cologne.

"Bonjour," said a gruff male voice.

They stopped. Looking down, he could see dark trousers and polished black shoes. The policeman had planted himself directly in front of them.

"Bonjour, monsieur," Dragoner said in a quavery voice an octave above his normal range. Then he sneezed.

"My sister has the cold, monsieur," Delilah said in badly accented French. "I think she ought to have remained in bed, but her physician insists that she walk every morning. For the sake of the babe, you understand. I made certain that she dressed warmly, even on this sunny day."

"You are English?" There was an edge of suspicion in his tone.

"American," she replied easily. "My husband's mother is French, and we have come over to visit his relations. We Americans are fighting the English now, you know, and their soldiers had come dangerously near to our plantation. Raoul thought it best that we leave for a time. And of course I must bring my sister, for she could not be left unprotected. Her William is serving in the American army, you see."

Dragoner sniffled and brought the handkerchief to his eyes.

"Ah. Then your relations live in this neighborhood?" He sounded more kindly now, the French being overfond of Americans and most especially when they were making trouble for the despised English.

"Only a cousin," Delilah said. "I thought we might visit her, but she is not to home. We are staying with my mother-in-law in the Faubourg Saint-Germain."

"Surely you cannot mean to walk such a distance, madame! May I locate for you a carriage cab?"

"How kind! But no, monsieur, thank you. We mean to walk another few minutes, to a small restaurant we passed on the way, and have ourselves a light breakfast. Hortensia must eat regularly, even when she has no appetite. Then we shall find a carriage. I'm sure we will have no difficulty. Everyone has been so helpful."

"In that case, I shall wish you good day. But should the lady find it troublesome to continue, there is one of my compatriots stationed two streets from here. He will gladly assist you. *Au revoir, mesdames.*"

The two feet moved aside, allowing them to pass, and Dragoner gave one last sneeze, this one brought on by the talcum powder. "Hortensia?" he murmured when he felt Delilah's tense arm begin to relax.

"I was improvising," she said a little breathlessly. "And I don't think he ever looked at your face, thank heavens. It was your belly that appeared to fascinate him. Shall we give his friend the go-around and turn off at the next corner?"

"Yes." He looked over at her. "That was well done, my dear."

Her eyes shone at the casual praise. "Thank you. I have a knack for subterfuge, don't you think?"

"*'She hath many nameless virtues,'*" he said.

"Oh, for pity's sake, sir. Don't start *that* again!"

They avoided the policeman they knew about and encountered no others before reaching the coach, which was drawn up in a side street near to the river. He spoke briefly to the driver, who had been snoozing with his chin resting on his collarbone, and permitted Delilah—she said it was only proper—to lower the steps and hand him inside.

Collapsing on the bench, his first thought was to rid himself of the basket. He removed the knife from the sling he'd tied around his thigh and gave it to Delilah, who tossed his skirts over his head and set to work sawing at the twine. The blade was dull now, after being applied to the anchor rope, but finally the last cord gave way. He felt the basket lifted from his stomach and reached to pull down his skirts.

Delilah, now sitting directly across from him, was holding up the basket and regarding it thoughtfully. "Well, the hair will grow in, I suppose. And he does have your eyes. Or perhaps it's a daughter." She flipped over the basket and examined the other side. "Too soon to tell. Really, Hortensia, you should have let the child come to full term."

And then, as he erupted in laughter, it came to him like a knife in the heart that he was irretrievably in love with his wife.

Had loved her, perhaps, for a considerable time. She had a way of sneaking up on a man, and disarming him, and leaving him bare-arsed naked to emotions he could not afford to in-dulge. Until now he had managed to fight them off, but he could no longer ignore what had happened to him or pretend, as he had been doing, that he remained indifferent to her.

Fain would I woo her, yet I dare not speak.

Must not. It was all the more urgent now that they separate for good. For *her* good.

The more he had come to admire and respect her, the less de-serving he had known himself to be. That was the one thing he was sure of now. And he had thrown away, that afternoon when he set out to prove himself beyond redemption, the one chance she had offered him to find out if they could make something of their marriage.

A year in her company. She had asked so little of him. He felt sick at heart to remember how savagely he had denied her.

She'd set the basket beside her on the squabs and was look-ing out the window, apparently oblivious to him flying off like grapeshot in all directions. "Where are we going now, sir?" she asked. "Do you mean to leave me with Madame de Staël in Clichy?"

"No." He coughed to clear his throat of a lump that had set-tled there. "We are on our way to the embassy. Wellington will be elsewhere, of course, on a Sunday, but perhaps we will be admitted. If not, whoever is posted at the door may be per-suaded to deliver him a message."

"I know where he lives," she offered cheerfully. "We could go there."

Delilah never saw a boundary but she wanted to leap it. "Let's not push him," he said, amused in spite of himself. "As it is, His Grace is unlikely to be pleased with us."

Chapter 20

"Now I see the myst'ry of your loneliness, and find your salt tears' head."

All's Well That Ends Well
Act 1, Scene 3

His Grace was in his office this morning, a young subaltern informed them when they applied for admittance at the embassy gate.

Delilah quite enjoyed his reaction to the spectacle of Lord Dragoner's dress and lavender slippers, and was only sorry that the cherry-festooned bonnet had been jettisoned in the carriage. She had helped him scour the rouge from his lips and cheeks, but when he began to peel off the gown as well, she had pointed out that a bare chest and oversized trousers held up with a neck-cloth were no great improvement, and that his bruises and bandages were bound to raise questions.

He had conceded, probably because he was tired of arguing with her. There was profound weariness in his eyes, and pain, which made her feel the more guilty for her own sparkling energy and good humor.

She wanted to celebrate. They had escaped! The two of them together, working together, had got out of the locked cabins and off the ship and all the rest of it, intact save for the injuries Dragoner had suffered along the way. Those were considerable, she must not forget, although he feigned otherwise.

The subaltern escorted them inside and held them in the foyer while another wide-eyed young soldier carried news of their presence to the ambassador. He must have been instructed to clear the passageway as well, for when at length the subaltern led them to the office, they encountered no one along the way.

The duke, his hands clasped at his back, was standing at the tall French windows behind his desk, gazing out over the lawn and gardens. He did not turn when the subaltern announced them and quietly withdrew.

They stood where they had been left, just inside the door, side by side like two children caught out in mischief and brought to hear their punishment.

For an extended time, the room vibrated with a tense silence. Then Delilah saw something move and looked over to see Madame de Staël seated near a low table spread out with cups and saucers, languidly waving her fan. Her swarthy face and dark eyes held no expression.

"Well, then, Dragoner," barked the duke, still facing away from them. "What have you to say for yourself?"

Beside Delilah, Dragoner stiffened. "Nothing for myself, Your Grace. But I would ask you to take my wife in charge until I have made certain that she can safely return to England."

"Yes, yes. I am perfectly aware that you have entangled her in your reprehensible scheme to entrap, as I understand it, the very same thieves you put to thieving in the first place. Sergeant Platt has told me the whole, save only what you and Lady Dragoner have been up to these last four-and-twenty hours."

"Eddie was here? Has he been injured?"

"A fleabite. He was shot at, but the bullet only parted his hair. And yes, he came here directly afterwards. Whereupon I was sent for—roused from my bed well before dawn of a Sunday morning—and arrived at the embassy not long before Madame de Staël, who had become concerned about Lady Dragoner. So here we all are, except for Sergeant Platt. He has gone out with a half-dozen troops in search of you."

Wellington finally turned, his eyes an arctic blue, and fixed a stern gaze on his scapegrace junior officer. "I presume you have an explanation for this muddle, Captain? One that accounts for your peculiar apparel?"

Delilah breathed a little more easily. If the duke were angry beyond recall, he'd not have made reference to an insignificant dress.

"The gown is what remains of a disguise," Dragoner said. "It has served its purpose. As for the rest, I shall, of course, most willingly explain. But if you will indulge me a short time longer, I must first see an end to what I have so unwisely begun."

"And just how do you propose to do that?" Wellington inquired in a frosty voice. "Am I expected to loose you to wreak havoc on the countryside?"

"On one man only, sir." Dragoner firmed his shoulders. "Ed—Sergeant Platt has told you, I am sure, about Jacques Batiste and his fellows. But he may yet be unaware, and you as well, that the Comte de Chabot has been pulling their strings. Mine, too, I am ashamed to say."

"Ah." Wellington sat at his desk and steepled his hands. "Interesting. And all the more trouble for the lot of us. I had thought we could skate by this without embroiling everyone of authority in Paris, including the king, in your tomfoolery, but it seems not. You have evidence that Chabot has committed a crime?"

"Witnesses to his involvement, yes. Myself, Lady Dragoner, and his henchmen when they are arrested. But it need not come to a trial, Your Grace. He gave orders for the death of my wife and made his thugs free to ravish her beforehand. I intend to call him out."

"Dear God, another duel!" Wellington's expression hardened. "I've already lost a score of good officers who cannot control their tempers, Captain. I don't mean to lose another."

Delilah could not help herself. "Thank you, Your Grace. A duel is the very last thing I wish, especially if it's to be fought on my account."

"Enough, Delilah!" Dragoner put a hand on her arm. "You cannot deny me, sir. This is a matter of honor."

"Humbug! Of course I can deny you. I *do* deny you. Hot-blooded young men are well enough on the battlefield, but in peacetime they are the very devil. This imbroglio was of your making, Captain, and in part I should like to see you resolve it.

Nevertheless, it has now become a matter of diplomacy, and I am left to pick up the pieces."

Delilah looked nervously from the corners of her eyes at her husband. His lips were set in a hard line, and the scarlet on his cheeks owed nothing to the traces of rouge.

"I must debrief you before proceeding further," said the duke, "but there is no reason for Lady Dragoner to be inconvenienced. Madame de Staël, will you be so kind as to escort the young lady upstairs?" He smiled at Delilah. "The embassy was formerly a residence, as you may know, and we have not yet converted all the rooms to offices. Perhaps you will enjoy a stay in the Princess Borghese's bedchamber."

It was a dismissal, she knew, and a firm one. She was not to hear the rest of what he had to say to Dragoner. Madame de Staël took her arm and led her away, but before the door closed behind them, she stole a glance over her shoulder at her husband.

Arms at his sides, his back straight as a spear, he stood facing the Duke of Wellington with as much dignity as any man wearing a dress could possibly muster.

Tears rose to her eyes. It wasn't fair. What had happened was more her fault than his.

"Come, my dear," said Madame de Staël. "You needn't worry. The duke, by his own admission to me, was kept apprised of what our dragon was up to. Until it all fell apart, of course, and now the gentlemen must sort out the consequences and find a way to deal with them. It is most annoying that they exclude us, to be sure, but that is the way of things."

Every bit of the energy that had kept her going had begun to seep out of Delilah's ragged toes. Only her feet had suffered from the ordeal she had passed through, and she knew they were bleeding inside her borrowed demiboots. She barely took note of the lavishly furnished room that had once sheltered a princess—one of Bonaparte's sisters, as she recalled—but she gathered her wits long enough to tell Madame the story of her involvement with the Comte de Chabot and what had happened afterward.

All the while, Madame de Staël was divesting her of her dress and her footwear. When she cast eyes on the injured feet,

Madame tugged the bellpull and gave orders to a servant, who returned with a basin and hot water and soap. At some point, clad only in a chemise, Delilah found herself in bed with the covers pulled over her and all the curtains closed.

"Later," said a disembodied voice, "I shall see that your clothes and other possessions are brought to you. For now, I must go home and reassure Lady Hepzibah that you have been found and are well."

"But Dragoner is not at all well," Delilah murmured to a closed door. "Who is to care for *him*?"

Sometime later, she didn't know how long because she had been sleeping, the door opened again. The click of the latch roused her, and she sat up, clutching the linen sheet to her breast.

It was Dragoner, looking confused to see her. He must have expected to be ushered into a room of his own. But he came inside, nodding thanks to a uniformed figure who vanished into the passageway, and halted a considerable distance from the bed.

She could scarcely see him in the dim light that filtered through the breaks in the curtains. Someone had found him a shirt to wear, and the knitted slippers were gone, replaced with a casing of bandages around each foot.

"You will wish to know what has happened," he said, his voice clouded with exhaustion. "There is some good news. Edoard returned a few minutes ago with Batiste in custody. He was found at Montmartre, the greedy sod, picking through his booty for whatever he could carry off in a wagon. Soldiers have been dispatched to look for the ship, which may well have run aground. If not, I expect that Beltrand and the others will make a clean escape."

"And Chabot?" she asked, flinching at the expression that crossed his face.

"For the time being, he cannot be touched. A matter of politics, you understand. Every aristocrat who supported Bonaparte fears retribution from the restored king or from the Vienna Congress, and to arrest any one of them would stir up a hornet's nest of trouble among the others. Or so the duke informs me. Our best hope is that when Chabot learns his brother has been taken, he will go into voluntary exile. Should that fail, the king will be urged to suggest he do so. It is all in Wellington's hands now, and His Majesty's. I have given my word not to interfere."

She hoped that her sigh of relief went unheard. "You ought to sit down, my lord," she said.

"Yes. When I can. But there is more to tell you, and when I do sit, I am certain to fall asleep. The most immediate problem is how to extricate Minette from the police. She may yet be at the house, or they might have arrested her. None of us can go there to find out, of course, and because it is Sunday, the duke has so far been unable to contact the proper authorities."

"I shouldn't be surprised if she has already managed to extricate *herself*," Delilah said.

"Nor I." He gave her a brief smile. "When I was dismissed, Edoard was providing Wellington a list of the places she would most likely go. He will make sure that she is found and brought to safety. Here, I imagine. We are all to stay here."

He moved, then, to the foot of the bed, and wrapped his hand around the canopy post. "You must pardon me, Delilah. My wits are scattered across several provinces. I cannot think what to tell you next. Perhaps it is time for you to pry the words from me. You have a gift for it."

A gift that he had always resented, she knew. But she sensed there were things he wanted to say, things that ordinarily he would have concealed from her, and that he did not know how to go about saying them. Her heart ached for him. He looked so . . . so unsure of himself, her dear, ferocious dragon. So lost. So *defeated*.

"Was it awful," she said, praying for guidance, "what the duke said to you after I was gone?"

He winced. "Bad enough, I suppose. On the face of it, we analyzed the mission and what had gone wrong, as soldiers will do after an encounter with the enemy. Except that on this occasion, I had scraped up a clutch of opponents because no others had presented themselves, and encouraged them to commit a crime when they were otherwise floundering about. Wellington rightly holds me responsible for the debacle that followed."

He swiped his fingers through his disordered hair. "The thing is, I so desperately required something to *do*. When the war ended, I became nothing. Ineffectual. A cipher. But I was kept on, and paid to produce information I could not find. I practically leapt on a pair of idiots keeping watch on my house because they were my only chance to make myself of use. And—I must admit to it—I was distracted from my duty by personal matters."

"By me," she said.

"By you." A singularly sweet smile drifted over his lips. "Most of all, by you. Perhaps I would have let go my obsession with the plot I'd helped to devise, had you not taken up with Chabot. Yes, I suspected him from the first, but dismissed the notion. Later, much as I wanted to, I could not figure a way to connect him to his brother's scheming. It appears now that he will escape scot-free."

"My fault, sir. If I had remained in England where I belonged, none of this would have happened."

"Not so. Some of it did not require your presence here. And in any case, the both of us are out of it now. Edoard as well, and Minette. Officially, Wellington has no idea what we have done or where we have gone. Unofficially, he will be in contact with the police, the minister of justice, and the king, smoothing feathers and quashing rumors. Edoard has kept a list of what was stolen and from where. With luck, most all of it will be recovered, although I suspect that Chabot fastened on the most valuable items and secreted them where they'll not be easily located."

Dragoner was finding it unbearable, she knew, to let go and leave the tying off of loose ends to others. His pride had been rubbed raw these last few days. And at the conclusion, he had been forced to stand—clad in a dress!—before the Duke of Wellington, begging sanctuary for his wife and asking permission to confront Chabot in a duel of honor.

What it must have cost him, to be denied the chance to redeem himself in the way men so foolishly went about proving themselves to other men. Thank heavens Wellington had the sense to rein him in. But in the end, he had been left with empty hands and a false certitude of failure. And that he had now exposed his soul to her, naked in his humility, brought tears to her eyes.

Something important had changed between them. She didn't know what it was or where it would lead, but hope began to spread white wings in her heart. And fear as well, because her pride demanded that he come to her willingly, not merely because he had nowhere else to go.

But never mind. Never mind. He must make the next move, if there was to be one. She had done all she could, and said to him all that she could say.

"Delilah. You have to know the rest." His voice shook with the effort of putting words together. "We are to remain here in hiding until we can be spirited away. You, of course, will return to England. Edoard, I believe, had in mind to wed Minette and go in service to a French aristocrat worthy of his skills. But that is no longer possible, and now it is my responsibility to see them both well placed. They are my friends, you see. The only friends I have. Will you provide funds to settle them in London, or wherever else they choose to live?"

The only friends I have. Her tears were falling in earnest now, but he wasn't looking at her to see them. Thank God his eyes were closed, giving her time to wipe her cheeks with the sheet.

"I have no money that is not yours," she said after a time. "You must decide what is to be done with it. But cannot Edoard continue to serve as your valet?"

"Whatever for? I am forbidden to appear anywhere in public until the duke—assuming he remembers that I exist and does not find it cumbersome to do so—scratches up my reputation from the sewers."

"Oh, he will!" she said immediately. "He has promised me that he will. And mark my words, I shall see to it he keeps to that promise."

His lips curved. "With you snapping at his heels, I expect he'll have no choice. But in the meantime, my orders are to go to ground. I am to stay out of sight and, more to the point, out of trouble."

"Then you should go to Dragon's Hill, don't you think? Or the river house, if you prefer, but there will be more to keep you occupied on your estate."

"Yes." He looked over at her then. "I hardly dare to ask. I have no right. But will you come with me, Delilah?"

And now, she told herself as the immediate yes rose to her throat, and now she must wrench the truth from him. This time, she would not take him on any terms but her own.

"To what purpose?" she asked without inflection.

"I—" He made a vague gesture. "That is, you suggested we spend a year together. I thought it was what you wanted."

"So I did, when we were strangers. I hoped you might come to like me. But I believe, sir, that you know me well enough by now, and the year I once asked for will no longer suffice. Only a lifetime will do. You must be my husband for every day and every night, or I'll have no husband at all."

"You would have me? Even now?" After a moment, he sagged against the bedpost. "But it would be a poor bargain, you know. I come to you without even a shirt to call my own, and no idea how to go about being a husband."

It was yes. He couldn't bring himself to say it, but the answer was *yes!* Her heart soared. But she met him on the rocky ground where he was standing, uncertain and needing reassurance, because she now had everything she wanted of him. And he was so weary, pushed to the edge of his endurance. There would be time for everything left unspoken. For the words of love she longed to give him.

"Well, then," she said. "Until I have trained you properly as a husband, I shall have to settle for a lover. You owe me a wedding night, as I recall."

It had been the right thing to say. He gave her a blinding smile. "Oh, a great many, I should think. But I'm sorry, Delilah. I don't expect I can give you one of them tonight."

"Indeed not. I'm far too tired to make the most of it." She held out her hand. "Come, Charles, before you topple over."

He stumbled forward and lowered himself beside her. Not under the covers, as she would have preferred, but his head rested on the pillow where hers had been and he gazed up warmly into her eyes. "I will keep all the promises I once made to you, Delilah. But no. I must remember. It is Delia." His voice caressed the word. "And to prove my good intentions, I shall even stop quoting bits of Shakespeare at you."

"Oh, but I wouldn't dream of asking so great a sacrifice." She lay back, her head joining his on the pillow, and turned onto her side to look at him. "In fact, Charles, I mean to go through all the plays and underline every passage where a man extravagantly praises his lady. You may then memorize the lines I've marked and give them back to me."

Chuckling softly, he wrapped his arm around her and snuggled his face against hers. "I doubt that even Shakespeare has written praise enough for you, lady mine. When my brain starts working again, I shall devote myself to coming up with words of my own. Already there are three of them dancing about in my heart. Perhaps you'll like them."

She was sure of it. But his voice had faded off near the end, and she felt the arm across her waist going limp. "Yes, Charles." she whispered. "Yes. But first we shall go home."

His breath was warm on her lips. "Home," he said.

Author's Note

After Napoleon's abdication in 1814, the newly elevated Duke of Wellington somewhat reluctantly accepted the position of British Ambassador to the Court of the Tuileries. A great admirer of Madame de Staël, he first made her acquaintance at her "salon" in Clichy, stopping by on his way from Madrid to England for the Victory Celebrations. There, in an uncommonly theatrical gesture, he was seen to drop onto one knee before her.

Returning from England in August, he spent several weeks inspecting the frontier fortresses in the Low Countries and found "many advantageous positions" for defense between Brussels and the French border. Ten months later, he had reason to be glad of that expedition, as he aligned his troops and artillery along the low ridges and slopes not far from the village of Waterloo.

The Divorce Act of 1857 marked the first significant attempt since the sixteenth century to alter England's divorce laws. Even so, little change was effected. Wives were now permitted to petition for divorce, but their rights continued to be strictly circumscribed. Protection of a married woman's property was not secured until 1882, and nothing was done to help abused, abandoned, or separated wives. Divorce remained altogether out of reach for the lower middle class and the poor.

Finally, I wish to thank the crew of the *Lady Washington*, a replica of a 1757 sloop featured not long ago in the film *Star Trek Generations*, for taking me aboard and answering my landlubberly questions. Special thanks to Justin, who walked with me through my characters' escape route, corrected my nautical terms, and showed me the ropes. Er, *lines*.

—Lynn Kerstan
www.romcom.com/kerstan